DIARY
of a
Teenage Empath

THE AWAKENING

Jeannette Folan

 FriesenPress

Suite 300 - 990 Fort St
Victoria, BC, V8V 3K2
Canada

www.friesenpress.com

Copyright © 2016 by Jeannette Folan
First Edition — 2016

Cover art by Alison Gerard and Estella Vukovic

ISBN
978-1-4602-9578-6 (Hardcover)
978-1-4602-9579-3 (Paperback)
978-1-4602-9580-9 (eBook)

1. YOUNG ADULT FICTION, GENERAL

Distributed to the trade by The Ingram Book Company

For Nathalie, whose profound wisdom, magnanimous heart,
and steadfast friendship nourish my life

Hey

Before you get into reading my diary, I thought you might also want in on my empath playlist.

You've probably not heard any of these tracks before. The artists are relatively new - not your typical mainstream variety - but they're GENIUS!

If you're anything like me, music is as important as air or water - only more powerful. It's like a drug. Lately, these songs have become my drug of choice.

You can listen directly at empathdiary.com. Links to downloading the songs are also there. Enjoy.

Jenny

Were our senses altered, and made much quicker and acuter,

the appearance and outward scheme of things would have

quite another face to us, and be inconsistent with our well-being.

John Locke, 1854

Preface

Until a few months ago, I thought there was something wrong with me. I couldn't shake myself out of my own head. Trapped inside was a jumble of noise, static, and flashing images, like I was staring out the window on a high-speed train flying past scenes of my own life. Only it wasn't my life. The visions that flickered in my mind were of me, but not in the context of any familiar events I'd experienced. Some of the images were completely imperceptible, and those I could see clearly, those I could understand, were completely disturbing. Images like being stuck inside a dark well, walking through a labyrinth of hot coals, falling from the highest branch of a tall tree, and being lost in fog so thick for so long that I finally dissolved into it.

When I was released from these visions and could engage in normal activities, I began having routine panic attacks. I couldn't tolerate being in a crowd, being touched, being near certain people, or sometimes just being.

I read somewhere that our thoughts control our feelings, not the other way around. In my case, it didn't matter. It seemed I wasn't in control of either. I could be thinking about lying on a warm beach surrounded by laughing children yet feel a rush of sadness so overwhelming, I cried. Other times I would be feeling completely neutral, with no thoughts at all, and then suddenly the idea would occur to me to cut off all my hair. Thankfully, I didn't. Thankfully, I'd been able to keep my outward behavior under control, even if everything inside of me was out of control.

The journey I took to discover what was happening to me led to some of the most magical moments of my young life. But it also led me to wonder if magic wasn't just another form of insanity.

Part 1:
The Awakening

June 1

The symptoms I experienced all pointed to some kind of mental illness. At first my parents suspected that my behavior was due to a teenage crush or hormonal imbalance. They would give me half a hug then shoot each other a look that conveyed more mockery than concern. But then they discovered the row of deep paper cuts on my arm, and four hours later, I was sitting in Dr. Foster's office. Most of Dr. Foster's questions were related to thoughts of suicide and self-harm. I told him I didn't have any of those thoughts or feelings. He asked what I was thinking when I gave myself the cuts. I considered lying, telling him some girls at school dared me to do it or that it was the new fad instead of tattoos and piercings. But I never liked how a lie felt. It was too much like wearing someone else's clothes that were three sizes too small. So without weighing the consequences of the truth, I said, "Just wanted to make sure I was still here."

At the end of the session, he handed my parents a prescription for some anti-anxiety meds. They seemed relieved, like the dentist just told them he could save the tooth and a few Aspirin would stave off the pain. But I told them on the drive home that I had no intention of taking a drug that the doctor said would affect my central nervous system and cause umpteen side effects; especially not from a guy who'd spent only a sum total of fifty minutes with me. Besides, I knew a few kids at school on the stuff, and they walked around like zombies half the time.

My mom wasn't swayed. She said that if she saw any signs of self-harm or depression, she wouldn't give me any choice but to take the meds. I knew there was no point in arguing. Once she decided on a path, she wouldn't deviate from it, even if you pointed out that it led straight to hell. So it seemed my options were to pretend to be 'normal' or become a zombie.

June 8

Over the course of the next week, I worked on my acting skills, trying to be like I used to be before being became a struggle. I played upbeat songs on my guitar, cooked colorful meals, and generally did my best impersonation of a finalist in the Miss America pageant. But it was clear to me — even if my parents were fooled — that my comfort zone was getting smaller. I wondered if the day would come when the only time I didn't feel anxious would be when I showered or slept.

It wasn't so much that I was anxious — well, that's not entirely true. I felt a low grade of anxiety that hummed in the background like our antiquated refrigerator. But more intense were the feelings of either being disengaged from everyone and everything around me or being so 'plugged-in' that I felt like a circuit board about to overload and disintegrate in a single 'poof.'

For now, the one thing that kept me going was the calendar. Only one more week of school, and then I could enjoy an entire summer of solitude. The thought of starting high school in the fall with hundreds of kids I'd never met before was as comforting as a woolen blanket infested with lice. The thought of being alone just floating around in my pool for two and a half months, however, was divine.

It was this thought that had me caught up in a reverie during my history class and made Mr. Gerard holler my name not once but three times before I replied. Everyone began to laugh, but I didn't care. My grades were better than any of theirs, even on my worst day. As if in agreement with my thought, Mr. Gerard gave me a subtle wink before dismissing class.

As I headed to the cafeteria for lunch, I noticed a cluster of people in the hall. Getting closer, I realized there was a fistfight going on between two guys. I didn't know either of them, but since they stood a foot above everyone else and were wearing their jerseys, I figured it was a safe bet they were on the basketball team. My chest immediately tightened and a feeling of dread swept over me. Instinctively, I averted my eyes and turned around to take the back hall out to the garden area, where I could eat my bagged lunch in peace.

Surrounded by the trees, flowers, and birdhouses, I immediately felt tranquil again. This space had become my sanctuary over the last two years, and it made me a little sad to think I wouldn't have it to escape to next year. Though I was sure Trinity High School would have its own sanctuaries, this one occupied a special place in my heart. It was not only the place I came to most days for lunch, but it was also where I became an avid reader, where I studied the clouds, and where I had my first kiss and first heartbreak — if you can call it that after only three weeks of dating.

As I sat there nibbling at my sandwich and carrot sticks, I contemplated the transition from junior high to high school. By size alone, it would be the equivalent of thriving in a small pond versus surviving in the open ocean. I'd been lucky, getting through the past couple of years relatively unscathed. I had a small circle I hung out with, more study buddies than personal friends, but they were all going to West High School next year, so my only hope was that I could blend into my new high school like a sole on the bottom of the sea floor.

Back home, things were stiff, but not as bad as they were a week ago. My dad mostly acted like nothing happened, while my mom covertly monitored my every move. She watched how much I ate, how often I went to the bathroom, which shows I watched on TV. She even checked on me in the middle of the night to make sure I was still breathing. On a few occasions, even though I knew she meant well, I found myself holding my breath as she hovered over my bed. I had to admonish myself to breathe until finally she would tiptoe away back to her own troubled night of sleep.

June 14

Somehow, between good acting on my part and ignorance on my parents' part, I was able to make it through the end of the school year without any 'episodes' and without any meds or visits to Dr. Foster.

My graduation party, however, which was originally planned as a huge backyard BBQ for seventy friends and family, including my dad's entire office staff, had thankfully been downsized to a Sunday brunch at the local country club for immediate family only. This included both sets of my grandparents, my father's only sister, and her son, Ryan, and my mother's sister, otherwise known as my crazy Aunt Maggie.

I had never questioned why she was referred to as 'crazy.' I only knew that since I was a kid, she'd pretty much been excluded from most family events. The last time I saw her, I was probably nine or ten years old, and I remember she had a way about her that was mystical, but not in that dark, creepy way. She was light and carefree — and yes, a bit eccentric. But I felt a kinship with her more than the other few members of my immediate family, which was why I insisted she be invited to my graduation party.

Upon seeing her there, I felt for the first time in a long time a reason to celebrate. She wore tight black leggings and a short, dress-length chiffon-style top printed in a splash of vibrant colors. When she opened her arms to greet me, the fabric billowed out like angel's wings. As we embraced, instead of my usual pang of anxiety, it felt like home.

Feeling so immediately connected to her made me resent my mom for having kept her from being a part of our family all these years. I could understand why they weren't close. My mom's stoic nature and general closed-minded attitude was a stark contrast to Aunt Maggie's open-minded, expressive, holistic nature. But that wasn't a good enough reason to have kept Aunt Maggie from her only niece, who would probably have benefitted a great deal from her wisdom and friendship. Now that I was old enough, I would make sure that changed.

For now, I simply enjoyed a day in her company. Though I knew it was rude, I almost completely ignored my other relatives, choosing to spend the time absorbed in her stories of travel and adventure.

June 21

The summer began exactly as I'd hoped. Lots of sun and little interference from my parents. Being an only child in the age of 'helicopter parenting' usually meant extreme turbulence and confrontations on every front, hovering over every aspect of life, including friends, music, clothes, activities, diet, and dating. These were the challenges of most kids I knew in school. Thankfully, my parents missed the sign-up for helicopter parenting and instead opted for the oblivious parenting course — or at least they did until my cutting incident.

I could understand why it had freaked them out. It freaked me out, too. But I wasn't kidding when I told Dr. Foster that I did it because I needed to make sure I was still here. For weeks leading up to that time, I'd felt like I was breaking apart; like my atoms and molecules were separating and dissolving into the air — or maybe being absorbed by other life forms around me. I simply didn't feel solid anymore.

When I cut my arm and watched the skin separate and the tiny drops of blood come to the surface — when I felt the sting of pain and watched as the flesh inevitably healed — it comforted me. I knew by witnessing and feeling that process that I was a solid, fully functioning human being just like everybody else.

Although I kept my promise to my parents and hadn't cut myself again, I couldn't keep from thinking and feeling that something in me still wasn't right. Changing my outside behavior didn't seem to change whatever was happening inside. I thought about it being a physical illness — because I definitely had physiological effects — but really I was concerned with my mental stability. Was I going crazy?

My ongoing symptoms, if that's what they could be called, included erratic thoughts, moodiness, intolerance of loud noises and crowds of people, a fear of violence, and anxiousness. According to my Internet research, these fit a variety of psychological conditions, including general anxiety disorder, panic disorder, social anxiety disorder, and bipolar disorder. The suggested course of treatment for all of them was a cocktail of pharmaceuticals and therapy. Somehow I didn't think that was the right path for me. And while I'd be okay talking through my experiences with a qualified therapist, I couldn't imagine there was one qualified for this; one who would understand me. I mean, this wasn't an issue of my parents being abusive, not loving me enough, or giving me enough attention. I didn't have a complex about my body or looks or intelligence. I wasn't paranoid. I didn't feel my needs weren't being met. What I felt was that something external was affecting me internally, and that whatever it was, it was beyond my control.

July 13

I was ecstatic to hear that Aunt Maggie had decided to come for a visit in two weeks' time, yet I seemed to be the only one excited about the news. Dad discreetly rolled his eyes while Mom began wringing her hands and sighing heavily every few minutes. They both implied that their indifference toward her was nothing more than a personality thing, but I suspected there was more to it than that. I believed something significant had occurred that resulted in the chasm between them.

July 26

On the day Aunt Maggie came it had threatened to rain, but as if in response to her arrival, the sun was soon shining. And as if in gratitude, she wore a yellow and orange sarong and a smile as bright as I'd ever seen. She embraced me the same way she had at my grad party. I could tell it made my parents uneasy, and while it was not my intention to push their buttons, I would not deny myself the pleasure of every moment with Aunt Maggie.

Each morning as I awoke, I found her sitting quietly in our sunroom, meditating. After a while, we would share breakfast together and chat about the local vegetation, artisans, and my plans for high school. Our talks were always easy, and most especially hopeful. I sensed there was never a negative or worrisome thought in her head — quite the opposite of what I had experienced with my own parents, who seemed to perpetually live in a reactive state of task-driven defensiveness and fear. Work, bills, money, schedules, commitments, obligations, and a general sense of dread for all the 'what-ifs' in the world. Somehow, Aunt Maggie had achieved what most people try but fail to do: live a positive life.

At the end of the first week of her visit, I decided to ask about the trouble between her and my parents. Rather than jump straight into the fire, however, I warmed up with something safer.

"Tell me more about your work, Aunt Maggie. What's the best thing about being a travel writer?"

"You mean besides being adventurous, and luckily, highly lucrative?" She gleamed with delight and added, "It's been a life beyond my expectations. I've travelled the world, experienced many cultures, and met fascinating people. I've published a few books, learned a few languages, and now am able to enjoy a more spontaneous lifestyle, going where I want to and writing when I want to for a few select magazines. All in all, I couldn't have asked for more."

"Why have you never married? If you don't mind my asking."

"No, I don't mind at all," she replied with a wave of her hand. "Do you want the soundbite version or the miniseries?"

"Miniseries, please!" I said, clapping my hands in child-like delight.

"Then we'd better refill our teas and move into the sunroom."

Once we had taken our seats overlooking the back porch and maple trees, she took a sip of her tea and let out a small sigh. "Did your mother ever tell you that I was engaged once?"

I shook my head. "They never tell me anything that happened before I was born."

"Well, they did their share of living," she said with a wink. "But that's not my story to tell. My story," she continued, "started in my last year of college. I had dated a bit, but nothing serious. Then out of the blue my senior year, this tall drink of water named Rick showed up at one of the campus events. It wasn't surprising I hadn't met him before. My major was journalism. His was psychology. There was no reason for our paths to have crossed. Anyway, we started dating, and before you know it, we were graduating and Rick asked me to join him in Phoenix, where he was doing a research project over the summer related to his grad courses about communication through sensory differentials, or something to that effect.

"I had planned on going to grad school, too, but thought I would first take some time to explore the world. You know, back-pack across Europe or build houses with Habitat in Mexico."

I nodded enthusiastically, imaging myself doing the same thing after graduating high school. As if reading my mind, she said, "Do it. The sooner, the better. You won't regret it. As for me, I figured that Arizona was as good a place to explore as anywhere, so I said 'yes' to Rick, and off we went.

"His project took up a considerable amount of time, so I would usually head off in his car Monday morning, spend five days hiking the Grand Canyon or make my way to Sedona or Yellowstone or Tahoe and be back in time for pizza and beer on Friday night."

"So what happened? How did the engagement break off?" I asked greedily. "Did he end up meeting someone else? Did you meet someone else?"

"Relax, Jenny," she soothed with a teasing sparkle in her eye. "You said you wanted the miniseries version, so sip your tea, take a deep breath, and zip it."

The suspense was making me anxious, as if I already knew the end of the story, and it wasn't a good one. But I did as I was told. "Sip it and zip it." I smiled.

"A few months had passed, and everything was going well. Better than well, for me, anyway. I was off doing what I wanted to do, and when we saw each other on the weekends, it was pure joy and laughter, sex, and intimacy." She let out a long breath as she said this and closed her eyes in reverie. Whatever scene she was playing out in her mind made her eyelids flutter and my own pulse quicken. When she finally opened her eyes, she stared into mine and held my gaze as if she were swearing me to secrecy. A moment later, she snapped back into gear and picked up the story.

"Usually, when we reunited on Friday evening, we would get some takeout and stay in bed until Sunday."

As soon as she said this, she started getting that faraway look on her face, so I bellowed out, "Earth to Aunt Maggie!"

"Yeah, sorry. From now on, I'll fantasize on my own time." She continued, "On Sunday afternoons, we would meet up with his research partners at the local sports bar and hang out until the pool of money ran out or someone decided to get a game of flag football going.

"On one particular Sunday, we were playing a game out in the front yard where a few of Rick's colleagues shared a house. About halfway through the game, one of the guys kicked off, and Rick caught the ball. Of course, couples weren't allowed on the same team, so I charged across the field at him with the intention of flagging him into oblivion, but instead of running away, he dropped to one knee, which in professional football means 'fair catch.' As far as I knew, we were playing pub rules, not pro, so I said, 'What the hell are you doing? To which he replied, 'I'm calling a 'good catch' … and you're it. Will you marry me, Maggie?'

"He dropped the football and from his jeans pocket he presented a beautiful band of white gold with a small diamond and two emerald baguettes. Even a hippie girl like me appreciated the luxury of such jewels. Plus, the choice of stones had a special meaning for Rick and me."

"Really?" I asked, my eyes nearly popping out of my head, pleading with her to tell me more. "What was it? It sounds sooooo romantic."

"No can do," she said, shaking her head with conviction. "Some things are meant to remain strictly between two people." Although I knew she was referring to her and her lost love, Rick, when she said 'two people,' she gestured between us, and I couldn't help but feel again like she was admonishing me to keep some secret she was about to share.

"After a romantically brutish proposal like that, of course I accepted. The game immediately came to a halt, and we all walked down to the pub to have a proper toast to the engagement. I couldn't help notice, however, that while some of the group were sincerely delighted for us, others took a step back from the circle, glancing down at the floor and whispering to each other with critical looks at Rick and me.

"I tried very hard not to let them diminish my joy. After all, I didn't know them that well. They weren't my friends; they were Rick's research partners, which is the exact thought that made me stop in my tracks as Rick and I walked back to our apartment. I didn't beat around the bush. 'Rick,' I said, 'have you ever had a romantic affair with anyone on your team? Or perhaps has one of them expressed an interest in you?'

"He turned to me and said, 'I have not had any kind of relationship with anyone since I met you. If there is someone with an interest in me, they have not, thankfully, brought it to my attention. Now what's this all about, anyway? Not getting cold feet already, are you?'

"'Of course not,' I told him. 'But the way some of your colleagues were acting after you proposed, it's obvious they aren't happy with your choice of bride.'

"The look on his face was a mix of relief and frustration. He said, 'Maggie, it's not my choice of bride they protest. It's my choice to get married now, before I've even started grad school, let alone be published or achieve anything in my field.' And then I said, 'I don't understand. Why should they care when you get married or what you achieve? What's it to them? I thought this was just some warm-up project to keep you ahead of the curve.'

"He said, 'Well, in fact, as it turns out, we are way ahead of the curve, and they are looking to me to take the lead on it. When school starts, our project hours will automatically be cut in half. Adding a new wife to the mix, especially such a sexy one, might put a strain, so to speak, on my focus and time.'"

I could see my aunt getting lost in the memory, and it felt sometimes like she was inviting me to peek at the pages of her diary. More than just words, her story came to life for me, so much so that I could feel my pulse quicken as I imagined this gorgeous man 'strained' against me.

My aunt finally recovered from her trip down Fantasy Lane and picked up the story again.

"What I didn't understand," she said, "was what the big deal was over a pre-grad research project that, as far as I could tell, wasn't being mentored by a professor or funded by the university, the government, or a private company. Which is exactly what I said to Rick just before he turned and walked away, muttering something that sounded a lot like 'Maybe this wasn't such a good idea.'"

"Oh no, Aunt Maggie, that must have been awful. Was that the end of it then?"

"Of course not!" she shouted. "All you young people think about is ending things at the first sign of an argument or conflict. Relationships take work! That's no guarantee they will last, but not working on them is a sure guarantee they won't last. The quicker you learn that, the happier you'll be."

"What about your relationship with my mom?" I couldn't help myself. The timing was too perfect not to bring it up.

To my amazement, she fired back, "Yes! That's exactly what I'm talking about. It's the perfect example of a no-guarantee relationship."

"So what happened between you and my mom? I mean, you're here now but…"

"That's another story — kind of," she said with another wave of her hand. "Do you want to hear the rest of the story about Rick or not?"

"Of course." I nodded eagerly.

"Right. So after all apologies were made and we engaged in a sufficient amount of make-up sex, I thought everything was back on track. Weeks passed, grad school was starting, and I decided to find a job in town, at least for the first semester, until I knew where and when I would return to school."

I was about to interrupt her again to ask how she could consider going somewhere else for her grad school when she was newly engaged but thought better of it. She clearly wasn't a 'little wifey' type of woman, and I guess, if I was honest with myself, no matter how much I wanted a relationship, I wouldn't change my course of direction in life for romance either.

"I was lucky to find a good-paying job during the day at a vet's clinic. I always had a way with animals, and it meant that I got to see Rick most nights, too, though he also spent some nights with his research group. This went along at its own blissful pace until around early November when Rick began missing our weeknight dinners and started spending more weekends with the research team, never including me on the Sunday afternoon pub parties or football games. I shouldn't say 'never,' but there was a noticeable decline in our one-on-one relationship, if you know what I mean."

Got it. Aunt Maggie was a sex-crazed young woman and not afraid to admit it.

"Again, I wondered if his interests had swayed to someone else, and one night, I'm embarrassed to say, I followed him from the campus to the house where we used to play football — the one where three of his research partners lived."

I sensed the story was about to turn into a bad reality TV show. "What did you find?"

"Nothing, really. Or at least nothing that I could make any sense of. I saw them through the kitchen window. The whole team was sitting around the table, and it looked like they were just ... meditating. But it was very strange; even a little creepy. I stood there a few minutes and finally, feeling completely foolish, went home."

"That was it?" I asked in astonishment. "So what was it that caused you to finally split up?"

"It was my fault, really," she said with resignation. "After my 'peeping tom' incident, I started asking him questions about his research project. He must have sensed I had ulterior motives and found a way to dodge most of my questions, which only made me more apprehensive. It went on like this for weeks until finally it was time to go home for Christmas, and Rick was supposed to be going with me so we could officially announce our engagement to my family.

"A few days before we were to leave, Rick decided that their research project had reached a critical point, and he didn't feel he could spend the time away. I tell you, Jenny, as I live and breathe, I could feel my heart sinking and the entire world shift on its axis. I have never been a needy woman, but that night, I begged him to change his mind. I knew somehow that if he didn't come with me then, he would not come with me ever."

"And did he?" I asked as my heart beat erratically and my palms sweated in anticipation of the answer.

"No. He did not." She sighed heavily and took a sip of her cold tea while staring vacantly out the window.

I stared out the window, too, looking at the sun-dappled leaves on the maple trees and feeling a sense of loss for a man I had never met. I tentatively reached out to touch her arm, and as if sensing it was there, she reached out, too, and held my hand in hers.

"I'm so sorry," I finally whispered.

"It's okay," she whispered back. "It just wasn't meant to be. But the magical moments we shared together for almost two years were the most authentic of my life. So it took some time to grieve that loss, and…"

She didn't finish her sentence, but it seemed she wanted to say more. After a few minutes, I hesitantly asked, "So Aunt Maggie, how did it actually end? I mean, did you go home and tell your family you were engaged, or did you break it off before you left?"

Shaking her head, she said, "Although he didn't want to, I broke it off before I left."

"And did you tell anyone what you'd been through when you got home?"

"Well, that's the second part of the miniseries. When I arrived home, I tried as hard as I could to avoid the subject of Rick and instead focused on the family being together for the holidays. Of course, everyone asked how he was and tried hard not to bring up the fact that they expected him to be there with me. But they knew something wasn't right.

"On Christmas Eve, when we all gathered together for dinner and the tree-lighting and gift exchange, your mom, who was then only dating your father, reached into her stocking and pulled out an engagement ring. I had only met your dad once before, very briefly, but I could tell he was petrified as he got down on his knee and asked her to marry him in front of the whole family. I remember it like it was yesterday," she said, laughing.

It was hard to imagine my dad being that romantic. I'd never seen him do a romantic thing in my life, except maybe the time he made a horribly under-cooked cake for my mom's birthday years ago.

"Obviously," my aunt continued, "she accepted, and the Christmas celebration quickly turned into an engagement party. Your dad, not being privy to the fact that Rick was supposed to have been spending the holidays with me, started asking about him and how his research was going. I thought he was only being polite, trying to make conversation, so I kept my answers vague. I certainly didn't want to spoil the festive mood by announcing the break-off of an engagement they never knew about to begin with. But then he brought up the name of one of Rick's partners, explaining how he had gone to school with her and how he had kept in touch with her.

"I remember bracing myself for whatever he was about to say regarding 'her.' Was she interested in Rick? Or maybe she'd told him about Rick and me being engaged? While my head was swimming in defensive alarm, he asked I how felt about Rick's work being so controversial and whether I supported him in his passion for quantum psychology. For a moment, I felt as if I was floating outside my body. I had never even heard of quantum psychology — which, by the way, is a form of modern psychology that aims to discover who you are by acquiring multi-dimensional awareness — so anyway, I didn't know how to respond or what to think or how to wrap my head around the fact that a near-stranger knew more about my fiancé's — or ex-fiancé's — work than I did when I had been living with him for over a year."

"So how did you respond?" I asked.

"Honestly, I don't remember," she said. "The only memory that vividly sticks with me about that moment is how your mother responded when she overheard our conversation."

This was it. I knew that whatever Aunt Maggie was about to say next would be the reason the relationship between her and my mom deteriorated. After a moment of staring out the window and turning her tea mug slowly around in her hands, she quietly said, "'Well, maybe Maggie has finally found the perfect guy. Someone as cracked-up and insane as she is.'"

Although I didn't think my aunt was exaggerating, I couldn't believe my mother could be so cruel and insensitive as to say something like that. Not to her own sister, not in front of her new fiancé, and certainly not in the middle of a family Christmas celebration. I was speechless. I wanted to apologize on my mom's behalf. I wanted to run and find my mom and yell at her for having crushed my dear aunt's feelings so carelessly. I wanted to make it up to Aunt Maggie somehow, so that she would feel welcome and safe enough here to come and see me again and again and again.

Instead, I started to cry. The tears came in a rush, streaming down my cheeks uncontrollably until the sadness gripped me with such force, I began sobbing and hyperventilating.

My aunt put her teacup down and held me in her arms. "Shhh, shhh," she cooed softly in my ear. "I know it hurts. I know what you're feeling. But these feelings aren't your burden. They are mine. Let them go. They belong to me, not you."

I felt the sadness slowly lift, and my sobs give way to a smile and faint chuckles of embarrassment over my highly emotional reaction.

When I pulled away from her, I looked into her tear-rimmed eyes and thought how very much alike we were.

August 8

Saying goodbye to my Aunt Maggie was like letting go of a life preserver in the middle of the Atlantic Ocean. She had stayed as long as she could, I understood that, but it didn't make the separation any less emotional. In the weeks she had spent with me (and it was obvious after only a few days that she had come to be with me and not my mother and father), I had grown not only to respect and love her, but also to respect and love myself more, too. How was that possible? That one person could manifest so much goodness in others?

All I knew was that I intended to keep our relationship strong, and also to keep myself strong because of all I had learned from her.

August 10

With only four weeks left before the start of high school, I immersed myself in the rituals I had learned from Aunt Maggie. Each morning I awoke early and engaged in meditation in the sunroom, followed by tea and a healthy breakfast. Every day I felt as if she were there with me, moment by moment, breath by breath.

In the afternoon, things got a bit harder. My parents insisted, quite uncharacteristically, that I get out of the house more and had arranged for me to spend the last weeks of my summer vacation volunteering at the local seniors' home. I wondered if this was punishment for my having formed a deep relationship with Aunt Maggie, but considering how much room they had given us to spend together while she was here, I didn't protest.

Most days at the home, I took the people restricted to wheelchairs out for some time in the garden, pushing them around the grounds as if they were on a Disney holiday. Those who could speak and hear well enough would make small talk about the weather, the flowers, or the hobbies they had enjoyed in their pre-convalescent lives. Many would simply stare off into the distant abyss of life after death with a look of longing and anticipation in their eyes. Still others would spend the entire time complaining about their aches and pains of recent or long-past medical issues.

When I got home, I usually felt as if I'd been hit by a truck. My body ached as much as my heart did for these discarded souls. The only things that got me through the days were my meditation practice in the morning, playing my guitar, and the knowledge that my volunteering would end as soon as school started.

Thankfully, between Aunt Maggie's visit and my volunteering gig, I didn't have that much time to be nervous about my first day of high school or be mad at my mother about her treatment of Aunt Maggie. I was still angry about it, though, because as Aunt Maggie had later explained, what stung the most is that my mom didn't even try to pretend that what she said was a joke or acknowledge that the remark had been hurtful. Instead, my mom began treating Maggie like she thought she really was 'cracked up.' And what's worse is that my dad did, too. And since he was fast becoming the favorite (and only) son-in-law, the entire family seemed to gravitate toward his point of view on most matters. So instead of it simply being a hole in the relationship with her sister, my aunt found that her relationship with her entire family was turning into Swiss cheese.

With her pain still lingering in my heart, I gave her a call to see how she was doing. No surprise, I found her packing for a month-long hike on the El Camino. A spontaneous adventure was what she called it; a chance to travel someplace new while doing some freelance work for *National Geographic*. But I knew from watching a movie about the Camino on Netflix called *The Way* that people had died walking that trail, and most people took months to train for the hike. Though I knew my aunt was in terrific shape, I told her I would worry about her until she called me upon her safe return.

In a rather harsh tone, she blurted out, "Don't you dare worry for me! If you think of me at all, I insist you picture me happy and healthy and at peace with the world. You must be mindful of your thoughts, Jenny. They are more powerful than you realize. Will you do that?"

Though I was taken aback by her serious and stern tone, I promised her I would. She wished me bunches of love and promised to call when she returned.

September 7

As if on cue, the weather on the first day of school was ten degrees cooler, and the clouds looked like they might empty their entire contents onto the school grounds in one veritable dump. The school buses were coming from both ends of the parking lot that merged into a large roundabout by the front doors. The perfected choreography of their movements reminded me of bright yellow worker ants marching off to invade someone's picnic. The kids scrambling off the buses, however, looked more like a swarm of houseflies buzzing around in all directions, with no evident purpose or plan.

Luckily for me, I didn't have to take the bus. Since my house was on the east side of River Road, it fell just within the one-mile range of the school, which was deemed walkable by the school district's transport administration. I was thankful to have the time alone, sans houseflies, but it meant that I had to leave the house a bit earlier — and that meant I had to wake up earlier if I wanted to keep up with my morning meditations. Not generally considering myself a morning person, I knew this might inevitably be a challenge once homework, tests, and extra-curricular activities got into full swing. But for now, I was taking it moment by moment, breath by breath.

As I walked into the main hall, I could see a backup of students in line to pick up their schedules. I was fairly confident I didn't need to join them, because I had printed my schedule off of the school's student website, but as I stood there in the growing chaos and clamor, I began to doubt myself. Why would so many students not have printed their schedules from the website? Maybe they were in the line to report their attendance? Or confirm they were scheduled for the electives they picked? Or maybe this was the line for freshmen to get their school IDs?

As my confidence plummeted, I looked around for a familiar face but recognized no one. And why would I? Out of the hundred kids in my old class, I'd be lucky to pick out ten of them in a line-up. On top of that, my eighth grade class was only one of five merging into this high school. Plus, the freshmen at this school represented only twenty-five percent of the total student population. Running the numbers in my head, I realized I knew less than one percent of the people here.

Normally, this would have been a comforting thought, but for some reason, I suddenly fainted.

When I came to, three things were obvious to me. One, that I'd just called attention to myself in the worst way imaginable. Walking down the hall with toilet paper stuck to my shoe would be less embarrassing. Two, that there was no reason for me to have just passed out unless something was medically wrong with me. Since I never took those stupid drugs prescribed by Dr. Foster and didn't ingest anything stronger than jasmine green tea, I became concerned as to what might have caused this episode. And three, I was staring up at the most gorgeous face I had ever seen.

"Hi," he said, smiling, revealing a perfect dimple. "I think you're okay, but I'd like to get you to the nurse's office just to be sure." My rescuer offered no name, and since my tongue was glued to the roof of my mouth, I couldn't ask, even if I were able to overcome the mental fog that enveloped me. With a swift sweep of his arms, I was propped up by his side, being escorted slowly through a parting sea of onlookers.

"I-I'm so embarrassed," I finally stammered. "I don't know what happened. Thanks for helping me."

"No worries," he replied sincerely. "You probably just got a case of the frosh first-day jitters."

Great. So he obviously isn't in his first year, he's discerned that I obviously am, and that I'm such a spaz, I can't even handle the stress of the first day of school. Way to make a first impression! As we headed down the long corridor of administrative offices, I tried not to glance up at his handsome face or lean too much into his warm body. Although I still felt a little weak, I noticed a surge of energy building in me. "I think I'm okay now, if you want to go. I mean, you don't want to be late for your first class."

"The teachers give everyone a break the first few days. It's really no trouble." Again, the sincerity in his voice, his smile, his stunning blue eyes, were so captivating it made me want to be still so I could feel him around me like my plush blanket coming straight out of the dryer on a winter day.

I snapped myself out of my daydream in time to notice him holding open the door for me to the nurse's office. Two students wearing corduroy pants and Big Bang t-shirts were breathing into paper bags.

The nurse took one look at me and reached for another bag, but my escort grinned and said, "Hey, Mrs. Gillespie, it's good to see you. Hope you had a nice summer. I brought you a new patient. Her name is Jenny." As Nurse Gillespie reached over to shake my hand, he reached for the door handle, and glancing over his shoulder, he said, "You're in good hands. Welcome to Trinity High," and he was gone.

Between the huffing of the paper bags, the nurse's stare, and the hasty departure of my white knight, I stood for a moment in a disoriented fog. Did he just introduce me by name? How did he know my name? Had I told him as we were walking here? Did someone recognize me when I was passed out in the hall? Did I forget I was wearing a 'Hello, my name is Jenny' sticker? Just to be sure, I glanced down at my shirt and was relieved to find I wasn't. But that didn't ease my troubled thoughts on the matter.

Noticing my uneasiness, Nurse Gillespie came out from behind the desk, wearing white orthotic shoes and hose circa 1950, and gently led me back to a dimly lit room with a vinyl-covered bed. The pillow had one of those disposable slipcovers on it, but thankfully there was no roll of hospital-grade paper across the bed itself. I always hated how that felt, like I was a piece of meat about to be wrapped up in butcher's paper. She sat me down with such care, I wondered if the look on my face was that alarming. I tried to snap back into my usual benign expression, even added a fake smile for good measure, but she wasn't buying it. She'd already reached for the blood pressure cuff and was shoving a thermometer in my mouth with the other hand.

After both devices finished registering the results, she shook her head with a smile. "Probably just first-day jitters. Did you eat a good breakfast?"

"Yes," I replied with more conviction than I intended.

"Do you think you'll be okay getting to classes, or would you prefer to lie here a while?"

"I'm fine," I said. "I totally promise." I wasn't sure why I added that, but I'd say anything now to get out of there and not be the kid who showed up in the middle of her first class on her first day with a note from the nurse's office.

"Well, what I really need you to promise me is that you'll come straight back here if you're feeling at all dizzy or nauseous, okay?"

She said 'nauseous' in that adult tone layered with the mild accusation that a girl who had fainted and was nauseous could only mean one thing. I almost started explaining that I'd never even been asked for a sext yet but thought better of it as I heard the first-period bell ring.

I got up, gathered my bag, and started bolting out the door, but not before asking her the burning question on my mind. "Who was that guy who brought me in here, Mrs. Gillespie?"

"That was Nathan. Nathan Leeds, dear."

As I quickly pushed my way through the swarms of students, I repeated his name in my head, forcing the image of his face into my memory so that would be able to pick him out again amidst the two thousand other unfamiliar faces I'd be seeing every day.

I reached my first class and took a seat in the back, looking carefully at the faces of the other students as they came through the door. Immediately, I rolled my eyes at my own stupidity. He wasn't a freshman, so why would I think he'd be walking into this class? Duh.

English, social studies, French, and consumers ed all passed by without incident, meaning that I didn't suddenly drop to the floor in the middle of class, and I didn't bump into Nathan Leeds in the halls either.

Lunchtime was divided up into two shifts: 11:15 a.m. or 12:10 p.m. I was happy to have the latter, because it made the afternoon all that much shorter. Approaching the windowed cafeteria, I felt a pang of disbelief mixed with a bit of panic. Despite the room being nearly as big as a football field, it was filled to capacity with mobs of students clustering and cramming in all directions.

I decided to keep walking past the cafeteria and find some quiet place to eat my Ziploc salad, but when one of the teachers opened the door for me, I got nervous and ducked inside with a nod of thanks. Standing at the top of five stairs that led down to the cafeteria floor, I had a near bird's-eye view of the chaos that ensued. I had never been in an enclosed space with a thousand people before. The noise level was exponentially greater standing in the actual room versus the hallway outside. And the mixture of greasy food, cheap perfume, and B.O. made me cover my nose and breathe shallowly through my mouth.

As more students poured in behind me, I got pushed down the stairs and into the crowd. I spotted another set of doors at the opposite end and decided to make a dash for them before I was herded deeper into the mob.

I had a nearly clear line to my goal with only a few obstacles to navigate around. I made it past the main set of garbage cans, luckily avoiding the spilled milkshakes and smooshed fries left from the first lunch period. Then I zipped through the first set of tables, hopping over some kid's foot that darted out either intentionally or unintentionally, but either way would have been a face-plant for sure. Starting a small maze through the second set of tables, I thought I was home-free until a flash of something caught my peripheral attention two tables in, and before I could register what it was, I heard my name called.

My head turned in slow motion, my eyes narrowing their focus on the source of the voice. It was him. The guy who'd been on my radar for the past four hours was now twenty-five feet away from me, calling my name. In my mind, I instantly pictured us sharing a casual lunch, becoming friends, becoming more than friends, exchanging birthday gifts, and taking long walks in the snow. In reality, I bolted for the door.

I couldn't believe what a chicken I was. *If he follows me, I'll say I didn't hear him.* But why would he follow me anyway? I didn't even know where I was going. *What if he asks me where I'm going?* I could feel my face begin to flush, and spotting a washroom up ahead, I ducked in and let out a heavy sigh. Most of the stalls were empty. I took the one at the far end and spent a minute looking over the school map I had tucked in my pocket. Past the cafeteria and down the administrative hall was a door that led out to a garden maintained by the school's horticulture club. I wasn't sure if I was allowed to go out there, but it was worth a shot. It was either that or eat my lunch on the toilet.

The staff monitor at the door to the garden greeted me with a somewhat wary look, as if suspecting I might make a run for it as soon as I got outside. Maybe he was a mind reader.

As I stepped into the hedged-in space with a flagstone path and small center fountain, I knew I had found my lunch room. Or maybe not. A bright yellow sign indicated no food or beverages were allowed. Well, I might go hungry today, but at least I found a haven of my own. Just as I wondered why no one else was out here, the door swung open and a group of four — two guys and two girls — came into the garden and plopped down on two of the benches across from me. I tried to check them out without actually making eye contact, and I think they were doing the same to me, which meant that we ended up staring directly at each other in the most awkward way possible. I smiled, and they smiled back, but otherwise they kept to themselves.

By the time last period started, I was starving and a bit light-headed. Fearing another fainting episode, I sat down on the locker room bench and devoured my salad before heading to the gym for P.E. The great thing about living nearby was that I didn't have to get caught up in the mass of girls trying to shower, change, pick up their stuff from their hall lockers, and make the buses before they took off. I could linger behind, shower at my leisure, wander the halls, sit in the garden, or go to the library and study before strolling the .95 miles home.

All in all, I thought everything was going to work out just fine at Trinity High. But then again, it was only my first day.

September 8

Day two was much the same as day one, sans the embarrassing fainting spell. Knowing that Nathan had the same lunch period as me put some pressure on my actually embarking on 'the pit,' as I now called it, but I knew eventually I would get past my dread and build up enough tolerance to eat a meal among my fellow houseflies. Today, however, was not that day.

Instead, I snuck my tuna salad sandwich into the library and hid in one of the back cubicles, eating in silence while reading last month's edition of *Shambhala Sun*. I was excited by how much I connected to the articles in this magazine. My aunt had left me her copy with the Dalai Lama on the cover. The featured article was titled 'Educating the Heart,' and in it the Dalai Lama was urging people to teach children compassion. Most of the articles spoke of peace, tolerance, health, and mindfulness. I couldn't disagree with any of the philosophies. I just didn't see that many people around me who shared them.

As soon as I finished eating, I decided to spend the last fifteen minutes of my lunch period out in the garden. To my surprise, the same four students were gathered there. This time, rather than the uncomfortable no-eye-contact pretense, they extended a formal introduction to me. I met James, Rhonda, Lee, and Erica.

Rhonda, who had a fantastic British accent, and James were juniors, and it was obvious they were a couple by the way they held hands and exchanged affections. Lee and Erica were sophomores and belonged to the horticulture club. They were responsible for the installation of the fountain and the rare orchids displayed in the garden.

I complimented them profusely on their work, explaining how precious the space had become to me after only two days. They smiled at each other as if in acknowledgment of some 'I told you so' secret, which made me feel closer to them than not. And as the period came to a close, I realized I felt more comfortable with them than any friends I'd known. It wasn't anything specific they said or did. It wasn't even how they treated me, though they were very polite and friendly. It was merely a feeling that came over me of peace, respect, and security. I felt I was safe with them, and I hoped they felt the same toward me.

September 11

As the first week of school came to a close, I found serenity in my routine. My time, especially with my new 'garden friends,' was blossoming beautifully. James, I learned, was in the photography club. His work had already won some local awards, and apparently he was also good at capitalizing on the local interest groups. Rhonda was a music fanatic. She didn't play any instruments, but she claimed to know the words to over two thousand songs.

Lee and Erica extended an invitation for me to be a guest at the horticulture club, where plans were being made to build a greenhouse on-site for growing organic foods to be served in the school cafeteria. "Mother Earth knows how much we need a good veggie stew over more pepperoni pizza, am I right?" Lee asked. Everyone high-fived him in agreement — including me.

As I walked home on the last day of my first week at Trinity, I thought back to Lee's comment about 'Mother Earth.' There was an article in *Shambhala Sun* I thought might interest him, and I made a mental note to bring the magazine to lunch on Monday. But more importantly, I thought about the possibility that I had found some friends who shared some of the beliefs I had — even if I had yet to find my own way to express them.

September 12

As the weekend started, I found that homework was grueling. Not in the intellectual sense, but rather because it seemed a tedious interference to what I wanted to be learning. I tossed the textbook aside and decided to check in on Aunt Maggie's Facebook page to see how her El Camino walk was going. I was surprised and happy to see she had posted some photos, considering she was so tech-illiterate, she had to ask me to set up her page for her.

Her most recent post was from three days ago. It was the sunset in the background and a quote by T.S. Eliot: "*We shall not cease from exploration, and the end of all our exploring will be to arrive where we started and know the place for the first time.*" I felt a surge of peace run through me as I read it and smiled at the thought of her adventurous, courageous spirit. I wanted more than anything to be like her, to live without the fears most people had, and seek new experiences and growth in whatever form they came.

This was now more than just an idea I had — it was a declaration I felt I was making to the universe about my life as I wished it to be. I sat quietly, feeling my intentions settle into my soul.

"Want to take a little field trip?" My mom stood with her arms crossed at my bedroom doorway, staring expectantly.

"Uh … sure. I guess. Where are we going?"

"There's an antique flea market in town this weekend down at the Old Orchard farmhouse. I want to see if they have an armoire for the guest room."

Two things simultaneously crossed my mind. One, that she never cared about the guest room before Aunt Maggie's visit, which meant that maybe she was softening to the idea of her coming more frequently. And two, that I detested antique stores and flea markets. Weighing the pros and cons, I said, "Great! Let me throw on some jeans, and I'll be right out."

As we pulled onto the Old Orchard property, I was surprised at how many stalls had been erected for the weekend sale. The farm, which had once been a full-fledged working farm, had been transformed into an apple grove and pumpkin patch about ten years ago. I spent most of my childhood years here at Halloween, picking pumpkins and getting rides on ponies too old and tired to be carrying the weight of most of the spoiled brats raised on McDonald's burgers and fries. I felt a pang in my side as I remembered watching them digging their little Reeboks into the ponies like jockeys in the Kentucky Derby.

I shook off the memory and got out of the car to catch up with my mom, who was already making a beeline for the first row of vendors. As she walked past each stall, glancing briefly at the items on display, I stood back and quietly trailed behind her, not quite sure whether she really wanted my input.

After about twenty minutes, she entered a double-sized stall with numerous pieces of large and small furniture. I saw her ask the owner about one of the armoires, and by the look on her face, I could see she was not happy with the price. Still, she called me over to have a look.

As I stepped into the tented area, I felt a bit claustrophobic. Despite it being an open-air stall, the smell of the mildewed wood and decay was overwhelming. Though the workmanship was impressive, the musty quality of the pieces made me feel like I was in a dark, damp tomb.

She opened the two large doors to reveal a split interior, half with a rack for hanging and the other with simple shelving space. She beckoned me forward to take a closer look. Despite my burning nostrils, I stepped in beside her and opened one of the drawers at the bottom of the armoire. The owner, sensing he had a sale on his hands, began regaling us with the history of this antique, built by Quakers in the early 1900s. His words became noise in my ears as I stared into the open drawer and envisioned a tiny Quaker baby wrapped in its mother's shawl, cold and sick with smallpox.

A wave of nausea suddenly came over me, and before I could remove my hands from the drawer, I was puking into the hundred-year-old, $2,000 armoire. After profusely apologizing to the man, who was screaming obscenities at us, my mom hauled me back to the car and loaded me into my seat. Rather than offer me some water or a tissue, she said, "I don't know what's come over you lately, Jenny."

Nor had I. But at this moment, I didn't have it in me to talk. All I cared about was getting away from this place and back to some fresh air that didn't smell like dead Quaker babies.

The ride home was strained. I kept waiting for her to ask if I was feeling better, and she kept waiting for me to explain what happened. Neither of our expectations would be met that day.

When we arrived home, far earlier than my father anticipated, my mother related the events to him while I sought refuge in my room with my iPad. Although I knew Aunt Maggie would probably not be picking up her emails on the El Camino, I wrote her anyway.

Dear Aunt Maggie. I hope you are safe and well on your El Camino adventure. I wish I was with you. I wish I was any place but where I am. Why do I feel like such an alien in my own life?

I'm not comfortable with my classmates at school except for a few kids I hang out with in the garden at lunch. I can't even visit an antique fair with my mom without puking into some vintage armoire. My studies don't interest me. I feel there's no point or purpose to my life. I wonder sometimes how I keep getting out of bed in the morning — then realize it's only the sheer guilt I would feel for my parents' remorse if I didn't get out of bed ... if I didn't wake up from some overdose of my mom's sleeping pills or a razor to my wrists. Sorry. Too many negative thoughts — that I would never act upon. But still ... I felt so content when you were here. And now I feel so lost. Come back soon. Love, Jenny.

September 14

Monday morning couldn't have come quickly enough. With all my homework reluctantly done, I started my second week of high school with only mild trepidation. The hope of building on my new friendships motivated me. Plus, I had to admit, I thought I might work up the courage to pass by Nathan at lunch.

As it turned out, when the fifth period bell rang, I realized I had left my lunch on the counter at home and would have to face 'the pit' if I expected any nourishment to carry me though the day. Standing at the top of the cafeteria stairs, I took in a big breath and held it as I made my way swiftly to the salad bar. Like a Navy Seal diver in training, I counted the seconds I could go without having to come up for air. Ten, eleven, twelve — grab the plastic box and heave in a pile of greens. Twenty, twenty-one, twenty-two — plop in some cherry tomatoes and cucumbers. Thirty, thirty-one, thirty-two — peppers, bean sprouts, radishes, balsamic dressing. By fifty, I was starting to feel woozy and took a deep breath into the sleeve of my wool sweater.

"Are you okay?" a low, familiar voice said behind me. I turned to face the mesmerizing, somber blue eyes and inviting smile of Nathan. Inhaling deeply, I felt woozier than before.

"Uh…yeah," I stammered. "Just thought I was going to sneeze. Didn't want to spread any germs on the salad bar." I sounded casually convincing, though my pulse was beating an unsteady samba.

"I saw you here the first day. I tried to get your attention, but I guess you didn't hear me. I haven't seen you around since. Do you not eat? Or do you just avoid eating here?"

"I avoid eating here," I replied honestly. "Crowds really aren't my thing."

"Mine either," he said with a congenial smile. "But the friends I hang out with make it tolerable. You should join us."

I stood speechless, holding my plastic salad box with my feet frozen in place. The kids in line, insensitive to the miracle that was happening to me, began moaning about moving it along. Nathan gestured toward the checkout counter, and I clumsily trotted over to pay for my lunch.

"So what do you say? Do you want to take a chance on crowd consumption?"

My knees were going weak. Of course I wanted to spend the next fifty minutes in the blissful company of this gorgeous creature, but my mind kept sending red alerts: *Can't breathe! Need air! Too crowded! Evacuate! Evacuate!*

"Maybe some other time," I finally said. "I'm meeting some friends and…" and I couldn't think of what else to say.

Letting me graciously off the hook, he replied, "Okay. I'll see you around," and walked away.

As I stared at his perfect form making its way through the throng of students, I realized I had no place to go with my plastic salad lunch. It was too awkward to sneak it out of there and into the library, and the garden didn't allow any food or beverage. I had a choice: either endure the chaos of a thousand buzzing houseflies to spend time with my blue-eyed angel or retreat to one of the bathroom stalls like a typical teen with an eating disorder.

Don't be afraid! I said to my panicked self.

Taking a shallow breath, I followed the path that Nathan took and promised myself just fifteen minutes to snarf down my lunch and then be safely off to the refuge of the garden.

"I changed my mind," I said hesitantly as I stood behind him at his table. "Is it still okay if I join you?"

Nathan turned, flashed a hundred-watt smile, and said, "Yeah. Of course. Great. Most of my friends seem to be MIA now, but you can meet them some other time."

It was weird having most of the table to ourselves. As we ate, it was as if we were the only two with audible voices set against a soundtrack of background murmurs and rumbles.

"So how are you adjusting to Trinity? No more fainting in the hallways, I presume?" he said with a soft chuckle that expressed more affection than sarcasm.

"No." I felt myself blush. "Things have been pretty great, actually. I met some cool friends. They're older than me, but we have a lot in common. We meet out at the garden every lunch. In fact, I'm meant to be there shortly, so I probably shouldn't stay long." I thought my explanation of an early departure was better than him discovering in fifteen more minutes that I was an absolute social freak who, being in such close proximity to his hypnotic gaze and vanilla-honey scent, would be rendered an inarticulate buffoon with salad greens stuck between her teeth and a napkin stuck to the sole of her shoe.

A clean and early exit was definitely the way to go. So after gulping down my lunch, I gave him a smile, and with a final deep inhalation of his aroma, I fled the pit and made my way to the garden.

As expected, James, Rhonda, Lee, and Erica were convened in the garden, debating whether or not global warming was an actual threat or just a scare tactic devised for political and financial gain.

Sensing I did not want to contribute to the discussion, they smiled and nodded at me, and the debate continued. After about ten minutes, the door behind me swung open, and as I turned to see who was invading our space, my stomach flipped like a Cirque du Soleil performer. It was him. Nathan. Beaming that smile and then greeting each of my friends with a sort of palm-to-palm touch. I felt a pang of foolishness thinking that he had come to look for me.

James turned to me, saying, "Jenny, this is our friend and fearless leader, Nathan. Nathan, this is…"

"Jenny," Nathan interjected. "We've already met a couple of times. Good to see you again so soon."

Completely dumbfounded, I could do no more than give a half-smile and nod.

"So what are you discussing today?" Nathan asked the group.

"The truths and fallacies of global warning," Lee replied.

"Ah," Nathan nodded, "an oldie but a goodie."

The discussion picked up where it had left off, and what became increasingly obvious was Erica's position about how the Earth *felt* in the process of climate change. It was as if she were speaking on the planet's behalf, and though it sounded strange, it also made perfect sense.

As the conversation began to lull, I wondered what James had meant when he called Nathan 'our fearless leader.' I cleared my throat, intending to ask that very question, when Nathan stood up and said, "So we're on for seven o'clock Friday night at my house. Jenny, would you like to come?"

I caught James and Rhonda exchanging mischievous smiles and wondered what this invitation meant. Was it a social invitation like a date? Or maybe they were all working on a project together? Either way, an invite from Prince Charming could not be refused. "I'm in!" I blurted out with too much enthusiasm. Before they could see my face flush, the bell rang and our party broke off to resume the rest of the day's mundane schedule.

September 17

It seemed that each day took an entire week to pass. It rained incessantly on Tuesday and Wednesday, making it impossible to spend any time in the garden at lunch. I thought I might see the gang having lunch with Nathan in the pit, but looking through the glassed wall as I headed to the library, I didn't see anyone I recognized at Nathan's table — not even Nathan himself.

My mind jumped to the notion that maybe these were all just imaginary friends I had conjured up to overcome my social insecurities. I pushed the thought away with a few deep breaths, remembering how Aunt Maggie told me to be mindful of my thoughts.

Slipping into my favorite cubicle in the back of the library, I got ahead on a few chapters for my social studies class while munching on chunks of apples and carrot sticks. Each bite I took thundered through the open space of the library like a giant stomping on bags of potato chips. I made a mental note to bring quieter fruits and veggies from now on.

Noticing it was nearly time for the bell, I tucked my lunch bag away and closed my book. As I did, a wave of sadness swept over me, taking me by such surprise, I had to lay my head on the desk and close my eyes. Trying to breathe deeply, I pictured my Aunt Maggie holding my hand and walking together on the El Camino trail. I'd read about this visualization technique in the *Shambhala Sun* magazine and had been using it any time I felt anxious, but it didn't seem to be working very well today. I forced myself to get up and head to class as the bell blared its warning. Passing by the front desk, I faked a smile to the two women who ran the library. Although they smiled back, I noticed the older woman, Mrs. Lockhart, looked as if she'd been crying, and as I passed some kids at a table near the exit, I heard one of them remark that Mrs. Lockhart's husband had just died.

I tried for the rest of the day to shake off my gloomy feeling and focus on my classes, but my mind kept darting around to Nathan, paper cuts, Aunt Maggie, the garden, Mrs. Lockhart, the antique armoire, Dr. Foster, and round again. As I walked home in the misting rain with my mind feeling like mush and my body limp and strained, I wondered if my fruits or veggies weren't contaminated with salmonella. It would certainly explain how awful I felt.

Dragging myself upstairs at home, I ran a hot bath and made a cup of chamomile green tea. Breathing in the essence of the tea and the steam rising from the hot, lavender-scented water, I began to feel like myself again. *Moment by moment, breath by breath. Thank goodness it isn't salmonella.*

Slipping into the tub, I willed my mind and my muscles to let go of all the worries and stress of the day, but as I closed my eyes, a question popped into my head: *What worries and stress do I really have? And why do they seem to hit me out of the blue when I'm not in a stressful situation?* If I'd fainted because someone pulled a knife on me, I could understand. If I got sick on a ride at a carnival instead of an antique fair, I could understand. If I was overcome with sadness while attending a funeral, I could understand. But these feelings and reactions I was having to random, benign situations, felt beyond my control, and this I could not understand.

When I opened my eyes, I realized I must have dozed off, because the water had gone completely cold and I could hear my mom's voice calling for me from downstairs in the kitchen.

"Jen," she hollered, "someone is on the phone for you."

"I'm in the bath," I hollered back, climbing out of the tub and wrapping myself in a towel. A knock on the door startled me, and

I stubbed my toe on the vanity. "What?" I snipped sourly, opening the door a crack.

"I thought it might be important," she said, shoving the phone through to me before turning away.

"Thanks, Mom," I called after her in a gentler voice, hating when I acted like such a brat. "Hello."

"Well, hello," a beautiful voice greeted me. "I hope I'm not calling at a bad time."

"Nathan? Is … is that you?"

"Well, I was going to say it was Ryan Seacrest, asking why you didn't audition this year for *American Idol*, but since you recognized my voice…"

"Ha, ha. You wouldn't be asking if you heard me sing."

"I doubt that," he replied. "In fact, I have a feeling you'd be in the top ten."

I looked in the mirror and watched my face turn bright red. Why was he calling, and how did he even get my home number?

"I hope you don't mind, but I got your number from 411, and I'm just calling to firm up our plans for tomorrow night. You're still coming, I hope?"

"Yeah. Yes. Sure. I'm definitely coming, but…" I took a deep breath, unsure of how to ask exactly what I was being invited to.

"It's just a casual get-together with some friends from school. James, Rhonda, Lee, and Erica will be there, along with one or two others."

"That sounds great," I said with a sigh of relief. "Should I bring anything?"

"Just your beautiful smile and your warm friendship."

Although it would have been a totally corny thing coming from anyone else, it made me happy when he said it. Maybe it wasn't going to turn out to be a date after all. Maybe it really was a casual get-together with his friends, and he was being polite by inviting me. But it didn't matter. For the first time in years, with the exception of Aunt Maggie, I felt like I was truly welcome.

After taking down Nathan's address with an eyeliner pencil on the bathroom mirror, I hung up and stood quietly wrapped in a wet towel and warm feelings.

September 18

Another rainy day on Friday meant that I didn't get to see my garden friends to ask them any of the questions I had tumbling around my brain about what to expect that night. I had thought about going to the pit to see Nathan, but I didn't want any chance of spoiling the flirtatious mood from our phone call yesterday. I was ready to play it cool if I showed up at his house and was introduced to his girlfriend, but I was also ready to accept that his gallant gestures and flirtations might actually be how he felt about me. Either way, it was only a matter of hours until I knew for sure.

Arriving at Nathan's house at a quarter after seven, I said goodbye to my dad and promised I'd call him to pick me up by eleven. While my parents seemed pleased that I was making new friends, they were equally skeptical, considering my track record with friendships.

Nathan answered the door when I rang and gave me a hug, as if we'd greeted each other this way for years. He took my jacket and then led me downstairs to a rustic basement, complete with cedar-planked walls and Indian tapestries. Everyone stopped their conversations to welcome me and introduce me to some other friends. Faith got up to give me a warm hug while Adam nodded from his chair.

I sat down on the small, unoccupied love seat and was surprised when Nathan squished in beside me. He offered me a drink from the array of beverages on the center table: organic apple juice, Perrier, Italian lemonade, and a pot of green tea. I opted for a mug of the tea, and he smiled at me while pouring it and clinked his own mug to mine.

He then addressed the group. "Thanks, everyone, for coming to another Friday night meeting. I'll be going through a few more formalities than usual for the sake of our newest member, Jenny."

Member? Did he just say 'member'? I thought this was a casual gathering for some friends. The term 'member' or 'meeting' had never come up. My mind began imagining these kids as members of the KKK or Church of Scientology. No wonder they called Nathan their 'fearless leader.' And no wonder he was being so nice to me. He was looking for new recruits!

Sensing my reaction to his opening remarks, he began cautiously with an explanation of the meeting. "Every month, we gather here to share our knowledge and experiences of our empath skills; that is, the unique sensitivity to feeling the positive and negative vibrations of all matter around us, including people, objects, or other living beings."

He looked at me for a response, but I had none to offer. I had hardly heard a word he said because I was so distracted waiting for them to don their pointy white hats. What was that term he used? Empath? Did he say something about feeling vibrations of objects? Everything around me suddenly seemed very surreal, and I had an urge to fake a headache, grab my things, and leave, but the close proximity to Nathan and his piercing eyes kept me glued to my seat.

"The usual format," he continued, "is to allow a five- to ten-minute update for each person on whatever issues they have encountered since our last meeting and then open the floor to discussion or exercises. It is imperative that I remind everyone of the trust of confidentiality that exists in this room. Nothing spoken or done here is shared with any individual under any circumstances. All those who agree, say 'agreed.'" I nodded and said 'agreed' along with them but still wasn't sure what I was agreeing to.

Turning to me, Nathan said, "Jenny, since this is your first meeting," (*and maybe my last*, I thought), "you can observe tonight, and if you want to stay after, I'd be happy to answer any questions you have."

I nodded, feeling like I'd been shot with a tranquillizer dart. But as surreal as this all felt, I also had a hunch it might have some relevance, considering the recent events in my life. His description of the sensitivity to people, objects, and living creatures made me flash back to the fainting, puking, and panic attacks I'd been experiencing but had no explanation for. Could it be I have these empathic skills he was talking about? I decided to stop jumping to conclusions and to sit back and listen. Then I would make a decision about whether or not these people were nut-jobs. But first, I had to inhale some of Nathan's intoxicating aroma...

Erica was the first to speak. Looking at me directly, she said, "All of us here are what are called emotional empaths, but I am also a geosentient, meaning that I can feel the effects of what is happening to our Earth. While there is much turmoil overall, such as the depletion of our glaciers, global warming, excessive waste of natural resources, I also feel the positive power of those trying to help heal our planet. There has been a great surge lately in green awareness and the consciousness of Earth's well-being. Although the problem is a global one, the solution is actually a local one, meaning that much of the healing needs to happen within each local community. So my goal now is to try to initiate community projects."

While I sat dumbfounded by Erica's eloquent report, not sure whether I believed her 'geosentient' story or not, everyone else began clapping and high-fiving her. Erica looked at me with sisterly eyes. She held my gaze until it felt like she was giving me a warm hug, and I had to look away as a swell of emotion overcame me.

Lee was the next to speak. "I want to first welcome Jenny to our gathering. I've gotten to know her a bit over the past couple of weeks, and I sense that she will be a great addition to our group." I smiled and nodded a thank-you across the table to him, feeling somewhat hypocritical and touched at the same time.

He continued, "As you might have suspected, Jenny, I have a way with all things botanical. In empath terms, it's called 'flora,' but I prefer 'green guy' instead. This week, I've been helping out at some local greenhouses that are trying to reduce their use of pesticides, especially in the tomato and vegetable plants being sold to the general public. There are many alternative products and growing practices, and it's my hope I can demonstrate that going organic is not only good for people, but good for their bottom line as well."

Again, the group applauded at the end of the report, this time me included.

Faith told her story of coming from a long line of gifted psychometric/medium empaths. She could only sense the spirit of the deceased on their belongings, but she was hoping that in time she would be able to see and hear the spirits directly, as her mother and grandmother could. I immediately thought back to the old armoire that made me sick to my stomach and how the image of that dead baby still sometimes flashed in my mind.

So far, Faith had not seen a way to employ her gift to serve society, besides perhaps opening up a shop somewhere to give psychic readings. Everyone laughed in unison and joked about various names for her shop like "Faith & the Hereafter."

When Adam began to speak, I sensed the mood changing. The shift was slight but perceptible. As with the others, Adam explained for my benefit that he was a telepathic empath, able to read a person's unexpressed thoughts. As he said this, he stared into my eyes, and though I thought he might have intended it to be flirtatious, it came across as threatening — as if he were warning me that any ill intentions I had would not be hidden from him.

Nathan interjected before Adam could continue, asking if anyone wanted a fill up of their teas or drinks. After a ten-minute break, with our mugs and glasses full, Rhonda spoke next.

"As Lee expressed earlier, I also want to welcome Jenny into our group. I've grown to like you so much in the short time I've known you, and I hope we go on to be great friends. My empath skills are somewhat daunting — to me and anyone who has come to know about them," she said in an almost apologetic tone. "I am a precognitive empath."

Everyone in the room simultaneously "Oooo-ed" and laughed until Rhonda, laughing herself, finally said, "Shut up, you neophytes! I'm trying to explain this to Jenny." She smiled at me across the table and continued. "My skill, if that's what one would call it, involves the ability to feel or sense something before it actually happens. It might be as benign as the phone ringing or as dramatic as a fire or accident. I only awoke to my ability a year ago, and so I have much to learn and cope with now. The most difficult part so far is determining whether my 'visions' are real or imaginary and what to do about them, if anything."

As if feeling guilty for their earlier outburst, everyone in the circle looked at Rhonda with a mix of awe and compassion. As for me, I didn't know what to make of her. On one hand, some of what the others had said made sense to me. I'd seen enough episodes of Cesar Millan, the dog whisperer, to believe that there were some people who were extra-sensitive to the feelings and behaviors of animals, and I suppose if I stretched that belief out a bit, a similar sensitivity to plants and other living creatures would not be too far-fetched. As for a medium, although I had never engaged in a reading myself, I had heard enough stories from people who were non-believers and then had an experience that changed their minds completely. But to believe a teenager could tell the future was more than my mind was willing or able to accept right now. It's not that I believed it was impossible; I just didn't have any experience to commit one way or another.

When James began to talk, I noticed that Rhonda reached for his hand as if to comfort him. He squeezed it and entwined his fingers into hers. "I am," he said with a deep breath, "a healing empath. Like Rhonda, I only awoke to my condition a little over a year ago." He looked off to some place far away for a moment and took another deep breath before continuing.

"What I have learned so far is that I have some ability to adjust the vibrational frequencies of people in such a way that their physical cells or organs are elevated to a higher energy level, and this results in some type of healing. I don't yet know how to control it — I mean, even when I think I have raised a frequency, I have no real way of confirming it."

Rhonda, still holding his hand, began shaking her head, saying, "That's not true. You've been able to manifest healing many times with immediate, visible results."

"But nothing life-threatening," he blurted at her.

Everyone sat respectfully quiet, and it was obvious there was a back story to James's situation that everyone understood but me. After a few moments of silence, Nathan cleared his throat and said, "Thanks everyone for coming and sharing your stories with Jenny. I know we're all still new at this empath stuff, but as I've said before, we're better off helping and learning from each other as we go.

"As you know," he continued, "we normally spend the remainder of our time doing a few exercises, but if nobody minds, I would like to wrap up tonight's meeting early so that I might spend some time with Jenny."

Nobody appeared to object, until Adam cleared his throat, saying, "If you don't mind, I'd like to stay behind, too, and see if I can help answer any of Jenny's questions."

I looked between Adam and Nathan, sensing a high level of testosterone percolating. In a slightly patronizing tone, Nathan replied, "How about if I walk her through the basics, and you can be available to answer any questions she might have about your 'specialty.'"

With a cocky sway of his head, Adam said, "I'm available 24/7," then he gave me a long wink.

Nathan cleared his throat, and everyone immediately raised their heads up, gazing at the ceiling. I wasn't sure why they were doing this, but I automatically did the same. Then seven voices said in unison:

Sever the cords that bind me to all people, places, and things

that do not serve my greater purpose and highest good.

Shield me from all low vibrations and negative energies —

whether they be from this universe or beyond.

Fill my body and soul with radiant, pure light

then grant me the wisdom and courage to share it with all I encounter.

A moment later, everyone was up saying goodbye, most stopping on their way out to wish me well or hug me. When it was finally just Nathan and I left in the room, I suddenly felt self-conscious and asked if I could help clean up while clumsily collecting a handful of mugs and glasses.

"Uh, it's all right, actually," he said with such warmth in his voice I almost lost my grip on the glassware. "I mean, that would be great, but maybe we could just sit and chat for a while first?"

I loved how he posed it as a question, as if I could still decide to clean up now if I wanted. "Sure. Of course," I stammered, putting the items back down on the table. He gestured for me to come sit across from him, and I obliged.

"I imagine you must have a ton of questions, so let's not waste any time. Out with them," he said with a gentle smile.

Of course, I had dozens of questions, but the first one on my mind rolled off my tongue. "Why didn't you talk about your gift like everyone else did? What gift do you have?"

"To answer your first question, I usually do give my own report at the meeting, but thought it was more important to spend the time with you one-on-one. As for your second question, I'm not yet sure of all of my empath skills. I am, most predominantly, an emotional empath, but I also have the ability of manifestation; but that's not really an empathic gift. What else would you like to know?"

He leaned forward as he said this, and the earthy, vanilla smell of him distracted my mouth from forming words. "I, uh, was just, um, wondering exactly what manifestation means exactly."

His smirk made me feel more flattered than foolish, and he steadily replied, "I can sometimes bring about that which I want to have or have happen."

"I don't understand. How do you do that?"

"Well, I don't exactly understand it myself; not the reason for it, anyway. It's based on the law of attraction. As for the mechanics, I simply clear my head of all earthly distractions and focus my entire being on the result I intend to bring forth. It could be something as simple as intending to ace a test or as complex as meeting the girl of my dreams." He looked into my eyes and held my gaze as he said these words, and I immediately diverted mine, though I knew that my face revealed all the emotions I was trying to hide in my eyes.

"It sounds like hocus-pocus." I chuckled, hoping I didn't come across too judgmental. "I don't mean any disrespect, but it's a bit like 'Criss Angel Mind Freak' stuff."

Nodding, he said, "I felt that way, too, for a while. And it makes sense, but that's because you haven't become fully aware yet of the 'real' reality. You're still living by the programmed version of reality based on how you were raised. Yet correct me if I'm wrong, something has changed in you in the last several months — something that's made you question your beliefs about who you are, why you're here, and what you're meant to do. Am I right?"

Of course he was. And though it was not an easy confession to make, although I was worried about how he would judge me and whether I was risking any kind of relationship, I felt compelled to tell him my story. So over the next hour, I revealed to him all that had happened since the time of my 'cutting,' including the other incidents that made me believe I was possibly going crazy.

"Like how we met," he interjected, "on the first day of school when you fainted."

"Yeah," I mumbled, still feeling stupid about the whole incident. "I'm still not sure why that happened."

"I think I know." His words came out hushed, and I had to lean toward him to hear what he was saying. "Approaching the school, you felt relatively calm, sure of where you were going and what you needed to do, but as you became surrounded by the hundreds of new students who didn't know where they were going or what they were doing, your confidence began to diminish. Nothing about you had changed, but because you were absorbing all the excessive emotional energy of the kids around you, it sent you into an emotional overload. And since your brain and your body didn't know what to do with all that extra intake, it went into defensive mode and shut down — the ultimate example of fight-or-flight in action, the result of which was your fainting on the ground amid hundreds of your classmates."

I believed his hypothesis was correct, but I still didn't understand why I had gone through this experience instead of any one of the other hundreds of my new classmates. When I asked him to explain this, he said, "Because they don't have the emotional empath skills you have."

I shook my head. "You call it a skill, but if what you say about me is true, it seems more like a curse or at the very least a condition that needs some sort of treatment." Maybe I was wrong to dismiss Dr. Foster's recommendations so quickly. Drugs might be a solution after all.

"I know it can feel like a curse, Jenny. I've been there myself, and sometimes when I allow myself to get ungrounded…" He paused and shook his head in a way that made his dark hair fall across his eyes and made my stomach flip. "Well, let's just say I can get pretty messed up, too."

Although I had many more questions to ask, I instead pulled away from his magnetic force, saying, "Speaking of messes, maybe we should get back to cleaning this one up." But as I stood up, he took hold of my arm and gently pulled me back to my seat.

"One of the strongest traits of being an emotional empath is that you feel so much of what everyone around you is feeling, you start to deny what you are actually feeling yourself." Before I could respond, he leaned forward, took my face in his hands, and kissed me once softly on my lips, pulling away only enough that I could still feel his breath on my mouth.

You start to deny what you are actually feeling yourself. His words resonated in my head, sending a warm sensation throughout my body, and realizing how rare it was for me to have complete ownership of my feelings, I allowed myself to taste his sweet kiss again.

I don't know how many minutes passed, but when we finally pulled apart, my lips were deliciously sore and my breath was ragged. I could barely bring myself to open my eyes, fearing that if I did, I would realize this had all been only a dream.

The sound of voices coming from somewhere off in the distance brought me out of my reverie. When I opened my eyes, Nathan was standing over me, extending a hand to help me up. "Come meet my parents," he said.

Parents? Holy crap. It didn't even occur to me the entire night to ask where his parents were. But they were obviously here now, so straightening my shirt and running my hands quickly through my hair, I turned to greet Mr. and Mrs. Leeds.

As Nathan politely made the introductions, I noticed the contemporary style of his parents' appearance and felt their down-to-earth nature.

They spoke to Nathan like he was an equal, a man instead of a child. And likewise, Nathan spoke to them with respect and courtesy, sharing the highlights of the night's events, most especially how I was the newest member of the 'Trinity Empath Club.' I wasn't sure whether to be flattered or embarrassed, but his parents responded with a warmth and kindness that I had never experienced with any other adults.

Wishing us a good evening and extending an invitation to me for dinner sometime, they retired upstairs, leaving Nathan and me alone.

"Your parents are so ... un-parentlike," I said.

"Yeah, they're pretty cool. We've been through a lot as a family, and it's made us realize what's important in this world, so we don't really bother anymore with the petty stuff."

I sensed something significant in his tone and asked what had happened in their family.

"My older brother, Daniel, committed suicide when I was twelve."

"Oh, I'm so sorry. I shouldn't have asked," I said, reaching instinctively for his hand.

"It's okay, but it's been hard. He was sixteen. The same age I am now, actually. He'd been troubled for a few years. My parents did what they could." He shrugged. "They got him to the best shrinks and tried every medication the doctors threw at him, but in the end, Daniel decided he didn't want to live with the pain anymore."

I wasn't sure what to say. I could feel a hole opening up in my chest and numbness radiate throughout my limbs. As if someone turned on a faucet, tears began streaming down my face.

"Hey," Nathan said, squeezing my hand, "you need to learn how to not let other people's emotional stuff into your field. You're an empath, remember?"

Wiping my face, I mumbled, "I had no idea until tonight what an empath even was, let alone finding out that I am one. So how do I do that? How do I keep out other people's emotional stuff?"

"I'm glad you asked. First," he said, letting go of my hand and stepping back into the open area of the room, "you need to learn some shielding techniques."

He instructed me to stand across from him and close my eyes. "'The Bubble' is the most basic and sometimes most effective exercise. Keeping your eyes closed, take a few deep breaths and imagine a large translucent bubble in front of you — the kind like you had when you were a kid with the little plastic wand you blew through. Do you have it in your mind?"

I nodded, noticing how his voice had become low and hypnotic.

"Good. Now imagine the bubble moving toward you until you are completely surrounded by it. You are now inside the bubble. Can you feel it?"

A smile spread across my face that I couldn't contain. I felt lighter, more relaxed, and at ease with myself.

"Although you can see everything around you, and you are physically visible to everyone, your energy — your energetic field, that is — is safe and protected in the bubble. This includes your thoughts, which are now completely your own, and your feelings, which are no longer affected by outside influencers. You are only you — all you — inside the bubble. Can you feel it?"

I did. It was like nothing I'd experienced before. It was an instant shift in my physical, mental, and emotional state. With my eyes still closed and a smile still spread across my face, I said, "How does this work? What magic makes this happen?"

"It's not magic," he replied. "Well, that's not entirely true. It's the magic of imagination, which is really just the brain's ability to manifest things in the non-physical world — or sometimes even the physical world when you get really good at it. But that's for another time. Right now, just keep your eyes closed and concentrate on being in your bubble."

"Okay," I said, taking a few more slow and steady breaths.

"Good. Now, no matter what I say, no matter how sad or horrible or emotional it may be, I want you to remain in your bubble-state. Any time you begin to feel a twinge of the emotional energy that I'm exerting, I want you to silently say 'I am safe and at peace in my bubble.' Can you do that?"

I nodded, reciting the words in my mind.

He then took a deep breath and began. "When Daniel was thirteen, he cut his wrist. Not enough to kill him, but it was certainly a loud cry for help. He had never been an outgoing person, but during that first year, he withdrew from the friends he had and stopped participating in sports and school activities. My parents thought it was a reaction to the death of his friend, who drowned in a freak accident. They thought that with some counseling, he would get better. But he didn't. Everything seemed to agitate him. He couldn't stand to be in a room if the TV or radio was on. He was depressed and lost all of his liveliness. It was then he was put on meds. Although the doctors could not agree on bipolar, anxiety disorder, depression, or a combination of them, he was given pretty much every pharmaceutical in the book. That year was probably the hardest on us all because Daniel was just a shell of himself."

He paused for a moment, and though my eyes were closed, I could tell he was looking at me for any signs of emotional change, but as instructed, I kept repeating my mantra. *I am safe and at peace in my bubble.*

"By the third year," he continued in a more serious tone, "Daniel had been in and out of the mental hospital several times. He had other self-harming incidents, too — hitting his head on the wall, cutting, and once he tried to overdose on his meds. I remember it was my twelfth birthday, and when I blew out the candles to make a wish, I wished that I could have my old brother back. The one who played catch with me in the park and taught me how to bunt and steal bases."

Despite the mantra in my head, I could feel my heart begin to ache and my body become tense as if ready for some battle.

"Keep breathing, Jenny," he said softly. "Do you want to stop?"

I shook my head, but only because I wanted him to keep talking. I wanted to know every intimate detail of his life, even if it meant I'd be emotionally wiped out because of it.

He went on, "Later that night, Daniel came to me in my room. He climbed into bed next to me like he used to do when I was really little. He talked to me about sports, school, our parents, and even girls (which he said someday I would worship more than baseball). Then he said, 'Promise me that no matter what, you will do whatever you have to do to stay the happy kid that you are; and that you'll keep bringing that happiness into Mom and Dad's life — no matter what.'

"I didn't know, of course, why he was saying this to me, but I did understand what he meant by it. Because throughout all of Daniel's struggles, my parents never left me behind. They never stopped playing games with me or helping me with my homework or cheering me on at my baseball games. I never felt neglected, even though they had a son who they could have rightfully neglected me for.

"I don't remember him leaving my room that night, but the next morning, my parents found Daniel in the bathtub, his wrists cut wide open, his life gone from his body." Despite my mantra and breathing and my imaginary bubble, I struggled not to open my eyes, take him in my arms, and kiss away all his hurt and grief. I felt for a moment like I was being kept prisoner in this bubble, not allowed to feel the sun or rain or to engage with the outside world that at this moment contained someone I wanted to connect with more than anyone I'd ever known.

I could feel my face scrunching up and the tears begin to infiltrate my eyes. And as much as I wanted to give in to them, I also wanted to show Nathan that I was strong and could stay focused in the exercise.

"Open your eyes, Jenny."

When I finally did, I saw that his own were filled with tears. He opened his arms in a pose of surrender, and although I was unsure what he wanted me to do, if this wasn't perhaps some test or initiation into the Trinity Empath Club, I broke through my precious bubble and wept with him in my arms.

Minutes later, still embracing each other, he whispered to me, "I'm so sorry. I shouldn't have put you through that. But I've been wanting to share that story with someone for so long."

I pulled away, looking into his somber eyes with my own still wet with tears. "It's okay—" I started, but he interrupted me.

"No, it's not okay. It was wrong of me to use this 'training exercise' as a way to unload my crap on you. I'm supposed to be teaching you, not taking advantage of you. It's just that..." He paused and looked way.

"It's just what?" I prompted him.

"It's just that ever since that day when I found you passed out in the school hallway, I felt there was something between us. Like you were an angel sent to help me heal all that was messed up in my life."

An angel? *His* angel? Despite the complete drain on my emotions from the last half hour, I was instantly elated and energized with the belief that he felt the same intensity and connection I felt that day and every day since.

We leaned into each other and exchanged a slow kiss that conveyed years of longing, hurting, and even celebrating life beyond our immediate understanding. It seemed almost as if some future versions of ourselves were coming back to this moment to solidify our bond.

With chills still rushing through my core, I broke away and said, "I have to call my dad. He's expecting me to phone him for a ride home."

"Of course," Nathan said, wiping his wet lips with the back of his hand, his eyes penetrating into mine with such force, I felt dizzy as I stood to retrieve my cell phone from my purse. With trembling hands, I punched the buttons for home and told my dad I was ready to be picked up.

"Jenny," Nathan called as I gathered my things to leave, "I can't accurately explain how I feel ... there is such clarity, and yet I feel so overwhelmed at the same time. You are ... an abundance. That's the best I can do for now. I hope you'll think about everything and let me know what you decide; whether you want to..." he hesitated and looked around as if the words would appear somewhere in the room. "...pursue the club or a relationship with me — or both."

As much as I wanted to answer him with a resounding 'yes' to both questions, I instead asked him another question that had been stuck in the back of my mind.

"You said earlier that you are sixteen. Yet as a junior, shouldn't you be seventeen?"

"Yes," he answered, "but I skipped fifth grade, so that makes me only a year older than you." His tone was intentional, a way of letting me know that I shouldn't consider a two-year gap in our grade-level as a factor in my decision about our relationship (as if it would be!).

When the headlights of my dad's car appeared a couple minutes later, I said goodbye — without another kiss — and walked out of what had been the most intense night of my life ... so far.

September 19

I awoke with a reasonably clear head and decided to investigate this empath thing for myself. My Google search resulted in 356,000 results. Really? How could I have never heard of this before? The first hit was a website that offered an empath quiz. The questions were about things like how being in public places can be overwhelming; feeling others' emotions and taking them on as your own; watching violence, cruelty, or tragedy on TV or in real life is unbearable; knowing when someone isn't telling the truth; picking up physical symptoms of another person; drawn to nature; need for solitude; loves to daydream; moodiness.

Whoever came up with this quiz must have been reading my journals. It was almost spooky how bang-on the list was to me.

Despite there being many more resources of information, I felt it was too much, too soon to dive into them and instead closed my computer to meditate on the other issue at hand.

I wondered if Nathan's 'proposal' wasn't just a heat-of-the-moment thing. Maybe he just wanted someone to worship him for a while — which I was getting fairly good at, albeit in my own thoughts. Before I allowed myself to get too caught up in predicting his wants, I decided I had better take a serious look at the offer on the table. The Trinity Empath Club consisted of the only friends I had so far at Trinity, not to mention that we had so much in common, and I was learning a great deal from them about myself already. I wouldn't want to do anything that jeopardized that — like dating their fearless leader. As for Nathan, I did want to have a relationship with him, but was I cut out for it? I spent the next several hours mulling it over, and by the time I turned out the lights, I felt I had my answer.

September 20

On Sunday morning, as I pulled on my hoodie to take a walk down to the market for some organic juice and muffins, I was startled to find Nathan standing at the foot of my driveway, looking a bit lost and anxious.

"I know you've made up your mind," he said, somewhat out of breath, "so I just wondered what you've decided."

The way he bit his lip; the way his dimple appeared and disappeared from his cheek when he was caught in a nervous smile; the way his eyes peeked out from under his dark hair — all of him called to me, and I didn't resist in answering. "How do you know I've made a decision?" I said, hooking my arm through his, obliging him to walk with me down the street to the market.

"Because I'm clairsentient, which is an extremely heightened level of empath." Noticing my uncertain expression, he said, "I can read people's vibrations and their energies, and I've been tuning into you, hoping I could tell when you made your decision." He turned to me, and a look of surprise came across his face, as if he hadn't intended for all that to come spilling out.

"I'm sorry," he said, holding up his hand in defense. "I didn't mean to invade your space or make you feel like I was spying on you — you know, emotionally. It's just that…"

"It's just that you've been spying on me emotionally," I jeered, realizing I was a bit more put off than I thought I'd be.

"Yes. Yes. Okay. I was, and I'm sorry. Truly, I am."

"Just promise it won't happen again," I said.

"I can't do that. As much as I'd like to be able to." He face was a mixture of defeat and shame.

"And why not?" I had stopped walking now, wondering if my Prince Charming wasn't actually some kind of psychic stalker. I never did find out how he knew my name on that first day of school. Could it be that he and his whole group of friends were really just anti-social freaks looking to increase the size of their cult-like following? The moment that thought popped in my head, I realized how 'pot-kettle' it was. *I* am an anti-social freak, after all! Just as my head came the full 360 on that inane string of thoughts, I realized that Nathan had been talking the whole time.

"Wait. Whoa. Nathan, stop. You have to start again. I wasn't listening to a word you said."

"Thanks for being so honest … I think. I was explaining how I can't promise not to 'spy' on you because I don't always know whose vibrations I'm picking up. Only when I 'scan' my space — or my social network, as I call it — can I get a better idea of where or who the energy is coming from."

"But a minute ago, you said that you were 'tuning into me,' and now it sounds like you're saying that you don't know if it's me or not. Which is it?"

"I know it's confusing — or rather, convoluted — but what I'm trying to explain, obviously less effectively than I would like, is that with clairsentient skills, it takes a lot of practice, patience, and awareness to be able to tell whose energy or vibrations you are picking up. The first day I met you, however, when I found you passed out in the hallway at school…" He reached for my hand and squeezed it lightly. "Jenny, the reason I came running to your aid the way I did was because I felt an immensely strong vibrational pull to you. When you were in distress, it was like all of my empathic alarms went off. And your energy, your frequency, somehow left a vibrational mark on me that is, as best as I can describe, like a phone number or a GPS coordinate. Ever since then, it seems that whenever I want to know how you are, I simply 'dial up' your number.

"But I want to be clear," he continued, "that nothing like this has ever happened to me before. Maybe it has with others, but not to me." He was searching my face for some reaction to what he'd said.

"If you're such a skilled empath," I finally said, "how come you can't tell what I'm feeling now?" He moved in slowly, bending his head to kiss me, but I quickly pulled away, blurting out, "I've decided we should just be friends."

Nathan stepped back, nodding. I could tell he was disappointed, but he said, "I think that's a good decision. It's the right thing to do. At the very least, it might help me see this whole vibrational connection to you more clearly."

"About that," I said. "I wonder why I don't feel the same energy boost around you. Don't get me wrong," I quickly added. "It's not that I don't have feelings for you, but they aren't the same as the other times I described to you, like the first day of school or the antiques fair."

"I don't know," was his simple reply. "But there is a lot to learn about being an empath. I mean, no one's published any studies yet, at least not ones that are identified or classified as empathic research. All we can do is to keep searching for answers on our own or find others who are willing to share."

Walking again side by side, I felt that same security and comfort with Nathan, as if we had been good friends from long ago. It was the same feeling I had when I was with Aunt Maggie. It was the way I thought all people should feel with their fellow human beings — even when the relationship didn't last very long.

Looking up at the sky, I saw a bank of clouds rolling by as fast as I'd ever seen, like they were being played back on high-speed time-lapse video. "Look!" I pointed up. "Don't they remind you of an ocean's tide rolling in and out of the sky?"

"What? You mean the clouds? Yeah, they really do look like that." He walked a few steps more, staring at the sky. "I probably don't take the time to look up as much as I should. But every time you look, it's entirely new, isn't it?"

We walked in silence for a few minutes. "What's funny to me, Nathan, is that everything you've told me about being an empath and energy doesn't feel like it's new. It feels more like something I just … forgot."

"I know, right? But that's part of the awakening process."

"Awakening? Awakening to what exactly?"

"Have you ever heard of Dr. Wayne Dyer?" he asked.

"The name sounds familiar. Could it be I read about him in a spiritual magazine, or was it something on TV I saw recently?"

"Most likely both," he nodded. "Dr. Dyer is — was — one of the most recognized spiritual minds of this time. He died not long ago. One of his most famous teachings — and there are many — is that we are spiritual beings having a human experience; not the other way around. And the 'awakening' is our realization of that truth.

"We are divine beings, Jenny. All connected to each other in ways we are only beginning to understand. One of those ways is by our energy, our vibrational attraction. You are awakening to that truth by your empathic abilities."

"But if we're all connected, then shouldn't everyone be an empath, at least to some extent?"

"That's exactly what I wondered! My belief is yes, to some extent, everyone has some empathic traits. But it's possible those traits aren't strong enough to present themselves in the kind of dramatic episodes you've experienced. It's also possible that there are some who understand instinctively how to control their gift, or there may be many empaths just like us who simply have not yet started the awakening process."

"When did you start?"

His face immediately turned sad, as if he had been jolted back to a painful memory. "I knew something was happening to me during the last year of Daniel's life. But with everything my parents were dealing with, I didn't dare reveal that I was experiencing some of the same symptoms he had that first year he was troubled."

"That must have been agony for you. How did you cope? How were you able to avoid going down that same path?"

"I was lucky to have found a mentor of sorts. He made me understand that the emotional swings I was experiencing were mostly coming from Daniel — that I was empathizing with him to an extreme level, because we were brothers, he said. And he tried to also explain that Daniel was experiencing the same thing, only on a more universal scale. He said that, in a manner of speaking, the world was killing him."

"You were only twelve," I said, bewildered by Nathan's bravery at such a young age. "How did that make you feel?"

He shrugged and sighed wistfully. "I felt like I had just remembered something I had forgotten … since the beginning of time. In a way, it comforted me. I stopped believing I was going insane. But in another way, it terrified me because I felt I had absolutely no control over my own emotions — and if that was what was driving my brother to the edge, I wondered how far behind him I would be. Either way, my awakening seemed like a nightmare."

"But this mentor, surely he could have done something to help your brother."

He shook his head, and the sadness in his eyes gave me a lump in my throat. "The counseling he did with Daniel helped somewhat, but it was too little, too late. Daniel was in too deep. He stopped fighting for himself long before Richard was involved."

"But that doesn't seem right. Why couldn't somebody have done something for him?" My voice was getting loud, and I began feeling panic spread in my chest. I couldn't control it as the flood of tears started spilling down my face, but I quickly realized that this was an empathic reaction. Though the tears still came, I started stomping my feet up and down the sidewalk, shouting, "These are not my feelings. This isn't my energy. I am safe and at peace in my bubble…" But then the hyperventilating began.

"I'm so sorry. I did it again, didn't I?" Nathan bellowed through my sobs.

I hated him seeing me like this. Anyone passing by would have thought he'd just told me my parents had died in a freak accident and I had to go live in an orphanage in Siberia. My words had become broken syllables of nonsense, and the snot running out of my nose had now reached my chin. "Make it stop," was all I could get out between sobs.

Stepping closer to me, he compassionately but firmly said, "You can make it stop. Separate yourself from the emotions. Put yourself inside your bubble. See the separation. My emotions are inside *my* bubble. I own them. They are not yours. Now give them back to me."

Through several deep breaths, I felt some relief as I imagined tossing back the pile of feelings to Nathan — from my bubble to his, like we were playing hot potato in the schoolyard. When I'd finally calmed down, I searched my pockets for tissues, and, making do with a couple old napkins, blew my nose and cleaned up my face as best I could.

"Why does it hit me so hard and so fast?"

"I think it's because you're ungrounded," Nathan replied matter-of-factly. "Do you know anything about the chakras?"

"I know there are seven and that they are the spiritual centers in the human body. Other than that, I'm clueless. I've only just recently started reading about them in the *Shambhala Sun* magazine."

"That's great. Definitely keep reading as much as you can. What I'll add now is that the chakras run along the spine, from the base up through the crown of the head. Each of the seven contains certain parts of our body, as well as the emotional and spiritual states of being. The energy that is carried through the chakras is called Prana. It's the life force that keeps us healthy. Keeping the energy flowing and balanced in your chakras is key to good health — especially for an empath who can get thrown off balance by the energy of others all the time."

"How do you know so much about this stuff?"

"Mostly through Richard, but I do some reading on my own, too, and — I'm a bit embarrassed to say — I take workshops sometimes. So are you ready for some grounding?"

"Are we going to ground ourselves right here in the middle of the street?" I imagined that this exercise would end up with the neighbors calling the cops on us for inappropriate behavior, and my parents would have to come bail me out of jail. If it ended in that, this grounding exercise would mean I was grounded for life.

I starting chuckling at my own ridiculousness, which prompted Nathan to ask, "Anything you'd like to share?"

"No, really … just my own silly head filled with silly thoughts. So tell me about grounding. How do we do this?"

"Well, first, doing grounding exercises outside in nature is very beneficial." He took my hands and walked me onto the grass next to a large oak tree. "Look at this tree. Look up at the branches and down the trunk, and imagine the roots splaying out deep into the earth. Now stand up straight and close your eyes. Picture the tree. Picture yourself as the tree. Your arms are the branches reaching high up in the air, and your body is the trunk standing strong and tall. Inhale the power and energy of the universe. Inhale it into your crown chakra and feel the energy flowing down through your third eye at the center of your forehead, down the throat chakra, then your heart center, down the third chakra, and finally your first chakra. Exhale the negative energy and inhale the positive energy. Do that again. Now imagine all that energy running down into the ground, forming roots of strength, vitality, and balance. You have connected yourself to the earth. You are grounded in its power. Feel it surge through you. Now open your eyes."

The whole process took about five minutes, and when he asked how I felt, I replied, "I little light-headed from all the deep inhalations, but otherwise it was very powerful. In fact, I feel so good, I wonder how I would have coped if I hadn't learned about being an empath. Thanks so much for showing me that exercise. And for not getting me arrested."

Nathan began laughing, quickly connecting the dots to my earlier silliness. "You should be doing that exercise every day, and sometimes more than once a day, if you're feeling 'off.'" Now he took me by the arm, saying, "Let's get you to the market, unless you think someone might be there reliving their mournful childhood, in which case I will whisk you away to safety at once."

"I don't need any saving," I said in my best supergirl voice. "I'm grounded, and I've got my bubble. See, I'm learning."

As we approached the market stalls, I scouted for some fresh herbs and picked out a couple organic pumpkin muffins and a java-juice from my favorite vendor. Nathan had disappeared around the corner. I gave a cursory sweep of the market then stood on my tip-toes, trying to see over the tops of the stalls. Finally, at the far end of the market, I spotted him at the flower stand. He looked as cool and charming as he had the day he walked me to the nurse's office — and every day since. I could see him negotiating with the young woman at the stand. Keeping him in view, I began snaking my way through the crowd until I was only two stalls away. As he spoke, his eyes lit up, and a smile suddenly burst across his face, showing off the perfect dimple in his left cheek. When he raised his eyes, looking in my direction, I ducked behind a wall of homemade maple syrups and organic cough remedies. Peeking out a minute later, I saw that he was gone.

"Caught you spying on me," Nathan whispered from behind.

When I turned around, I was greeted with a face full of autumn flowers.

"You bought flowers? For me?" I said in surprise, though what else did I think he'd been doing at a florist stand?

"Actually, no. They're for my other girlfriend. I just thought I'd ask your opinion before I buy them for her."

"Girlfriend? I thought we were just going to be friends for a while?" Although I didn't want to hurt his feelings, I wanted him to respect my wishes. Yet I admitted to myself that I equally wanted him to be my full-time, go-to-dances, exchange-gifts-at-holidays, make-out-every-chance-we-could boyfriend. Perhaps he was detecting my underlying desires through his acute clairsentient abilities. If so, this might end up being a rather annoying relationship.

But still, I wasn't sure which way to move. My first — and only — relationship felt nothing like this. I hadn't even had an imaginary relationship as intense as this one. Nathan was surpassing my wildest dreams of a boyfriend — yet we'd only met a few weeks ago. I couldn't project how intense this was going to get, especially considering there were two emotional empaths involved, and I didn't know if I trusted myself not to make a mess of the whole thing.

"You're right," he said, serious and straight-faced. "I'll give these to my mother." And he turned to walk away.

"Hey!" I shouted after him, grabbing the flowers from his hands. "Thank you. I don't want it to seem like I'm rejecting you — or the flowers. I'm just not very experienced at this, and I have a feeling…" I hesitated to say out loud what I feared he might be feeling too.

"Yes?" He spoke softly, leaning into me as the crowds of shoppers scurried around us. "What is the feeling?" His eyes penetrated through me until I felt a rush surge through my body, making my pulse quicken and my brain stop cold in its train of thought.

"Never mind," I mumbled, turning away before I gave in to the urge to kiss him.

He walked beside me in silence as we left the market and headed back in the direction of my house. After a few blocks, he said, "I think we're both on a teeter-totter over what to do. I don't want this to ignite like a firework and burn out in the blink of an eye. But I also don't want to miss sharing the Fourth of July with you. Does that make sense?"

I wasn't sure I understood, so I shook my head.

"Let me try to say it another way. Life is unpredictable, and life is short. I found that out at a very early age. And I feel I've spent enough of my life hiding under my bed because I was afraid of what would happen if I didn't; if I had to actually go out and live life. I don't want to do that anymore. I especially don't want to do that now that I've met you. So despite what I said earlier about thinking it was a good idea for us to be just friends, I don't really want to. I want to live my desires — not hide from them. So I hope that you'll please think about..."

I lunged into his arms and held him close. "I don't need time to think. I know exactly what you're feeling, and not because I'm an empath. I've been hiding under my bed for a while, too, and it's ... torture. It's suffocating me. I only started to feel safe when..."

"When you met me?" he asked with a sexy smirk.

"Actually, I was going to say since I connected with my Aunt Maggie, but I met you right after that, and now that I am out from under the bed, you're definitely taking me places I never thought I'd go."

"So does that mean you'll be my girlfriend?"

"Only if you promise to be patient and understanding and supportive and not pressure me too much or put too many expectations on me."

He stopped me with a kiss. "For someone who says they have no experience in relationships, you sure know what to demand as a girlfriend."

October 7

The next couple weeks passed in a general routine of monotony sprinkled with bliss. The weather, turning wet and colder, meant the time in the garden at lunch was ending, so I dedicated my time to the library, reading about chakras, empaths, and anything related I could get my hands on.

On Fridays, I dared to join Nathan in the pit for lunch, but the noise and general emotional chaos, not to mention the idiotic behavior of some of the students, was still hard to cope with, no matter how I tried. Something about the pit always burst my bubble.

On Wednesday in the library, I saw Rhonda and waved her over. She flung herself down on the seat next to me and whined, "Is there anything worse than having your birthday weekend turn out cold and wet?"

"Your birthday is this weekend?" I exclaimed in a tone of delight that almost didn't sound like me. "I thought it was supposed to be sunny and unseasonably warm?"

Rhonda looked over the top of her glasses with a 'did you forget who I am' stare.

"Oh, right. I didn't realize empathic precognition included foreseeing the weather conditions."

"It doesn't ordinarily. But I can 'fore-sense' a bummed-out mood with James, and since I know he blew a wad of cash on fireworks for my party, there's only one conclusion I can make from that."

I nodded, realizing I still had a lot to learn about the variations in empath abilities.

"And what do you mean 'is it my birthday this weekend?' You're coming to my party with Nathan, aren't you?"

"Sure, I'll be there. I, um, guess I forgot."

"You're a bad liar," she said, smacking me on the top of my head before bouncing out of her chair and out the door.

*

When Nathan called me that night, I confronted him about Rhonda's party.

"I didn't think you'd want to go. It's going to be loud, lots of kids and music, and as close to the pit as anything you've experienced in your teenage life."

"But you could have at least asked me," I said, annoyed that he'd decided for me.

"Yes. You're right. I was just trying to protect you."

"Okay, but I thought you were supposed to be teaching me how to live out from under the bed — not pushing me back under it."

"I'm so sorry," he said sincerely. "That was wrong of me. Of course, we should go. We'll have a good time. I can pick you up at eight ... if you'd like to be my date."

"Thank you," I replied formally. "I would like that very much."

October 10

The night of the party, keeping Nathan's words in mind about comparing it to the pit, I made sure to go through my grounding and shielding exercises before putting on my black jeans and angel-wing emerald sweater that Aunt Maggie helped me pick out when she visited. I wondered how she was doing, if she'd finished walking the El Camino, and when I'd see her again.

Nathan picked me up just before eight o'clock, and I ran out the door before my parents could insist on meeting him, telling them I would be home by eleven thirty.

The party was everything Nathan had warned it would be. Loud with dozens of teenagers milling about the house, dancing to the music blaring from the Bang & Olufsen speakers, and drinking what someone referred to as 'Raucous Rhonda Birthday Punch.'

Feeling grounded and shielded, I looked over my shoulder at Nathan and said, "If you can't hide from 'em, might as well join 'em." And off I went to get some punch and give the birthday girl a hug and kiss.

I found Rhonda in the kitchen pulling trays of mini pizzas from the oven. "Happy birthday!" I said, holding out a small gift bag to her.

"You weren't supposed to bring a gift," she scolded, giving me a kiss on the cheek. "But thank you!"

"Open it," I said, happy we had a moment alone to do so.

Inside the bag was a small wooden box that contained a leather strap necklace with a crystal ball charm. It seemed like an appropriate gift for a clairvoyant empath.

"Jenny, it's beautiful. It's brilliant! I couldn't have asked for a more lovely treasure." She hugged me as if she really meant it, and I felt a bond begin between us that I was certain would outlast many friendships in my life.

Filling a platter with the pizzas and another with cheese and veggies, she asked, "How are you and Nathan doing?"

I was somewhat surprised by the question and unsure how to answer.

"That bad?" she said, wrinkling her nose as if smelling spoiled food.

"No!" I protested. "I'm just too new to the whole relationship thing to have a qualified opinion. He's great. He's gorgeous and attentive and…"

"And you're not sure of any of it, are you?" she said, offering me a piece of baguette slathered in brie.

Taking a deep breath, I finally answered, "He's more than I ever imagined I would find. I just don't know what he sees in me and if I can live up to whatever that is." There. I'd said it.

"Jenny, what you need is a good look in the mirror. I'm not talking about beauty, which you've got. I'm talking about the spiritual mirror, which you've got in abundance." She held my hand and placed it against my heart. "The frequency of your heart chakra is as high as it gets. In terms of vibrational enlightenment, that's like the equivalent of … the Dalai Lama. *That* is what Nathan sees in you."

I closed my eyes and took a deep breath, trying to imagine my heart chakra vibrating at such a high frequency, but all I felt was a bit foolish.

"Enough of the serious stuff," she said, tugging on my sleeve. "Come help me celebrate my birthday."

The rest of the night flew by with dancing, talking, and even a few fireworks that James managed to shoot off in between the storm clouds. Although I'd only had one cup of punch, I felt giddy and playful, more relaxed with Nathan than I had before, and surprisingly, more at ease among the crowd and noise, too.

"That's great. Your exercises are working — plus, it helps that the crowd is so euphoric. Like you said earlier, if you can't hide from them, you might as well join in." Taking my hand, he spun me around then swayed with me to the beat of the music.

"I think this should be our song," he whispered.

"Mmm. I wrote a song a bit like 'Exchanged' once."

"Wow. I didn't know you wrote music, too."

"Well, I'm no Steve Collom, but I do have a fan club."

Nathan let out a burst of laughter, and I lightly punched him in the gut. "I'm sorry," he said, "you just caught me off guard. I don't doubt that you have a fan club; in fact, I'd like to sign up. Who should I contact to become a member?"

"That would be the president of the club, Fiona."

"Fiona? As in…"

"Princess Fiona, yes. She and her husband, Shrek, are my biggest fans; along with Nemo, Ariel, Mickey, and several dozen other … stuffed animals."

Nathan smiled like the sun, spinning me around in his arms. "I'm sure you have more fans that just your stuffed animals."

"No. Not really. I only give very intimate concerts. Held in my closet. With no one but my stuffed animals in the audience."

"Well, perhaps I could buy a ticket for the next concert. Would that be possible?"

"We'll see." I wrapped my arms around his body as we swayed to the music. He pulled me close and stroked my hair, whispering the lyrics in my ear.

"I remember when this song came out," he said, still holding my head to his chest and moving slowly together. "It was exactly two years after my brother died. I was fourteen and still having a really hard time. Simple things like shooting hoops or going to a ball game were suddenly awkward and strange, like I had never done any of it before.

"I remember this one time he took me see the Sox against the Yankees. It was the season Derek Jeter broke Lou Gehrig's record for hits. Daniel caught a foul ball hit by Jeter and waited two hours after the game so he could get it autographed. That might not seem like a big deal, but Derek Jeter played for the Yankees, not the Red Sox. According to most Sox fans, what my brother did was like committing treason. It was unthinkable. Even more mind-boggling is that on the bus ride home, he gave the ball to me."

"That's a great story. Do you still have it?"

He shook his head. "No. I put it in his casket, thinking that he should have it so he could remember me. Stupid, I know. Now I wish I could have it back just so I could remember him like he was, so generous and…unexpected."

October 16

The following Friday at the Trinity Empath Club meeting, I introduced an article I discovered in *Psychology Today* about research done on the brains of Highly Sensitive People (HSPs). "As I read the article and then went on to read the website of Dr. Elaine Aron — she's one of the authors of the actual research — it said that an estimated twenty percent of the population are HSPs, and as I read on, I realized than an HSP sounds a lot like an empath. In fact, the self-test on her website asks a lot of the same questions as the empath self-tests, so now I'm wondering if there really is any difference between the two."

Nathan was about to respond, but Adam jumped in. "It's like this, Jen." *Since when am I 'Jen'?* "An HSP meets a friend in a coffee shop, and the friend says that they are really sad because their dog just died. The HSP, being tremendously sensitive to the person's emotions, will feel as sad as their friend and might even start to cry. An empath, standing clear across the room, not having heard any of this exchange or knowing either person, will suddenly be overwhelmed by sadness and possibly cry themselves. Simply put, an HSP's system responds at the biological and psychological levels, whereas an empath's system is wired to respond at the energetic level, which usually results in change to the biological and psychological systems, as well." As he said this, he leaned forward and put his hand on my knee. I gave him half a smile before looking around the room for other input.

In a somewhat insulting tone of surprise, Rhonda said, "That's a great way to describe it, Adam. I never thought of it like that before, and that analogy really hits home with me, because sometimes I'll get an idea about something completely irrelevant to my life or, I think, irrelevant to anyone I know. But now I wonder if, in my process of awakening, my senses are broadening to cover a bigger scope beyond my immediate circumstances."

"What kind of ideas do you mean?" I asked, intrigued more each time she shared something about her precognitive gift.

"Inane ideas, really. Like the other day in class, this diagram popped into my head of the human body as if I were looking at it on my mobile, you know? And I sensed that I was looking at a map of my own body, and the heart center on the image was lighting up, giving me some kind of warning or information that I was supposed to act upon. And that was it. Like a mini-movie or dream that plays out in my mind in a second."

"What class were you in?" Nathan asked.

"Oh, it was my I.T. class. Do you think that has any relevance?"

"Well, it's interesting either way. I mean, perhaps you were picking up on someone else's idea for an app. Or it could be that the image that you thought was your body was really someone else's, and their heart was in some kind of duress."

"Good lord," Rhonda moaned. "I hope my teacher's not going to have a heart attack. I mean, he's a real wanker, but he doesn't deserve to die." Everyone laughed but quickly got back to the subject.

"It's great that you brought up the HSP study, Jenny," Nathan said with a smile that made my head spin. "And if that statistic is correct that twenty percent of the population are HSPs, we should probably keep ourselves alert for any signs of it at school. At the very least, we can educate people by sending them to that website you mentioned."

"And Jenny and I can do up some little cards to hand out with the information," Rhonda added enthusiastically. Everyone gave a few claps and nods in agreement, and then James raised his hand somewhat hesitantly.

"I did a little research of my own," he said, barely audible. "It has to do with heart mapping."

I noticed Nathan look at him with compassion in his eyes, and like at the last meeting, Rhonda reached over to hold his hand, which James pulled away before continuing to speak.

"Did you know there is a place called the HeartMath Institute? And one of its senior researchers, a Dr. Rollin McCraty, describes how the heart sends out a large electromagnetic field outside of the body, and that it is scientifically measurable. If you wire up two people, you can measure a person's heartbeat being detected by the other person's brain, and it can even have a physiological effect on that person."

"Is that how your empathic ability works?" I asked. "Is your heart the source or magnet for sensing others' illnesses?"

Everyone froze like statues, and I knew I had somehow asked the wrong question.

"I have no idea how my 'ability' works," he said with some sarcasm, "but ironically, this HeartMath Institute has done studies that show how the human heart can predict a future event three to five seconds before it happens. This isn't just empaths we're talking about. It's all of us! Every human can sense in their own heart what is going to happen — good or bad — several seconds before it transpires."

He elaborated about the test and then talked about how HeartMath researchers have shown that physical aspects of DNA strands could be altered by human intention. Although I wanted to ask more questions, I sensed by the silence of the group that it was best to leave the subject alone.

Finally, Nathan said, "I think we'd all like to learn more about it, James. Send us the links in an email, and we'll pick it up again at another meeting."

James nodded and bowed his head as Rhonda reached once again for his hand.

As they did the first time I attended, the group gathered at the close of the meeting, joining hands and reciting:

Sever the cords that bind me to all people, places and things

that do not serve my greater purpose and highest good.

Shield me from all low vibrations and negative energies —

whether they be from this universe or beyond.

Fill my body and soul with radiant, pure light

then grant me the wisdom and courage to share it with all I encounter.

As everyone was saying goodbye, Rhonda asked if she could give me a lift home. Although I longed for some alone time with Nathan, I sensed there was something Rhonda wanted to share with me, so I gladly accepted her offer and said goodnight to everyone, promising to call Nathan the next morning.

After dropping James off at his house, Rhonda cranked up the radio and began screaming along to "Say My Name" by The Mole.

"You seem tense," I shouted over the blare of the music.

"Do I?" she shouted back.

I reached to turn down the volume and said, "Yes. Tell me what's wrong."

"Nothing and everything," was her reply.

"What's that supposed to mean?"

"Nothing is wrong with me. Everything is wrong with James."

"I could tell during the meeting, and even at the last meeting, that he is ... sensitive about something. But aren't we all?" I chuckled at the absurd irony of calling an empath 'sensitive.'

"James is a bit different. His story isn't filled with rainbows and unicorns, I'm afraid."

"What is his story, if you don't mind my asking?"

"Well, I doubt he would tell you himself, but since everyone else in the group knows already, I don't see what harm it would do."

I waited for her to start talking and noticed that she'd turned away from the direction of my street and headed downtown instead. Pulling onto Commercial Street, she said, "I hope you don't mind. It's always easier to talk with a cup of hot cocoa in my hand," and parked in front of Arabica Coffee Shop.

Remembering Adam's HSP versus empath story from earlier, I quickly did an extra shielding visualization and repeated my mantra before stepping through the door.

As we sat down with our hot cocoas — hers with extra whipped cream — Rhonda let out a long sigh. "I love this place. It's the only coffee shop in town with a real fireplace and comfy living room-style seating. I usually come here to journal. So, about James," she said, taking a big gulp of her drink and wiping a whipped cream moustache from her lip. "You heard at our first gathering that he only realized his empath skills about a year ago."

I nodded and braced myself for what she was going to say next. I found myself doing that more now than ever before and decided to ask her or Nathan about how tense everyday life was becoming knowing that I am an empath, always on guard against any emotional turbulence.

"Unfortunately, about two months before that, his mom had a heart attack and died on the operating table a day later. He blames himself, believing that if he had paid more attention to the signs, to the changes he was experiencing, he would have been able to save her."

I shook my head at the tragedy both he and Nathan had faced at such a young age. "Well, that explains why he said the things he did about not being able to heal anything life-threatening. Do you think that he would have been able to save her?"

"I'm not qualified to answer that, but I have seen him do some pretty amazing things in the last year."

"Like what?"

"Well, just after his mom died, James was sent to foster care because his parents were divorced when he was a child. His father took off and was never heard from again. Until the courts could find his dad or a suitable relative to take James in, he had to live with this old couple, and it was while he was in their care that the old man became sick. He complained of a pain in his stomach and they took him to the hospital, but the doctors could find nothing wrong with him. They sent him home, but the pain got worse. James sat by the old man's bedside and tried to comfort him. When he put his hand on the man's abdomen, James said it felt hot and tingly, like there was some electrical current running from the man's body into his hand.

"James wasn't sure what to do, but he told me that this same sensation had happened before — once even with his mother. This time, an idea came to James that he must be feeling some connection with the person at the molecular level. So, while still touching the man, he visualized a bright light radiating from above into the top of his head, through his body, down his arm, and into his hand where he touched the old man. He sent healing light into the man's body, and after only a couple minutes, all the pain was gone. And the man never complained of any pain again."

"That's incredible! That's a miracle!" I blurted out, nearly spilling my cup in the process.

"I think so, too, but according to James, 'The old guy probably just had a bout of gas that finally passed when pressure was applied to his stomach.'" We both laughed at her scary-good impersonation of James.

"So James doesn't live with them anymore?"

"No. He was only with them a couple of months. Then an aunt came forward from his father's side of the family, and James has been living there ever since."

"That must kinda suck, living with the sister of your dad who ran off when you were a kid. Is he all right there?"

"Oh yeah, he likes it, all things considered. I mean, he and his mom didn't live around here, so when he moved in with his aunt, it meant leaving his school and all his friends. But I'm thankful, because if he never came to Trinity, I never would have met him."

"You guys do make a great couple," I said, thinking how nice it would be if Nathan and I grew as close as James and Rhonda. "Can I ask you something else, Rhonda? In confidence?"

"Shoot."

"What's up with Adam? I mean, sometimes he acts all tough and standoffish, then suddenly he gets flirtatious and touchy-feely. It kinda creeps me out, to be honest."

Rhonda let out a belly laugh and snorted so hard, I thought hot cocoa was going to come out her nose. "Oh dear, oh dear," she continued, "that's just Adam, I'm afraid. Didn't you know that his 'telepathic abilities' allow him to read when a girl has the hots for him, and apparently that's every girl at Trinity."

"Wait. Are you saying he isn't a telepathic empath?"

Still laughing, Rhonda said, "Well, we haven't seen much by way of real evidence, but he's harmless enough, so we let him hang around." Giving a sultry wink, she added, "And he's certainly not hard on the eyes either!"

"And he did have a good explanation of the HSP vs. empath scenario," I said.

"Yes, but if you Googled it, I'll bet you'd find it word-for-word on one of the first empath sites. Come on, let's get you home before your parents think you've run away."

October 28

By the end of October, my parents had become adamant about meeting my new friends, so I decided to ask everyone over for a little Halloween party. As it turned out, they all had plans, but Nathan said he would gladly skip the haunted house and corn maze to meet my parents. Great. Now it was going to seem like a formal 'meet my boyfriend' instead of a casual 'meet my friends' gathering. I wasn't quite sure how to handle it, but I knew who to ask.

*

"Aunt Maggie, I need some advice!"

After getting caught up on the highlights of her El Camino trip and the handsome Greek man she met en route, she laid it out straight.

"Darling, you're a young woman now. It's only natural that you would be seeing a boy at this age. Your parents are most likely expecting this. Didn't you tell me there was a young man you dated last year for a while? What happened when your parents met him?"

"Um … they didn't. I never introduced them for the same reason I don't want to introduce Nathan as my boyfriend."

"Which is?"

"Sheer embarrassment. They are either going to get all protective and paranoid or they're going to act like children and start gushing and fawning over him. Oh my god, what if they pull out my baby photos? I'll just die!"

"Take a deep breath, Jenny. You're getting over-dramatic, and that's not like you. What's really going on here?" Her question cut through to my soul, and she waited in silence for me to answer.

And waited.

And waited.

As my words were finally forming, they came spilling out on a wave of tears.

"Oh, Aunt Maggie, it's this guy, Nathan. He's … different. When I'm with him, I feel like I've known him forever — for longer than my life. And when I'm not with him, I still feel safe, like we're still connected in some way."

"Hmmm," she said softly. "And this Nathan … have you 'been with him' yet?"

"Aunt Maggie! I'm fifteen! Of course not!"

"Okay. Just asking. Because you know you can talk to me when the time comes. I was fifteen once too … for about five years."

Laughing through the last of my tears, I asked her again in all seriousness what I should do about introducing him to my parents.

"Here's what you do. You go to your parents tomorrow and you tell them straight, 'Hey Mom and Dad, I want to bring a guy over to meet you whom I've been seeing from school. I ask that you please both be cool about it and not do anything to embarrass me — like pull out my baby photos. If that sounds okay with you, he'll be here at eight. If not, we can make it another time."

"Geez, Aunt Maggie, that's good. You should have been a shrink."

"I am, darling, I just don't get paid for it!"

After some more laughter and promises to talk again soon, we hung up, and I decided there was no time like the present to face my parents about Nathan.

Much to my relief, they barely reacted at all when I gave them my little speech. They didn't even seem surprised to learn I had a boyfriend. Agreeing to be on their best behavior, they wished me goodnight, and I went upstairs to bed, but as I shut the door to my room, I heard the faint sounds of giggles and cackles coming from the den. All I could hope is that they were getting it out of their systems now.

October 31

When eight o'clock came and the doorbell rang, I nearly jumped out of my skin. "I'll get it," I hollered, racing down the stairs from my room. But my father was already in the foyer, and in my haste to beat him there, I fell down the last two steps and face-planted just as my dad swung the door open.

Both my dad and Nathan came rushing to pick me up and assess the damages. Fortunately, it was only a skinned knee and a small bump on my forehead, which unfortunately grew to the size of an egg over the next few minutes. I guess I didn't have to worry about my parents embarrassing me — seems I could do that all on my own. My parents tried very hard not to dote on me, but I could tell they wanted to rush me off to the ER without delay.

"Maybe we should get you to the ER just to be safe," Nathan said, examining my head like a pre-med student.

"That's a very smart idea," my father said while giving me a thumbs-up behind Nathan's back. "I'll get the car."

"And I'll get my purse and Jenny's jacket," my mother chimed in before dashing from the kitchen. This couldn't be happening.

"Happy Halloween," I said to Nathan in a pathetic attempt at some humor.

"Well, I'm happy anywhere you are," he replied, giving my bump a light kiss.

"And here I was worried my parents were going to ruin our night."

"Why would you think that?"

"Oh, because they're my parents," I retorted. He looked at me skeptically. "Trust me. You'll understand when you get to know them."

"Well, that sounds promising." He was leaning down to give me a kiss on the mouth when my mother popped up from around the corner with my jacket and what looked like my large overnight bag.

"Um, Mom. I'm just getting checked out at the ER, not getting checked in for long-term care."

"Well, I just tossed a few things in the first bag I could find. You know how long you have to wait sometimes to be seen in those ERs, and you never know..."

I shot an 'I told you so' look to Nathan as he helped me up from the chair. When he winked at me in return, my knees buckled and I nearly went down.

"That was you," I said defensively, "not the bump."

*

Thankfully, we didn't have to wait long before being seen by a doctor, but the line-up of gurneys in the hall for the CT scan was like bumper-to-bumper in morning rush hour.

"It's Halloween," one of the nurses bellowed as she passed by. "All the crazies come out at Halloween."

My parents and Nathan were hovering over me on the gurney as the chaos of a busy night at the hospital swirled around us. I started to feel a bit claustrophobic.

"Hey, Mom and Dad, would you mind going down to the cafeteria and getting a coffee or something."

"Well, I don't think you're supposed to have anything, dear, before they take you in..."

"I think she means she wants us to get lost for a while," my dad interrupted, taking her by the arm and giving me a smile as he pulled her away. Despite how hard my dad tried to act smooth, he always came across like one of those goofy nerds who wears two different-colored socks. I only then realized that was one of the things I loved about him the most.

After my parents were out of range, Nathan smiled and said, "Hi," brushing my hair away from my bump. "How are you feeling?"

"Besides foolish, you mean?" I said with half a smile. "Actually, I'm feeling really tense. I don't think it's because of my head. It's more like I feel something..." In that instant, a loud bang sounded from behind us, like someone had shot a gun. Nathan threw his body on top of mine in protection.

"What's happening?" I croaked from under the weight of him.

"I don't know. Just be still and breathe. Do your shielding exercise. Say your mantras."

Barely audible from the panic in my voice and his smothering weight, I gasped, "Shielding? How can an imaginary bubble stop a bullet?"

Down at the end of the hall, a nurse and security guard wrestled a man to the ground who had been brought in for blowing off a firecracker in his hand while heavily intoxicated. Apparently, he thought it would be funny to try to blow off the other hand while in the hospital. When the commotion was finally under control, Nathan stood up and asked if I was all right.

"Am I all right? I'm in the hospital with a self-inflicted head wound on the night I introduce my boyfriend to my parents while simultaneously thinking I'm being shot at as my boyfriend smothers me and suggests I protect myself with a mental image of a bubble." Hearing how ridiculous I sounded, I started laughing uncontrollably, doubling over from the spasms in my side and snorting so loud, some of the other patients gave me dirty looks.

The same nurse from earlier walked passed again and glared at us. "Yup. All the crazies come out on Halloween."

Nathan joined in with me this time, and we both laughed until we cried.

November 1

I awoke the next day in my bed, feeling sore from the fall but otherwise happy. Nathan called in the afternoon to see how I was doing and asked if I wanted him to come over. As much as

I wanted to say yes, I really felt like curling up alone on my sofa in my pj's and watching an old movie. Plus, I had a few chapters to read for English and biology before school tomorrow. Nathan wished me a relaxing day and promised to come for dinner next weekend.

"A do-over," he said with warm humor.

"Sure. And I'll let my dad answer the door next time."

November 7

The following Saturday, Nathan showed up as promised, and my parents, though not without obvious glee, treated him like a regular school friend. They asked about his interests, his family — I was thankful that Nathan skipped mentioning his brother's suicide — and then allowed Nathan and me to take the lead on the conversation for the rest of the dinner.

We talked about the green projects underway at the school, thanks to Lee and Erica, and were thrilled when my parents offered to volunteer with us at the upcoming Earth Day recycling project.

When dinner ended, Nathan and I cleared the dishes and went down to the basement to watch a movie. My parents made a point of saying goodnight and shut the door to the den where, I presumed, they would be replaying and analyzing every moment of the evening.

Although I had saved several potential movies on Netflix for us to watch, we instead plopped down on the sofa and started talking.

"Your parents are pretty okay. Not quite as nutty as you made them sound."

"Give them time. They've been on their best behavior. But you made them feel relaxed, so thanks for that."

"And you made *me* feel relaxed," he said in a deep, soothing voice, "so thanks for that." He reached out and brushed my hair away from my face. The look in his eyes was a mixture of tenderness and desire. He held his stare as he leaned closer to me, one inch at a time, until I could feel his breath on my lips.

The anticipation of his kiss gave me a fluttery, sinking feeling, and I was immediately brought back to the Rock n' Roller coaster when I was ten years old. I had finally grown tall enough to ride it, and the rush of being on that roller coaster for the first time is one I thought would never be topped. Until now. Although we had kissed before, this time was different. He wanted me to feel desire perched on the edge of fulfillment; wanted me to feel it in every cell in my body. We didn't move, not toward each other or away. Our eyes, closed now, allowed us to focus more acutely on the sense of our proximity. The warmth radiating from our lips, the feel of each other's breath, the smell of our skin and hair, all created an intoxicating blend that induced a craving so strong, I didn't know what would happen if I acted on it. I didn't think about it. Not how much I still had to learn about Nathan or that my parents were only one flight up and two rooms away. I didn't think at all. In that moment, I was one hundred percent consumed by my senses, and like the first time Nathan kissed me, I realized that these feelings were completely my own.

It was strange being so connected with my emotions. No outside influencers or invaders. This was all me. The liberation of that realization was what finally pushed me over the edge, and I moved, ever so slightly, to Nathan's lips until my lips brushed his like the stroke of a feather.

I felt him smile as I licked away the tickling sensation from my lips, then he reciprocated my gesture, dancing his tongue around the edge of my mouth. This time, it was my turn to smile, and soon my tension gave way to uncontrollable laughter until both Nathan and I were laughing and rolling around on the sofa out of breath.

"Come to me," he finally said, putting his hand on the back of my head and drawing me to him with a look that thrilled me and scared me all at the same time. When our lips met, they burned with an intensity that initially made us both pull away in surprise. But like that first roller coaster ride, the rush was so extreme, we had no choice but to give in to it.

*

"Tell me about manifestation," I said after we'd finally come up for air. "You said you clear your mind and focus on the end result. Tell me more, especially about how you can manifest an A on a test." I laughed and nudged him playfully.

We were snuggled up now, feet-to-feet on the sofa, warm under a woolen blanket my grandmother had knitted. He shifted into his teacher mode. "To begin with, manifestation is not an empath thing. It's a law-of-attraction skill that anyone can develop. One of the terms used to describe the mechanics of manifestation is 'Quantum Jumping,' which basically means that you can alter or control the outcome of a desired result — like the grade on a test — by sending your positive energy into that dimension."

"You mean into the future?"

"Not exactly. It's more like a different version of you that already exists in another dimension; a parallel universe." He looked at me, waiting for any questions, but my mind was trying to wrap itself around the concept.

"When we are able to connect with that other version of ourselves ... the one who aced the test, got the scholarship, won the girl ... then we actually make the jump into that other dimension, although our awareness of ourselves doesn't really seem to change."

"But how do you connect with a parallel universe?"

"Practice, practice, practice." He laughed and wrapped his legs around mine under the blanket. "Seriously, it has a lot to do with believing that the possibility exists — because the universe doesn't respond well to doubt. Then you sharpen your senses to fully participate in the event, not as if it's a future event, but as if it's already happened."

The way he spoke with such clarity and certainty made me feel like this was something that was not only possible, but something that had already happened — as if I were having déjà vu at a deeper level of knowledge and understanding instead of just sensory.

"Teach me how," I said, sitting up and grabbing his hands to pull him up. "I want to learn. Take me through an exercise."

"Okay, no need yank my arms from their sockets! Just tell me something you want to achieve but have been afraid to."

"Um...let's see. I have to give a speech next week for English in front of the whole class, and I know I'm going to blow it. I can't do stuff like that — be the center of attention."

"Good. Let's start by getting you into a relaxed position." It came out more seductive than he intended, and he blushed while at the same time getting a devilish grin that made his dimple pop to life. It left me dumbfounded every time. As I sat back on the sofa, he pulled the lever on the side, popping out the footrest that shifted me back into a reclining position.

"Now close your eyes and relax," he said in a low voice. "Try to see the insides of your eyelids. Usually there are tiny vessels that appear as squiggles or shapes floating on the black background of your eyelids. Let yourself get lost in those shapes."

As I closed my eyes and relaxed, I saw the squiggles he was talking about, but I also saw tiny flashes of light flickering in the margins of blackness, followed by swirls of purple and green. They were strange yet comforting, and I allowed myself to be entranced by them. Like the first time he took me through the bubble exercise, his voice became smooth and hypnotic. "Breathe in slowly ... and exhale slow and easy. That's good. Continue just like that. Now picture yourself in school walking down the hall. See what you're wearing, how you have your hair, what shoes you have on. You walk into the classroom and take your seat. Feel the way your body rests in the chair. Feel the book and papers in your hands as you put them on your desk.

"Now listen to what's around you. The teacher is talking, someone whispers to another student behind you, someone else taps their pen on the desk. Smell the odors around you. Perfume, hair products, B.O. from the kid who just came from gym class.

"When your name is called, no one seems to care. They continue to doodle in their notebooks and play with their hair or bite their fingernails. Now picture yourself standing there, casually talking about your subject. Nothing different than what you do with your friends. You feel relaxed, safe, and comfortable in your skin and your surroundings. Picture it now. Hear your voice and its confident tone. See your teacher and classmates as they smile and nod at you. Feel the confidence and ease flow through your body as you conclude your presentation. Then hear the applause! Your face breaks out in a smile. You take a deep breath and a small bow before taking your seat, knowing you just aced another project."

The whole time Nathan spoke, I allowed my senses to follow his direction, feeling, seeing, hearing, and smelling all he instructed me to. At the end, I was energized with a pumped-up elation, as if I'd just won a race. My heart was beating faster than normal, my muscles were flexed with energy, and I realized I had a smile on my face just as he described.

"Yes!" I shouted, opening my eyes and stretching my arms overhead. "I did it! I did a great job!"

"That's it!" Nathan high-fived me and hugged me. "That is exactly the frame of emotion you need to be in for manifestation. If you can live it in your mind, body, and soul, then imagination can become reality."

"Let's hope," I said, still pumped up with adrenaline from the exercise.

"Not hope," Nathan clarified seriously. "With certainty. You must be certain. As sure of it as you are of your own name. Manifestation goes beyond hope or even belief. It's about certainty. It's a knowing of what is true before it's proven true in this domain. Do you understand?"

"I think so, yes. But the skeptic in me wants to ask … has anyone actually proven this method works? It's not that I'm doubting you when you say you've made it work, but has it been scientifically tested?"

"Well, I can tell you about a guy named Dr. Denis Waitley who trained Olympic athletes using a visualization technique he called Visual Motor Rehearsal. When he hooked the athletes up to biofeedback machines and asked them to run their event with only their imagination, they found that the same muscles fired in the same sequence as if they were running the event in real life. He concluded that the mind couldn't distinguish whether the event was happening in the physical world or just in their minds.

"There is other research out there, too. Some have shown success for weight loss and others for rehab of muscular/bone injuries. I'm still just learning about it all myself. I find it fascinating."

*

That night after Nathan left, I went to sleep replaying the manifestation exercise in my mind. What I wore, what I saw, how everything smelled, how it sounded in class and how I felt. I replayed the scene over and over until it felt like a memory instead of a wish. When I woke, I felt I understood.

November 11

When the day came for my presentation, I was oddly calm. Instead of being anxious about what would happen, about what could go wrong, I kept the feeling of certainty, relief, and pride that I had a done a good job. And that feeling stayed with me throughout the entire ten-minute speech. When it was over, although I was happy, I didn't feel surprised by the outcome. A sense of assurance and gratification filled me. And when Nathan asked me if I nailed the presentation, I shrugged. "Of course I did."

November 20

With all the time I'd been spending with Nathan and learning about being an empath, I'd hardly touched my guitar. Most days I didn't think anything of it; in fact, the less I played it, the less I felt the urge to play it. But today I felt inspired. So after school, I set out my 'audience' of stuffed animals and held a comeback tour of greatest hits. With every strum, my body resonated until at last my heartbeat and breath matched the rhythm of the song. The warmth that radiated through my body felt like the sun blazing on my skin after a long, cold winter. Vitamin D major!

By the time my parents got home from work, I was so elated and energetic, they asked if something special had happened at school. They eagerly waited for my answer but looked confused and a bit awkward when I said that I just had a great session with my guitar. I shrugged to myself, thinking that you probably had to be a musician to understand one. With my buzz only slightly diminished, I did a quick load of laundry and got dressed for my third Trinity Empath Club meeting.

*

Rhonda picked me up and, no surprise, she was singing at the top of her lungs to a song I'd never heard. James was in the front seat, so I got in the back and greeted them both with a silent-movie 'hello,' knowing they couldn't have heard me even if I screamed.

The meeting began jovially. Even Nathan and Adam were sharing a laugh over something as they fixed their cups of tea. Nathan welcomed everyone and explained that Erica and Lee would not be joining us; they were at a meeting to promote the school's greenhouse and vegetable garden initiative. He then opened the floor to whoever wanted to speak first. Faith shot up her hand.

"I learned a couple new exercises for emotional empaths I'd like to share with everyone. The first I call 'the brush-off.' It starts like the basic grounding exercise, opening your crown chakra to receive the positive energy from the universe, but as you exhale, you physically brush off the negative energy from your arms, legs, torso, and head down and away from you." She stood and demonstrated the movements, saying, "The added gestures really enhance the intention of the exercise." Everyone nodded and praised her as she sat back down.

"Obviously," she continued, "this is a great little exercise when you can steal away somewhere private."

Adam interjected, "Or if anyone does see you and asks what the hell you're doing, you could just say 'cat hair.'"

Everyone laughed, and I noticed Faith blushing before she continued.

"This next little trick is one you can do if you're with someone or several people and are getting a sense of negative or even hostile energy coming at you. I call it 'the warning,' and basically it's just a simple command you give to whoever's energy is trying to infiltrate yours. It doesn't matter who the person is, because you're actually addressing their energy.

"So to do this, I picture myself with one hand on my hip and the other waving a finger in the air as if to gesture 'no.' It's kind of like what my mom used to do to me when I was little and reaching for something I wasn't supposed to touch." Again, she stood and demonstrated 'the warning,' saying, "While I'm picturing myself doing this, I say in my head, 'Tsk, tsk. Do not cross into my space! You don't belong over here. Now go back to where you belong!' It's quite funny, actually. It makes me feel like a kid on the playground chasing away a bully. I find it works remarkably well, but like any of our exercises, intention is the foundation of their success."

Everyone applauded as Faith took a bow and smiled sheepishly at Adam.

Next, Rhonda and James gave a book report on *Empath Intuition* by Dr. Michael Smith, followed by Adam, who introduced the topic of how anyone can send and receive telepathic messages. When no one responded to his introduction, he said, "Allow me to demonstrate," and held out his hand for me to join him in the center of the room. Without even looking at Nathan, I could sense his hostile energy and thought it would be a good time for Adam to practice 'the warning' exercise.

"First," he began, "believing telepathy is possible is essential to its success. Do you believe, Jenny?"

I nodded and said, "I do."

"Next, you need to turn off your physical senses, removing as many distractions as possible. I'll ask everyone to please remain quiet; and Jenny, I'll ask you to put this on." He pulled out a black sleeping mask from his back pocket so casually, I wondered if he carried it around with him just in case anyone he randomly met needed a telepathy demonstration.

Once the mask was on me, he continued. "I want you to calm your mind. Think of nothing except the empty space between us, void of all physical objects, clear and open, ready to be the channel for our thoughts. When your thoughts are calm, when you sense your mind is open, exhale away any final bits of debris in the path between our connected minds."

I quickly became absorbed in the blackness. My focus on the space between us was intensely acute and yet took no effort. I wasn't just in a void; it felt like I *was* the void. Even as Adam began speaking again, it seemed he was calling to me from somewhere inside the depths of this mental cavern.

"Staying idly as you are in the vast space, I'm going to send you an object. Keep breathing, keep your mind still. There's nothing else for you to do."

A full minute passed in the black of nothingness, my only awareness being my own breath. Then out of nowhere — literally nowhere — a bright red apple appeared in front of me. The expression on my face must have indicated that I had connected with a thought, and before I could say anything, Adam said, "I believe red delicious are your favorite."

I tore off the mask as my jaw dropped open in disbelief. I'd read his mind! As I looked around the room, I saw a few skeptical faces — Rhonda, James, Nathan, as well as a dazzled one — Faith.

"You guys," I implored with sincere awe in my voice, "I pictured a red apple!" Although they applauded, I didn't understand why everyone else wasn't as amazed as I was, but on the heels of my telepathy high, I felt a bizarre rush of power mixed with fear. To think that, like Adam said, telepathy is something anyone can learn to do, made me wonder how many other intuitive skills could be taught. Could I one day move objects with my mind? Could I bend spoons and transport myself to other places? A strange and startling world flashed before me. Lost in my thoughts, I almost didn't hear when Nathan called my name.

"Is there anything you'd like to share tonight, Jenny?" he asked.

"Besides your wicked telepathy skills," Adam chimed in, raising his hand to high-five me, which I accepted awkwardly before clearing my throat to begin my own report.

"I guess I just wanted to tell everyone about a manifestation technique I tried that Nathan taught me." I saw a huge smile spread across Nathan's face, but he was also shaking his head as if in disapproval, so I asked, "What? Should I not be sharing this?"

"Oh no, I think everyone would love to hear about your experience. It's just that I was going to talk about manifestation tonight, too, so it's just funny that we had the same idea."

"So let's tell the story together." And so for the next ten minutes, Nathan and I relayed the background, the process, and finally the success of how I manifested a perfect speech in my English class. At the end, everyone cheered and applauded, congratulating me on my rapid growth and enthusiasm.

As before, Nathan closed the meeting with the empath prayer, and as the group said their goodbyes, Adam approached me and leaned his forehead to mine, saying, "I'm in your head now, Jenny."

As I pulled away, I saw Nathan clenching his jaw and fists. I stepped over to him and took his hand, hoping it would deter him from giving Adam a punch in the head.

"Am I giving you a lift home, Jenny?" Rhonda asked.

"Yes, if you don't mind. But can I have a couple minutes first?"

Sensing Nathan's tension, she nodded and waited with James for me at the door.

Turning to Nathan, I said, "Hey, whatever is going on between you and Adam, please don't put me in the middle of it."

He shook his head. "The guy just gets under my skin sometimes."

"That's because you let him. That's what he wants, Nathan. He's just a button-pusher, and every time you react this way, he wins. So how about you shift some of that negative energy into positive energy by giving me a kiss before I leave?"

He smiled and bit his lip in a way that made me want to bite it, too. And I did. Again and again, in a heated few moments before saying goodnight.

November 29

My newfound talent for manifestation meant that I was excelling in most of my classes, except P.E., which ... why would I bother wasting my manifestation power on badminton? I also practiced the techniques on my social anxiety, figuring that if I could overcome my fear of public speaking, maybe I could also get past the emotional repulsion of the pit. I really wanted to become a more resilient version of myself so I could spend more time with Nathan during school, since we didn't seem to have a lot of chances to see each other outside of school lately.

Even during the long Thanksgiving weekend, Nathan and his parents went to stay at his aunt's house while I spent mine at home as usual. Aunt Maggie was about to leave on a trip to Crete with her Greek god for a couple of weeks while writing an article for *The Sunday Times Travel* magazine and doing whatever it is they do in Greece. Feeling somewhat abandoned, I allowed myself a small Thanksgiving pity party.

As I thought about all I was thankful for, I pictured Nathan, with whom I felt I could share almost anything; Rhonda, who offered a great womanly perspective; and Aunt Maggie. There was no substitute for the wisdom, understanding, and love she offered. It was that thought that prompted me to ask my parents if we could invite her to come and stay for Christmas and New Year's week.

"I'm sure she's already got plans, Jenny," my mother responded when I ran the idea past them.

"And you know how she hates the cold," my father added, as if being helpful.

"Well, I want to ask her anyway. Will she be welcome here if I do?" I could feel the spirit of Aunt Maggie's straightforward communication style surge from me. The question left little room for my parents to put forward any diplomatic excuse, so after half-hearted nods of agreement, I hurried to call Aunt Maggie and book her for a holiday visit.

*

"I have a better idea," Aunt Maggie said. "Why don't you come and spend the holidays here with me? You're certainly old enough to travel by yourself, and a young woman of your age should start to see the world!"

Although my parents were not pleased with Aunt Maggie's proposition, in the end I think they viewed it as the lesser of two unpleasantries. And so I began making plans to spend Christmas break with my favorite aunt.

December 7

"I'm glad you're going," Nathan said when I broke the news to him about my holiday plans.

"You are? Gee, thanks. That's just what every girl wants to hear from her boyfriend."

He smiled in that devilish way only he could pull off with his sexy dimple and hypnotic eyes. "Are you going to let me explain, or should I slip the noose over my neck now?"

"The floor is yours. Speak," I commanded.

"I was hesitant to tell you that my parents and I take a cruise over the holidays. It's a rough time of year for us since Daniel died, and it seems to take the edge off a bit if we're out of our usual routine, away from home."

"Of course," I said. "But why were you hesitant to tell me? Surely you'd know I would have understood."

He shrugged. "I guess because this is the first time that I don't want to go with them. I wanted to stay and share the holidays with you." When I looked into his eyes, there was a glimmer, a twinkle of life that replaced the somber expression I had seen there since we met.

"That would have been nice," I said, wrapping my arms around him and inhaling his intoxicating aroma. "But we can make any day a holiday. Hey, what do you say we make a holiday of our own? A Christmissed holiday!"

He pulled away, looking into my eyes with such intensity, it made me feel light-headed. "I love it, and I also…" he cut himself short and looked at the ceiling, finally saying, "…and I also think we should pick a date now. How's the Saturday one week before break?"

"Wow. That's less than two weeks away. Are you sure that's enough time for you to shop for all my presents?"

"All your presents?" He gulped with a look of fear clouding his face.

"Ah, I'm just teasing. One perfect, thoughtful gift will do."

"That I can manage. I hope."

December 9

The flip-side of our advanced Christmissed holiday was that I would have to find one perfect, thoughtful gift for him as well. And that would mean a trip to the mall. The thought of being surrounded by hundreds of Christmas shoppers made my whole body tense. I wondered if it would be unromantic to pick something out online.

As I contemplated what the perfect gift for Nathan might be, my mind wandered back to our Christmissed conversation and how he had paused so abruptly when he said, "I love it and I also..." And I also what? Whatever he was about to say wasn't how he thought we should pick a date. That much was obvious. Maybe he was going to say *and I also think we shouldn't exchange presents.* That would explain his uncomfortable expression when I brought up the gifts. Or, I pretended for just a moment, maybe he was going to say, *and I also love you.* I tried to let that projection wash over me, playing it out in my mind and seeing what my reaction would be. A sudden sinking feeling made me quickly shake off the image, and I sat down at the computer to see what Amazon had to offer.

Clothes? Gadgets? A book? Art? A watch? After two hours, nothing jumped out at me, so I decided to call it a night and see if anything popped up in my dreams, which as of late had been extremely vivid.

*

On the plane to visit Aunt Maggie, I stared out the window, in awe of the massive array of clouds that formed like pink and purple mountains from another world. I had never seen anything so beautiful and was not surprised when tears began falling down my cheeks. The peace I felt in that moment was one I had not experienced since childhood, when I would spin myself in circles on our front lawn and collapse on the grass, staring up at the heavens as if they were home.

I flipped on my iPod and was taken further into my reverie as Barber's "Adagio for Strings" filled my head with the sounds of angels. I was so lost in serenity, I was startled when Nathan took my hand in his.

"I'm glad you're with me." I smiled through my joyful tears.

He leaned over and kissed a tear from my cheek and then another. "With each other and for each other, always."

Climbing to our cruising altitude high above the heavenly clouds, I closed my eyes and slept peacefully with Nathan's hand in mine.

December 10

When I awoke, I realized I was running late for school. Oh, how I wished I could crawl back under the covers and relive that dream again. Despite feeling better than I had some months ago, I still felt happier and more at peace in my dreams than I did in real life. Although it bothered me, I pushed the thought away, convincing myself that I would feel better as soon as I got the hang of this empath thing. If only there were a way to use manifestation to change being an empath.

The walk to school, while gorgeous in the fall, was going to be brutal once the snow fell. Maybe I could convince Rhonda to give me a lift to school. I noticed she was driving most days now. I laughed out loud picturing her screaming out "Say My Name" that night in the car.

A horn suddenly blared behind me, and I jumped a half-foot off the ground. Expecting to see a car full of loser kids, I was surprised when Rhonda leaned out the window and shouted for me to jump in.

"That's so weird. I was just thinking of you."

"You don't say." She smiled and winked, tapping her hand on the steering wheel in time with another song I'd never heard.

"Yeah, in fact, I wanted to ask you a favor. I wonder if you'd mind giving me a lift to school on snow days, or extremely cold days, or days ending in Y."

"No sweat. Consider it done. But you have to do me a favor in return. I want you to have lunch with us every day this week."

I shook my head. "Ask another favor. I'm not ready for the pit full-time just yet."

"It's not full-time, Jenny. It's fifty minutes a day for one week. Your friends will be with you, and if you don't come, you can start waterproofing your snow boots."

Her tone had changed from playful to pissy, so I surrendered. "Okay. Okay. You win. I'll see you in the pit."

"At 12:10 sharp!" She pointed a finger at me as we pulled into the student lot.

*

The morning flew by, and when the bell rang announcing fifth period, I considered feigning a headache and spending lunch napping in the nurse's office. But Rhonda wouldn't be fooled, and I hated walking in the winter weather almost more than I hated the pit. So I dragged myself down the hall, grabbed my lunch sack from my locker, and entered hell at Trinity High. Before I got down the stairs, I felt a hand on my shoulder. "Knew you could do it," Rhonda cheered. "Come on, let's get you some grub."

"Not so fast," I said, holding up a hand. "I'm here as you requested, but I'm not submitting myself to the sewage that passes for food in this pit. I have my own lunch. I'll meet you at the table."

Despite the time with Nathan, the friendly banter, and my delicious tomato and cheese sandwich, it was a painfully long and tense fifty minutes. And so it was for the rest of the day.

December 11

On day two of my pit promise, Rhonda bought me a slice of apple pie. I didn't want to eat it, but she seemed to be trying so hard to include me in their lunchtime rituals that I thought it might hurt her feelings if I rejected the offering. I smiled a 'thank you' before taking a big bite and chewing what tasted like sugary glue and Styrofoam. I was a second away from spitting it out but instead guzzled half a bottle of water and swallowed it down in one big gulp.

I couldn't disguise the look of repulsion on my face, and it was then that I noticed everyone staring at me. A moment passed in suspension before the entire table started cracking up, slapping me on the back and taking snapshots of me on their mobiles.

It took me a minute before I realized that the 'sweet gesture' was really a 'pie prank,' because everyone but me knew how gut-wrenchingly awful the apple pie was in the pit. It was easy to forgive Rhonda, and by the hearty laughter and feeling of com-radery around the table, I felt like I had just passed a club initia-tion, which, all things considered, could have been much worse.

Above the ongoing jibes and laughter and the general chaotic noise of the pit, a massive explosion sounded from some-where down the hall, shaking the building like an earthquake. Immediately, a thousand noisy kids fell into silence. Then, as another loud bang was heard, chaos filled the room. The adult supervisors, trained in emergency response, shut and guarded the doors as the P.A. system sounded an alarm followed by a recorded message: *This is not a drill. You are to calmly walk to the nearest exit and report to your designated station outside the perimeter of the building. Do not leave the school property. All students must be accounted for. Repeat — do not leave the school property. Report to your designated emergency station outside of the building or go to one of the emergency staff for help.*

As the message began repeating, the doors of the pit were opened, and throngs of students pushed their way out into the hall, where we were corralled toward the exit leading to the student parking lot. All around me, students were guessing what had happened. A bomb? A terrorist attack? A gang retaliation? Something crashed into the school or fell from the sky? I could feel my pulse quicken and my body tense as I was pressed into the herd of panicked students shuffling out to safety. Although I thought Nathan was right behind me, I couldn't be sure, and I couldn't turn around to look, but I occasionally felt his hand touching my back or shoulder, and it comforted me, though only slightly.

When we finally got outside where I could breathe and move, I turned around to find Adam behind me instead of Nathan. I looked behind him to see if Nathan was anywhere in sight, but he wasn't. "That was intense," Adam said in an awed tone. "Did you feel the shockwave from that blast?"

Pulling away, I spat out, "This isn't some Hollywood action movie. People could be hurt. What's wrong with you?"

*

When the school was emptied and the fire trucks and emergency vehicles arrived, I finally spotted my friends two stations down from me. Although we weren't allowed to leave our spot, Nathan, Rhonda, and the others shouted to me, asking if I was okay and apologizing for letting me drift away from them in the commotion. I nodded as my teeth chattered from the cold. I didn't know how long we'd have to stay standing outside like this with no coats, hats, or gloves, but each minute that passed tempted me to sneak over to Nathan's station and hide in his warm embrace.

Finally, after what seemed like hours but in reality was a brief forty-five minutes, the all-clear bell sounded and the P.A. directed us to return to our fifth-period location. Though I didn't like the thought of returning to the pit, I would at least be with Nathan and my friends.

When we all got back to our table, Adam made a stupid remark about offering to keep me warm, and Nathan shot me a look that asked if he should smack the guy. I shook my head and smiled at him so that he understood Adam wasn't worth the trouble. One day I might regret that.

After forty minutes had passed, the P.A. sprang to life again, this time with the principal's voice instructing us to gather our belongings from our lockers and board our buses or proceed home. School was dismissed for the remainder of the day. The rest of the announcement could barely be heard over the cheer that erupted from the pit, but nothing seemed to be said of what the emergency was about. Although the buses were called to the school for early pickups, Rhonda offered to give James, Nathan, Lee, Erica, and I a ride home.

"I can walk,"I said reluctantly."You'll be too crowded otherwise."

"Please…" Erica said, giving me a hug. "It wouldn't be the first time I had to sit on Lee's lap in that car, and it won't be the last."

We agreed to meet out at Rhonda's car after collecting our stuff from our lockers, which meant I only had an extra minute or two to find out as much as I could about what happened, as I suspected all of us were going to do in whatever way we could. My locker was on the second floor, and as I made my way down the hall to the stairs, I did something I'd never done since starting at Trinity High. I spoke to every student I could, classmates and strangers alike, asking if they'd heard any details about what had happened. My efforts were rewarded with blank stares, grunts, and the occasional inane speculation of fallen meteors.

When I left my locker, I decided to take the back stairs down to the main hall, and there I saw that the entire hallway leading to the library had been draped off with construction tarps. A small cluster of kids had gathered to check out the scene but were quickly shooed away by one of the school's security guards, who just happened to be an old hall supervisor from my junior high school. I smiled and waved at him as I approached and non-chalantly asked how he and his family were doing, as if we were bumping into each other at the market instead of meeting in the middle of a major catastrophe. I shook my head, saying, "It's just terrible what happened."

Without questioning my knowledge, he replied, "It's a shame, isn't it? Mrs. Lockhart was such a lovely woman. Lost her husband only a month or so ago."

I nodded then took a shot at acquiring more information. "The sad thing really is how it happened."

This time he nodded to me and leaned in to make sure no one else was in earshot. "I'm told the roof was supposed to have been inspected over the summer, but apparently there were some delays and ... there's probably no one to blame, but this is just the type of thing that makes you wonder how safe any of us are in the world. It's a miracle only a few kids were in the library at the time and that they escaped with minor injuries."

So the roof had collapsed and Mrs. Lockhart had been killed. As these realities sank in, I felt the blood leave my head and the walls start to spin. "Hey, are you okay?" I felt his hand on my arm and tried my best to snap back into reality.

"Sure," I replied with my best fake smile. "It's just been an intense day." I patted his arm and walked away in the direction of the exit to the student parking area, where Rhonda and the others were waiting for me.

As I suspected, everyone had tried to learn something about the incident, and although they had confirmed that there was a collapse in the library, there was no mention of Mrs. Lockhart or other injuries. I sat quietly in the back seat with Nathan, Lee, and Erica, not offering any additional facts. It took only a few minutes to get to my house, and as I got out, I leaned forward and said to Rhonda, "I'll be calling you later." I could tell by the way she tensed up that she knew perfectly why.

*

"You knew something was going to happen in the library," I said accusingly to Rhonda on the phone later that afternoon. "That's why you insisted I came to the pit this week."

"What do you want me to say?" she replied.

"I want you to tell me why you lied to me; why you would withhold information that could have saved the life of that nice woman? Why would you do that?"

"Oh, I see," she said defensively. "You think I should have gone to the principal and said 'Hey, Joe, I have a premonition that the library roof is going to collapse, and since I'm a precognitive empath, you can take my word to the bank.' Is that what you wanted me to do?"

"Yes!" I shouted. "You could have said something! You could have *done* something!"

I could hear her breathing heavily on the other end of the phone. "Jenny, you don't understand that I don't yet know what I know. I have no way of understanding the difference between a thought fueled by some news report or action movie versus a vision given to me by the universe. I can't yet tell the difference. And if I cried wolf every time I had an image of something bad happening, I'd be locked up in the mental ward by now."

"But you felt sure enough to keep me away from the library this week!" I hollered.

"Yes. Yes, I did."

As her words sank in, I realized that I could have been one of those kids who escaped with minor injuries, or I could have met the same fate as Mrs. Lockhart. It was hard to speak. On one hand, I wanted to thank Rhonda for keeping me out of harm's way. On the other hand, I wanted to hate her for not doing the same for everyone else.

Neither of us spoke for a long time, but the exchange of feelings was palpable, conveying equal parts of sadness, gratitude, regret, and forgiveness.

"Thank you," I said finally, breaking the silence.

"You're welcome," she replied.

"I'd like to go to her funeral, if we're allowed," I added.

"I'd like that, too."

December 19

On the afternoon of Christmissed, I took a hot bath and thought back to the day I had soaked in this tub and got a phone call from a stranger (or a Ryan Seacrest impersonator) that changed my life. How had it changed me? Besides the obvious fact that I now had a boyfriend and a strong circle of friends, how was I different? I pondered that question while playing with the bubbles in the water until an answer finally emerged.

I was no longer afraid to find out who I am.

*

Nathan was picking me up at seven o'clock, and though he wouldn't tell me where he was taking me, he suggested I wear something nice. "Prom nice?" I asked. "Or going out to a fancy restaurant nice?"

"A festive fancy dinner nice," was his reply, and so I painfully rummaged through my closet for the most festive outfit I could pull together. It was moments like this when I wished I took more of an interest in fashion or shopping.

"What can I do?" my mom asked from the doorway of my room. The question caught me off guard, and it took a moment for me to register that she was offering to help me get ready for my date.

"I'm supposed to be 'festive' tonight, and I just can't seem to find anything but black, black, and gray."

"Well, black can be festive with the right accessories and foot-wear." She sounded like one of those guest hosts on a daytime talk show doing a makeover.

"What do you suggest?" I asked, leery of what her answer might be.

She took out my short, flared black dress and laid it on my bed, then rummaged in my drawer for a pair of black tights with a subtle lace design. Next, she pulled out a pair of black leather ankle boots from the back of my closet that I'd thought I'd given to Goodwill last year. And finally, motioning for me to wait, she left my room and reappeared three minutes later with a dark silver wrap that shimmered with thousands of tiny sequins. In her other hand was a box that contained her Swarovski crystal teardrop necklace and matching earrings.

"Really, Mom? I thought these were your best pieces. You only wear them to weddings."

"I know," she said, pulling my hair back and holding it up in a bun. "But you only go out for your first Christmas dinner with your first love once."

"It's actually 'Christmissed,' Mom. And he's not my first love."

"Oh? You mean there's been another?"

We both started laughing, and I felt strangely compelled to hug her and whisper a 'thank you' into her ear.

*

When the bell rang at seven, my dad insisted on answering the door. As I came down the stairs and laid eyes on Nathan, I nearly lost my footing, he was so gorgeous. There he stood in a black suit that snuggly showed off the muscular contours of his body, a steel-blue shirt that matched his eyes, and a shimmering silver tie that I wanted to grab so I could pull him close and kiss him until my lips hurt.

He helped me with my coat and promised my parents he'd have me home around eleven.

"Where are we going?" I asked, thankful the car was toasty warm, considering I was wearing the thinnest of garments.

"Well, if you insist on knowing, I'll tell you that we're dining under the stars."

Not wanting to be ungrateful for whatever planning and efforts he'd made to make tonight a special occasion for us, I pretended not to be mortified at the idea of dining *al fresco* in near freezing temperatures.

Sensing my reluctance, he put his hand on my knee and said, "Don't worry. You won't be cold. I promise." And true to his word, I wasn't, because our night under the stars was actually inside the Southworth Planetarium. There in the middle of the domed theater was a white linen candlelit table set for two.

"Merry Christmissed, Jenny."

I turned and kissed him, feeling myself floating up to the heavens. "Merry Christmissed to you, Nathan."

He took my hand and led me down the stairs to the table, held my chair out for me, and signaled to a waiter, who appeared with two glasses of sparkling cider.

"How did you do all this?" I asked, truly bewildered.

He shrugged. "Remember the mentor friend I told you about, Richard? Well, he used to be on the board and is still a big contributor, so he pulled a few strings for me. Speaking of strings..." He signaled again, and two guitarists appeared and began performing a beautiful song I'd never heard.

"This is surreal." I sighed. "You amaze me."

Reaching across the table and taking my hand, he looked intently into my eyes. "If anything I do is amazing, it's because I am inspired by you." For the next hour, we talked and laughed and listened to the soothing music under a starlit sky.

"I hope you find this Christmissed gift as perfect and thoughtful as you'd hoped it would be."

"More than perfect, better than thoughtful. But I have to ask, how were you able to hire musicians? They must have cost you a fortune! I'm sorry, that was rude of me."

He laughed. "They're from the high school band. I gave them twenty bucks each."

"You've outdone my wildest expectations, though admittedly, I didn't really have any expectations."

"You could have fooled me," he said playfully. "I was prepared to dig into my college funds for emeralds and rubies after the directive you gave me that day."

"Oh … I didn't mean for it to come out that way. It's just that after seeing my dad give my mom potholders and slippers for fifteen years, I thought it best to be up-front about the thoughtfulness involved in giving a gift to someone you care about."

"Well, I certainly do care about you. In fact…" His lips parted, and I suddenly got that sinking feeling again.

"Hey! I almost forgot your gift!" I blurted out. Reaching into my oversized purse, I pulled out a square box wrapped in vintage brown butcher paper and tied with twine. "For you," I said, handing him the box.

"The wrapping is very … you," he teased.

I held my breath as he opened it, hoping I wasn't wrong in my choice of gifts. "I found it on eBay," I said as he pulled out the contents of the box. "I know it's not *the* baseball, but it's signed by Derek Jeter, 2009. I thought it would make you feel closer to Daniel; remind you of him in the best possible way."

Nathan's head was bowed down looking at the baseball in his hands, and I could see the tears dropping from his face. I didn't want to ignite his sorrow, though it was foolish if I'd thought this gift wouldn't do that. But it was intended to make him smile, which, to my relief, he did a few moments later, saying how he could feel Daniel smiling down on him.

"Jenny, it's almost scary sometimes how in tune you are. I was at the cemetery earlier today talking to Daniel about you. And I thought again about how much I'd wished I had kept that darn baseball. Thank you."

After we finished dinner, a delicious lasagna that he said his mom baked that afternoon, he pulled out my chair, held out his hand, and walked me to the front row of chairs in the gallery. Once he made sure I was comfortable, he walked over to the control booth and hit a few buttons. The theater went dark for a moment, then the stars reappeared and a voice came booming from the heavens. Nathan came down and sat in the chair next to me, and I whispered, "What is this?"

"You don't have to whisper. We're the only people here. And this is the astronomical story of the Star of Bethlehem."

"You're unreal," I said, taking his hand and leaning back in my chair.

"No," he whispered. "I am very real, and I am very much falling in love with you."

December 20

The next day, I was packed and ready for my trip to New Mexico. My flight was leaving early afternoon, and while my parents still weren't thrilled about my going, they did their best to act normal by fussing over my packing, security issues, and 'in case of emergency' plans (the emergency being that I was left stranded somewhere). I didn't protest, though I knew they were being ridiculous, and instead just went along with them, comforted in the knowledge that I'd be in another world by the end of the night.

As promised, Nathan dropped by for lunch, bringing a veggie pizza for us to share and a poinsettia for my mom and dad. Earlier, when my mom asked what Nathan gave me for Christmas, I told her that he gave me the stars and briefly explained about the planetarium, the dinner, and the private showing of the Star of Bethlehem. I could tell she was impressed, but when she asked me what I got him and I replied "An autographed baseball," I could tell she was not. She said that a baseball wasn't a very romantic gift, and he might construe it as a sign that I only wanted to be friends. If only she knew.

*

Saying goodbye to Nathan was more difficult than I thought it would be. I had either seen him or spoken to him almost every day for nearly three months, and now I felt like I was going to be cut off from the one thing that tethered me to the planet.

"Don't worry," he said, wrapping his arms around me and stroking my hair. "We'll see each other again before you know it."

"It's twelve days, Nathan. Thank God I'll be with my Aunt Maggie, or I don't know what I would do with myself."

"I feel the same. I mean, I'll miss you terribly, but I can't wait to hear all about your visit. If your Aunt Maggie is half the adventurous spirit you describe, you're probably not going to want to come back."

"Oh, I'll be back, all right. Just make sure you don't forget this." Jumping into his arms, I kissed him as passionately as I ever had as he whirled me around the front yard with my legs wrapped around his waist and snow falling softly on our heads.

*

The airport experience was worse than I expected. Maybe on another day it wouldn't have been as bad, but this was the holiday rush, and everyone seemed to have taken an anti-goodwill-toward-men pill that morning. The lines to check in extended as long as a parade of Chinese dragons on New Year's in Beijing. The parents in front of me were oblivious to their children, who stepped on my feet more than once and nearly got their fingers crushed in their own luggage cart. Forty minutes later, I faced another back-up for the security check. I made sure to pick a line other than the Oblivious family and was rewarded for my efforts with a bickering couple who not only stood on my heels the whole time but also had the worst breath I'd experienced since Johnny Dalton belched his pickled egg lunch in my face last year. I wondered if they'd back off and give me some space if I farted in their direction.

I closed my eyes and tried to mantra myself out of a panic attack. The emotional stew boiling around me was making me sweat, and I had to wipe my brow with the back of my sleeve every few minutes. Knowing my mind and body were reacting at an energetic level to the feelings of everyone around me didn't help when I couldn't break their hold on me. My bubble technique worked for only a few seconds before it popped me back into travel hell, so it seemed all I could do was move along like the rest of the cattle through the chute and hope I came out undamaged on the other side.

I must have looked as bad as I felt, because the female TSA agent asked if I was all right. I nodded weakly and gave her a half-smile but couldn't summon enough energy to wish her a Merry Christmas. She apparently felt the same and waved me through to an X-ray machine at the end of the row. I stripped myself of every item possible, stopping just short of public indecency, to make sure that I didn't trigger the system and end up in a pat-down situation. Thankfully, the plan worked, and as soon as I put myself back together again, I bolted for the nearest washroom, where I hoped I could unplug myself from this empath fuse box before I overloaded.

Please don't let there be a line for the bathroom. Please don't let there be a line for the bathroom. Thank you. Thank you. Thank you. I took the wheelchair stall at the far end and prayed someone actually in a wheelchair didn't come in for the next five minutes. *Deep breath in ... one, two, three, hold and out ... one, two, three. Again, two, three, hold and out, two, three. I am a tree, two, three, hold. I'm strong and tall, two, three. I inhale the power and energy of the earth. The energy flows into me now — through my crown, my head, my throat, my heart, all way down through the bottoms of my feet, which root me to the earth and give me strength, vitality and balance. I am connected and grounded in its power.*

Who was I kidding? I felt barely glued together. I splashed a gallon of water on my face and, realizing they only had automatic air hand dryers, dabbed myself off with my scarf and made my way to the gate area, where I buried my head in a magazine until they called for boarding.

*

Despite the tumultuous experience leading up to the boarding of the plane, the connection through Chicago went smoothly, and the ride to Albuquerque ended up a comforting déjà vu. The massive array of clouds formed pink and purple mountains, and the background soundtrack of "Adagio for Strings" played in my ear. The only thing missing was Nathan by my side. I closed my eyes and tried to remember what he said in my dream. *We'll always be together?* No, it was more than that. *We are always for each other...?* That was close, but not quite right. With my eyes closed and the adagio climbing and falling in intensity, I began to drift off to sleep, but before completely losing consciousness, the words caressed my final thought: *with each other and for each other always.*

*

When I saw Aunt Maggie waiting by baggage claim, I ran into her arms and held her so tight, she couldn't breathe. "Easy, sweetheart, or you're going to break me in two. Dimitri already tried that once," she winked.

"And how is your Greek god these days?"

"He's good. Living full-time now in Voula. It's on the coast about a half-hour's drive from Athens."

"Oh, and how do you feel about that? I mean, did you know he was going back there full-time?"

"Sure I did. When I met him on the El Camino in Spain, he was living in California, but said he would be returning home to Greece to retire. And I'm fine with it, so stop looking so glum for me." We grabbed my bags as they came around on the carousel and headed out to her car, which I was not surprised to find was a Kia Optima hybrid.

"So how far away do you live?" I asked.

"About an hour north of here in Santa Fe, in between the Rio Grande and the Santa Fe National Forest."

"Do you like it here?"

"I love it! I bought the place about fifteen years ago, right around the time you were born, actually. I got it cheap. It's worth a fortune now, but I'm not ready to sell."

As we drove the hour to her home, she regaled me with stories of the history of the region, that Santa Fe meant 'holy faith' in Spanish and that its original residents were Pueblo Indians in the eleventh and twelfth centuries. The Santa Fe River had provided water to the entire area year round until around 1700. About ten years ago, it was recognized as the most endangered river in the country.

Pulling into her driveway, I couldn't see much of the outside of the property, since the sun had set hours ago, but it was obvious by the exterior lighting that the place was huge.

"Come in. *Mi casa, su casa*! I've got you set up in the guest room, and the fire is already going because it can get down below freezing at night, as you can probably already feel."

"There's a fireplace in my bedroom?" I asked, gaping at the gorgeous bank of twelve-foot floor-to-ceiling windows that covered the entire back half of the house. A fire was lit in the living room, and over the mantel hung a stunning painting of a woman wrapped in a red shawl with her back exposed and her head glancing over her shoulder, eyes peering at whoever was painting her. It took me a moment to realize the woman in the painting was Aunt Maggie.

"That was painted when I was twenty-five, not long after I broke up with Rick. The painter was an art student I had a brief affair with. I was pretty promiscuous for a while."

"And pretty. *Really* pretty," I said, still gaping at the painting. "You were like … gorgeous."

"Still am," she retorted with a kick of her heel.

"I didn't mean to say that…"

"I know, sweetie. But under these crow's feet and graying hair lies a sensuous sex goddess."

"Yeah, yeah. Enough with your sex life, already. You're making me…"

"What? Envious? I guess that means you and your Prince Charming haven't consummated the relationship yet?"

"No! How come you keep asking me that? I don't have any plans to do any such thing for quite some time."

"Well, in my experience, it's the *not* having plans to do it that usually leads to the doing it."

"Are you talking about your first?" I asked, trying to move the conversation away from me.

"Of course I am. Now sit down while I make up some tea and we can catch up on life."

When she returned with our teas, a smile covered her face, and she bent to hug me warmly, saying, "Your being here makes this the best Christmas I could have ever hoped for — even though I don't really believe in Christmas."

"What do you mean you don't believe in Christmas? You were raised a Christian like my mom, after all."

"Yes, but at some point, the population decided that Christmas was more about material consumerism than celebrating Christ's birth. That was the first nail in the proverbial coffin."

"And the second?" I asked.

"Was when I realized that Jesus was only one part of the picture. A pure and loving, holy part to be sure, but not the only one to celebrate, to follow, and to learn from."

"I noticed your Buddha statue on the table. Are you a Buddhist now?"

"No. But the Buddhist teachings have certainly expanded my mind and my perception of self; more than Christianity ever did."

"So what are you? What religion do you follow?"

She took my hand and leaned closer to me as if she were going to tell me a secret. "I am a child of God, of no particular earthly religion, but of all universal faiths."

"That's an interesting way to put it. It sounds … complete. You aren't against any religion, you're just for God."

"And that's really a good way to put it, my dear. Now how about we get back to talking about your love life?"

December 21

Aunt Maggie's stories kept us up until almost midnight, which was two o'clock in the morning east coast time. I was thinking I would sleep until noon the next day but was surprised to wake at eight o'clock to the smell of coffee and cinnamon rolls.

"It's carob coffee, actually. No caffeine. You'll love it!" Aunt Maggie looked as fresh as a daisy. I wondered where that expression came from, since daisies smelled like cat pee to me. The carob coffee was indeed delicious, and the rolls were warm and gooey without being too sweet.

"So what do you feel like doing today?" Aunt Maggie asked. "We could go hiking, shopping, check out some art galleries or museums. Whatever you want to do."

"I think I'd like to see Santa Fe. Could we just walk around the city and hang out?"

"Of course! And we can pick up some grub and cook together tonight."

"I'm not a very experienced cook, but I'm game for whatever."

As we drove into Santa Fe, I was mesmerized by the vast landscape and open skies. I thought back to my night at the planetarium with Nathan and imagined that the stars in New Mexico would put on a show far more brilliant than a projected skyscape ever could. When I told Aunt Maggie about my Christmissed with Nathan, she lit up like a string of lights and begged me for intimate details, but I assured her there were none.

Walking around downtown, we stopped in a number of art galleries where the paintings and pottery of the landscape and culture spoke volumes of the passion and dedication of the people to this land. Seeing me admire one particular small painting, she told me that it depicted a mystical place not far from Santa Fe called Ojo Caliente, one of the oldest natural health resorts in the United States. "Its mineral springs are said to have healing powers and have been a gathering place for thousands of years."

"Can we go there?" I asked.

"Why? Are you in need of healing?"

I shrugged. "Something like that."

After lunch at the delicious upscale Café Pasqual's, Aunt Maggie suggested we burn off our meal by walking up to the Cross of Martyrs, a site dedicated to the twenty-one Franciscan friars killed in the Pueblo Revolt of 1680. Although the hike was relatively easy, I found myself straining during the ascent.

"Perhaps you're not used to the elevation, dear. We are almost seven thousand feet above sea level."

"Perhaps," I said and pushed on.

When we reached the large cross at the top of the crest, I felt a sudden pang of remorse. It was a bit like a panic attack, but more physical. I thought back to the antique armoire and hoped to God I didn't start vomiting in front of Aunt Maggie. Instead of focusing on the cross, I turned my attention to the stunning views of Santa Fe and the mountainous landscape in the distance.

"What's in that direction?" I pointed directly north.

"Immediately in front of us is the 285 highway, which crosses over the Rio Grand and the Rio Chama, then passes by Ojo Caliente, goes straight up through the Carson National Forest, and finally on up to Colorado."

"The Ojo Caliente? Do you think we could go there?" I asked again, feeling a strong pull to take off there right now.

"Sure. Of course we can. It's been a while since I soaked up the springs. Perhaps we'll even bump into my old friend Shirley MacLaine. I'll make a reservation for us this week."

Feeling the tension start to fade, I followed her back down the path to find a market for tonight's dinner.

*

With a beautiful meal of mini fish tacos and roasted eggplant with tomatoes and feta cheese on the table, we sat down in time to watch the sunset out of the wall of windows in her dining room. "At this time of year," she explained, "the sun sets around five o'clock, which is about two hours earlier than I usually eat, but I find that my dinner isn't complete without this breathtaking Santa Fe sunset."

Breathtaking was the perfect word for it. A heavy cloud hung above the horizon, and as the sun sank down into it, the most magnificent fire-orange rays shot down to the earth, giving the mountains a purplish glow.

"I imagine your food must sometimes go cold," I said, realizing I'd barely touched my meal in the last ten minutes.

"That's why I normally have salads," she replied, and we both laughed, staring out at the final minutes of the most beautiful sunset I'd ever seen.

*

"So come on," she nudged, "tell me how your life has been, besides the romantic Christmissed soiree."

"What do you want to know?"

"Well, the last time we spoke at length, you were convincing your parents not to show Nathan your baby pictures."

"Wow! Has it been that long? I guess we'd better start exactly where we left off then."

For the next hour, I talked practically non-stop about my Halloween night at the hospital, about Nathan, my friends, especially Rhonda, and all about the roof collapse at school. The only part I held back was the part where I and all of my friends were empaths. I wasn't sure why I did that, because I was fairly certain she would be open and accepting to all of it. I think I just felt embarrassed by the whole thing. Like if I said it out loud, people would think that I thought I was special in some way, when actually I felt more like a freak. But she wasn't just 'people.' She was my Aunt Maggie, so I decided if the moment presented itself, I would tell her. Until that moment came, I wanted her to get to know me without the freak part.

As the evening passed, we cleared the dishes, talked some more, made popcorn, and settled in on the sofa to watch one of Aunt Maggie's favorite movies, *Ghost*. She couldn't believe I'd never seen it before, and I had to remind her that it came out years before I was born.

"That's no excuse! Have you ever seen *Gone With the Wind*?"

"Yes."

"*It's a Wonderful Life*?"

"Yes."

"What about *Casablanca*? *The Godfather*? *The Wizard of Oz*?"

"Yes, yes, yes. You can stop. I get your point. But are you really suggesting that *Ghost* is in the same category as some of the best movies of all time?"

"Just watch."

For the next two hours and nine minutes, I was glued to the screen, holding my breath at times, laughing at others and finally bawling like a baby. When I looked over at Aunt Maggie, I was relieved to see her wiping her eyes as well.

"We are two saps, aren't we?" she cried, reaching over to take my hand. "So what do you think?"

"I think it's a beautiful, funny, and touching story. I'm so glad I got to see it for the first time with you."

"Me too, sweetheart. Now what did you think about the subject matter?"

"Oh, you mean ... do I believe in psychic mediums? Although I've never met one myself —" I was fibbing just a little, since Faith wasn't technically a psychic medium "— I'm open to the idea that there are people who exist with such gifts."

She chuckled under her breath and patted my knee as she got up to stoke the fire.

"Have you? Ever met a psychic medium?" I asked.

"Oh yes," she replied, drawing out the words for emphasis.

"And did they help you communicate with someone?"

"They did, indeed."

"Can I ask who?"

"Oh, many people. Grandparents, friends, great-aunts and uncles…"

"Wow. And how did you know it was real? I mean, weren't you skeptical at all?"

"I was at first," she said, "more scared than skeptical, actually. But in time I began to accept the possibility that it was real, until I finally trusted it as so."

"Is there anything you found out that was dramatic or profound?"

"Well, let's see … I did learn that my parents wished I had been a boy and that my great uncle was the real inventor of the blacklight in 1935."

"And how did that make you feel? To learn your parents wished that you were a boy, I mean."

"No big deal." She shrugged. "They didn't name me Mark or force me to play sports or anything. I wasn't wounded by it, if that's what you're asking."

"I guess if I could meet a psychic medium, I'd ask about Nathan's brother who died four years ago."

"And what would you ask?"

I shrugged. "Just whether he was okay and if he had anything he wanted to say to Nathan."

"What was his name? The brother?"

"Daniel. His name was Daniel."

"Well, dear," she said with a sigh, "I think it's time we turned in. We'll figure out our plans for tomorrow in the morning. How does that sound?"

"Perfect. And thank you so much for such a fulfilling day. I love being here with you."

"Ditto," she said, giving me a kiss on the forehead and a hug goodnight.

December 22

The next morning, Aunt Maggie woke me up at the crack of dawn — 7:10 a.m. to be exact — and told me to toss some things in my bag for an overnight trip.

When I asked her our destination, she merely replied, "The big hole." So off we set in her Optima for God knew where, but an exhilarating feeling rushed through me that made me feel both alive and secure.

"The big hole," as it turned out, was none other than the Grand Canyon. The seven-hour drive got us there at three o'clock, and as we drove around the south rim, along Hermit Road and the long Desert View Drive, I felt a calm and comforting sensation pass over me. Looking out from the Desert View watchtower, I tried to catch my breath, both for the stunning view of the canyon as well as the climb up the seventy-foot tower.

"I don't know if I ever would have come here if it weren't for you," I said. "I've seen so many pictures of this place, but I didn't think it would impress me this much to see it in person."

"Ah, but seeing is only one of our senses, and something of this magnitude demands all of our sensory attention, yes?"

"Of course, you're right, Aunt Maggie. The Grand Canyon is a multi-sensory experience, for sure." As if on cue, a massive bald eagle soared almost immediately in front of us and let out a series of high-pitched piping calls. "That sounded more like a canary than an eagle. Maybe it was the female's mating call."

"No, that is sadly just the way eagles sound. Speaking of mating calls," Aunt Maggie laughed, "are you getting anxious to talk to Nathan?"

I exaggerated an appalled look, saying, "It's only been two days! I can live without speaking to him for more than two days."

She shot me a 'don't try to fool me' look. Conceding, I finally said, "Okay, okay. He said he'd try to call my cell on Christmas Eve from whatever port he's in, and if he can't reach me, he'll try again the next day."

"Sounds like a good plan," she jeered, taking my hand and leading me to our next stop in the Grand Canyon.

With only a couple hours to go before sunset, we made brief stops at Lipan Point and the Tusayan Ruin, an eight-hundred-year-old Pueblo Indian site, stopping lastly at Grandview Point to watch as the sun set the sky ablaze in a pallet of colors so vivid, only a poet could have put it into words.

*

We slowly made our way along Desert View Drive, oo'ing and ah'ing as the last moments of color painted the sky. We pulled off Route 64 onto South Entrance Road, thinking we'd spend some time at the Visitor Center. The center, however, closed at five o'clock, so we decided to come back in the morning.

"Where's our hotel? I assume you made reservations despite the spontaneity of the trip?"

"What hotel? I packed us a tent." She said it with such a straight face, I almost believed her. Then, at the next driveway, she turned in, and the El Tovar Hotel appeared before us. She pulled the car beneath the portico, and a dark-skinned boy with long black hair tied in a ponytail stepped up to open my door. He greeted me in the Tewa language, saying *"Bepuwave,"* which I later learned means "Welcome." Quickly, he hustled over to open Aunt Maggie's door and extended the same greeting to her. She popped the trunk, he grabbed our bags, took our car keys, and led us into the lobby.

The interior was comprised of dark wood in a cabin-like structure. The ceiling angled up with large wooden beams and the walls, adorned with moose, elk, and deer heads, made me squirm. I was trying not to be one of those teenagers who made a face at anything that wasn't from their own generation, but more than the aesthetics, this place just gave me the heebie-jeebies.

As we made our way up to our room, the boy who met us at the car introduced himself as Ahote. He was Hopi Indian and explained that his name meant Restless One. He gave me a full smile as he said this, and I couldn't keep myself from blushing. He was truly beautiful, and I reprimanded myself for wondering how old he was.

Like a true tour guide, he began regaling us with the history of the hotel. In 1905, it was built and owned by The Fred Harvey Company, apparently a well-known name in this part of the country.

He said that famous people had stayed there, like Theodore Roosevelt, Albert Einstein, Paul McCartney, and President Bill Clinton. But the most impressive trivia he wanted to share was that the ghost of Fred Harvey himself was said to be seen walking around the hotel, especially during the holiday season, when he allegedly would invite the guests to the Christmas gathering. No wonder I had the heebie-jeebies.

Beautiful or not, I couldn't wait for Ahote to go away. I noticed my aunt was unusually quiet and pensive during his narration, and when he finally left us in our room, she shut the door behind him, saying, "That boy couldn't take his eyes off you. Nathan had better watch out!"

"Aunt Maggie, first, you're delusional. Second, doesn't this place kinda give you the creeps?"

"Why, because of all that ghost stuff? That doesn't bother me one bit. But apparently it does bother you. Want to talk about it?"

"Not really. I mean, I've just never been in a place where there have been ghost sightings."

"Oh, I bet you have. You just didn't know it. But rest assured, no ghost roaming through this place will do you any harm."

"And how can you be so sure?"

She looked at me as if she were about to say something and then thought better of it. Finally, she shrugged and said, "He's been roaming these halls for over a hundred years and hasn't done any harm yet."

We settled in our room, which was, to my relief, decorated in the usual nondescript hotel style: two queen beds fitted with blue sheets and bedspreads, generic Indian art prints on the walls, and a view of the canyon that was now covered in the early darkness. We each took turns showering and threw on some fresh clothes before heading down to dinner in the hotel dining room.

As we passed Ahote in the lobby, he gave me another over-zealous smile, which my aunt noticed immediately and would certainly chide me about all through dinner. As we ordered our meals (me the pumpkin ravioli and her the braised bison with grilled Brussels sprouts), she grew quiet and looked off in the direction of the kitchen as if she were expecting someone she knew to appear.

I glanced over my shoulder and asked, "What are you looking at?"

She shook her head and gave me a half smile, saying, "I just thought I recognized someone, that's all."

"Aunt Maggie, are you okay? Are you tired from the long drive? Should we go back to the room and order something up instead? You look a bit ... off."

"Oh, stop," she chortled with a wave of her hand. "I'm fine. Don't start treating me like I'm your old aunt who needs looking after. I just walked the El Camino, for God sakes!"

"Yes, you did," I laughed. "Which is more than I probably could have done. But you do look tired and ... distracted."

She stared at me for a long moment and let out a sigh. "I guess I do have some things on my mind. This time of year seems to..." she paused, searching for the right words, "...stir things up." We sat in silence for a while and then she was staring over my shoulder again. This time the waiter appeared with our salads. "But let us now focus on each other's company and this delicious meal shared together on what I hope is the first of many visits here." After finishing our meals, we lingered in the dining room, chatting about the seven natural wonders of the world over hot cocoa and volcano cake.

"Did you know that there are mystical wonders of the world, too?"

"No. I never knew that. What are they?"

"Ah, we have the whole days' drive tomorrow to talk about that. What do you say we go get a little fresh air and check out the night sky before turning in?"

"Should we get our coats from the room first?" I asked, hoping she would say yes.

"The vigor of the cold will do us good. Come on, we won't go far."

The hotel was illuminated for ambiance, not security, so there was hardly any light pollution. Staring up at the sky, the stars were so abundant, so thick, that it was hard to discern any of the constellations that were easy to spot back home.

"Rick used to love astronomy. He would take me up to the roof at the science building at college, and we'd lay out on a beach blanket, watching the shooting stars or a lunar eclipse. I don't know how many times we fell asleep on that blanket."

"I'll bet that's not all you did on that blanket," I teased.

"Now you're getting the hang of it!" she cheered. "Think sex first!" With both of us laughing hysterically, we almost didn't notice the shooting star sailing by to the west of us. My aunt grabbed my arm and let out a small gasp. When I turned to her, I realized she wasn't looking up at the sky anymore but instead peering into the darkness around the side of the hotel. As my eyes adjusted, I saw it: a small figure dressed in a dark, hooded cloak, moving in a way I would not describe as human. Now it was my turn to grab my aunt's arm.

"Come on," she whispered, tugging my sleeve.

"Come on where?" I protested.

Rather than reply, she kept pulling me along, around the side of the hotel toward Hopi House. She stopped short and held out her arm to keep me from advancing further. (As if I intended to!) She stood still, eyes pointed to the ground, concentrating like a hunter waiting for the deer to make a sound. A moment later, the spell was broken, and she turned to me with a shrug, saying, "That's that."

I grabbed her by the shoulders. "That's what? What just happened?"

She laced her arm through mine and turned me back in the direction of the portico. She walked along nonchalantly while

I felt as wound up as a rubber band airplane. "Tell me, please," I begged.

"It's like this," she began before a long pause that got us nearly to the front door. "I am a psychic medium, and that was the ghost of a woman who died here in the early 1900s."

*

"I don't know what question to ask first," I huffed, kicking my shoes off next to my bed back in the room. "Why a woman ghost appeared instead of that Fred what's-his-name or why you didn't say anything about being a psychic medium last night while we were watching your favorite ghost movie?" I put sarcastic emphasis on the last part, and for the first time ever, I saw my aunt recoil from me.

"No, wait," I pleaded, "I didn't mean to sound like such a brat. I'm sorry, but please give me a few minutes of freak-out time, okay? I mean, it's one thing to see this stuff in a movie or to hear about someone's experience with a psychic medium, but to see an actual friggin' ghost and learn that your own flesh and blood can communicate with them all at the same time is beyond disturbingly scary."

"You should probably sit down and put your head between your legs. You're starting to hyperventilate. And to answer both of your questions: Fred Harvey's ghost lives inside the hotel, whereas Pirl's grave is outside near the parking lot area, so she occasionally surfaces there. As for why I didn't say anything before, I certainly never expected to see a spirit here today, or I would have. It was actually my intention to bring up the subject on our drive home."

"And how exactly do you know the spirit's name and that she died here?"

"She told me."

"She told you? When? She didn't do anything but flit past us."

"I know, but she still told me."

"How? Did she speak to you with words?"

"No. It's more like a memory pops into my head."

"I don't understand. Be more specific." The edgy tone was back in my voice, and I laid my head back on my knees as my aunt walked over to stroke my back.

"First, Jenny, let me say that nothing in your world has changed. Spirits have always walked this earth, and I've been a medium to them since before you were born. The only difference now is that you became aware of this truth."

Her words made sense, but I couldn't engage with her yet. I felt a resistance to accepting the possibility of communicating with spirits from the afterlife. The feeling was so strong, I couldn't even bring myself to look at her for fear a ghost would appear beside her.

"What are you afraid of?" she asked me directly.

I shook my head, searching for some logical explanation for my feelings. I let thoughts and images play through my mind, until finally a graphic vignette formed, and it wasn't pretty.

"I can hear the wheels turning in that head of yours, Jenny. Anything you'd like to share?"

Again I gestured a denial, but the words tumbled from my lips anyway. "I'm afraid that if you have this medium gift, then what if I have it, too? I mean, what if it's hereditary?"

"What makes you say that?" she asked curiously. I thought back to how Faith had described coming from a long line of psychometric/medium empaths, and despite my promise to myself to tell Aunt Maggie about my 'gift,' I found myself frozen, unable to do anything but shake my head.

"Okay," she said, "let's just say for argument's sake that it is hereditary. What so scary about that?"

"What's so scary about that?" I shouted. I jumped up and started pacing around the room with the vignette of ghosts and dead babies flashing through my mind. "I'll tell you what's so scary about that! First, I'm a teenager; which means that I'm on an emotional, hormonal rollercoaster already. I don't need any more drama. Second, I'm in my first year of high school, which means the social pressures to fit in are fairly intense. Being a freaky psychic medium is the opposite of fitting in. Third, I'm in the first real romantic relationship I've ever had, which all by itself is pretty scary and…" I was about to spill the whole truth about being an empath but instead finished the sentence by saying, "… and I think that's enough for any teenager to handle without adding Casper the Friendly — or maybe not-so friendly — Ghost to the mix. *That's* what's so scary about it!"

"Good," she said, raising her hands in a victory pose. "Knowing what scares you is half the solution to overcoming what scares you. And whether you are a medium or not, no one is throwing you into the deep end of the pool. The universe won't do that to you. Well, not yet anyway." She came to me and threw her arms around me in her usual soothing manner, and it worked. I felt comforted. For now, anyway.

December 23

After a turbulent night's sleep and a slow start to our day, we headed out for a few last hours of Grand Canyon sightseeing before the seven-plus-hour car ride home. We hadn't broached the ghost subject since last night, and I hoped it was one we could avoid for now. In the meantime, I picked up a conversation I'd started with Aunt Maggie at dinner the night before. "Tell me about the mystical wonders of the world."

"Ah, yes. When I said there were seven wonders of the mystical or paranormal world, I should have prefaced it by saying that not everyone agrees on what they are. The lists vary. So perhaps it would be better to say that there are numerous wonders of the mystical world — but I have my own favorites. Since we have a seven-hour drive, I'll tell you about them all, and you can decide for yourself which sound most intriguing to you. One of them is actually on several lists: the ancient world, modern world, architectural world, and mystical world."

"Wow." I gaped, truly surprised at such a marvel. "What is it? Can't be the Grand Canyon, because it's not architectural."

"No. It's the Great Pyramid of Giza."

"Oh yeah, I read about it a couple years ago in school, but I don't remember much."

"That's understandable. It's a bit before your time and not in your zip code. It was built in 2560 BCE in what is now Cairo, Egypt, for an Egyptian pharaoh. I forget his name, but it's believed to have supernatural properties."

"You mean like the whole pyramid power thing or something more specific?"

She shrugged. "Who knows. People experience different things in mystical places, and not a lot of people document their experiences — at least not outside the *National Enquirer*."

I was surprised by her flippant attitude but intrigued about the stories, so I asked her to tell me about the other mystical wonders.

Over the next several hours, I learned about Machu Picchu: not a place to go if you're afraid of heights but thought to be one of the most mystical places on earth. Stonehenge: supposedly, healing rocks brought from Africa to Ireland then moved to England by Merlin (a wizard) or aliens, no one knows for sure.

Chichen Itza: the Mayan people predicted the world would end in 2012. Thank goodness they were wrong! But the site is thought to be mystical, haunted, and was a place of human sacrifice. The Colosseum: said to be haunted by the thousands of people and animals slain from around 80 AD for five hundred years. And the tomb of Marie Laveau in New Orleans: famous for being haunted by ghosts.

"Have you been to any of those places?" I asked, hoping she wasn't going to start talking about ghosts.

"I've been to Stonehenge, Chichen Itza, and New Orleans. Machu Picchu is next on my list."

She didn't offer more, and I didn't want to get into any ghostly details, but I also didn't want to shut her out. I thought back to the story about how my mom had called her a freak and treated her that way until she was pretty much excommunicated from the family. It was even possible, I thought, that my mom knew about Aunt Maggie's gift and that it was the basis for the whole unraveling of the relationship. I couldn't let history repeat itself.

"So what was New Orleans like?" I asked. "Is it all voodoo and black magic?"

"You don't have to look far to find the paranormal in that city, that's for sure. But it's understandable, considering that the dead are all buried above ground. Some believe there are twenty ghosts to every living person in New Orleans."

"That's crazy! Did you see any when you were there? What was it like? What made you go there?"

"Well, aren't you full of questions all of a sudden. Does this mean you're not freaked out any more?"

"No. I'm still a bit freaked, but I trust you'll handle me with care."

"Of course," she said, patting my hand. "Just this once."

*

I must have dozed off at some point. I was dreaming of riding in a tube-like train with Aunt Maggie and Nathan. But the train stopped moving suddenly, and it made me so angry, I wanted to put my fist through the window.

The dream got fuzzy, and I woke with a start, my fists clenched and my heart racing. Aunt Maggie didn't seem to notice. She said we were in Albuquerque and pulled into a gas station that offered Subway sandwiches. We both got out and stretched, shuffling our way into the store, where she paid for the fill-up and ordered a vegetarian sandwich for each of us to go.

There were booths along the window across the back of the restaurant part, two of which were occupied by two couples. As we waited for our sandwiches, something happened between the couples, and within seconds, an argument had broken out.

"You apologize to my wife," a tall, bearded man said to the shorter, stocky guy at the next booth.

"Screw you," the guy retorted.

"You wanna step outside and discuss this?" The big man cracked his knuckles and spat on the floor.

I grabbed Aunt Maggie's arm and tried to pull her somewhere for protection, but a flimsy rack of chips and cookies was all that stood between us and the brawl that was about to ensue.

The kid behind the counter stood there smiling, as if he'd just won a ticket to a mixed martial arts match. Terrified, I mouthed to him "Call the police," but he didn't notice me. His eyes were glued to the two men now rolling up their sleeves while their wives shot dirty looks at each other over the back of the vinyl-covered booth seats.

The big guy took the first swing, but the short guy was fast and able to duck before the fist made contact. They shuffled then, cursing at each other as they pushed and punched until the big guy swung hard, missing his target again and instead putting his fist into the window. It was hard to tell if the loud crack was his bones or the glass. While he was trying to recover, the other guy took a hard swing that landed square on his nose. Blood began spurting down the front of his shirt, but it didn't deter him from going after his opponent again.

My heart was pounding in my ears, and a wave of nausea swept over me. I didn't think about what the right thing was to do; I just reacted, screaming louder than my voice should have been able. "STOP!"

To my amazement, they did. Even the wives appeared frozen at my command. My head was throbbing so hard, I was seeing double as I grabbed my aunt's arm and escaped to our car.

She pulled away in a relatively calm manner, considering what we'd just witnessed. It was at least ten minutes later when I began to comprehend the events.

"Are you all right?" my aunt asked with concern.

"I'm not sure," I replied, feeling like I was both drunk and hung over at the same time. I flashed back to the two men, the searing anger radiating from them, a dark and trembling vibration so powerful it took the wind out of me now as I replayed the fight in my mind.

"Shhhh," my aunt whispered, soothing me with her hand on my back. "Let it go. These aren't your feelings, Jenny. I get it. Now breathe and let them go."

"What do you mean 'You get it?'" I said with tears welling in my eyes.

She exhaled in a burst of resignation or perhaps impatience. "You're an emotional empath, Jenny. I get it."

"You do? I mean, you know? How?"

She laughed softly. "Of course I know. Of course I understand. I'm an empath, too, sweetheart. Your suspicions are correct about things running in the family."

"Of course," I grumbled, thinking about Nathan and his brother, Daniel. I should have known. All this time, I'd been afraid to tell Aunt Maggie what I'd been going through, when I should have known she was the one person who would understand.

"Do you want to tell me how it started? When you realized it or what you've been going through?"

"Not tonight," I muttered and drifted back off to sleep.

December 24

I didn't remember arriving back at Aunt Maggie's home or getting into my bed there, but I woke in my pj's shortly after sunrise to the smell of carob coffee and blueberry pancakes.

"Good morning," I said sheepishly with the memories of last night fresh in my mind.

"Good morning to you. How are you feeling?"

"Not great. A bit embarrassed and ashamed, actually."

"For heaven's sake, why?" She plopped two pancakes on a plate and extended them to me across the kitchen island.

"For one thing, my behavior at the Subway last night was reckless and juvenile. One of those guys — or wives, come to think of it — could have had a gun, and there I was screaming at them trying to break up their fight like some playground supervisor. And for another thing, I'm ashamed that I judged you for keeping your psychic medium thing a secret from me, while all along I was keeping my emotional empath thing a secret from you."

"You're an astonishingly insightful and thoughtful kid. All's forgiven, honey. Really. I understand what you're going through."

"Why didn't you tell me about being an empath when you stayed with me last summer?"

She reached across the counter and held my hand, shaking her head. "If there's one thing I learned about being an empath, it's that you can only believe what you *feel*, not what you see or hear, or what other people tell you is true. As empaths, we must *feel* the truth for ourselves."

I nodded as she spoke those words, knowing they were true but still feeling a tiny bit disappointed that she'd held out on me.

"I suspected," she continued, "that you were a highly sensitive being, but each empath is different. We awaken to our gifts when the universe senses it's the right time for us to do so. And that is not by the decision of another human being — even a close friend or relative. You become aware and accept it when your soul is ready to; and then your close friends and relatives are there for support and guidance. As I am here now."

I nodded again, appreciative of her honesty and wisdom, but really too exhausted to get into it. I was empathed-out.

"Finish your breakfast," she said, "then go get some more sleep."

*

When I woke again, the sun was low in the sky. There was a fire glowing gently across the room, and Vivaldi's *Four Seasons* played quietly in the background. I looked at the clock. It was after 3:00 p.m. I'd slept through almost all of Christmas Eve.

Christmas Eve! I realized Nathan was supposed to call me today, so I searched frantically for my cell phone to see if I'd missed his call. Not finding it anywhere in my room, I threw on my bathrobe and flew downstairs.

Aunt Maggie sat in front of the fire reading with my cell phone by her side. "Take it easy, dear," she said, patting the cushion beside her. "He hasn't called yet."

143

"Oh," I said, surprised she'd remembered and yet not surprised at all. "Thanks." I took the phone from her and plopped down on the sofa beside her. I checked the phone log and text messages but only found a brief 'Merry Christmas Eve' text from Rhonda.

"How did you sleep?"

"Like I hadn't slept in a hundred years."

"Interesting, considering you're only fifteen, but dramatic events will do that to you," she said. "You should have seen me after September 11. I slept eighteen hours a day for almost a week and barely ate a slice of toast each day. I lost twelve pounds, which was great for my figure but not a diet I would recommend."

I looked at my aunt with renewed respect and admiration. She had found a way to survive, overcome, and ultimately embrace being an empath/psychic medium. She was living her life out loud, while I barely had a leg out from under my bed.

"Don't be so hard on yourself." She patted my leg and offered a pillow to lay my head on. "Like anything else in life, it takes practice to become proficient."

I closed my eyes as she stroked my hair, imagining how many more of my days would be consumed with shielding exercises, meditation, and study just to be able to exist in the 'real' world. It was exhausting.

The vibration of my phone startled me, and Aunt Maggie handed it over with a smile. "Looks like someone keeps his promises. Tell him I said hi."

"Nathan! Hello, where are you?"

"In Bahia Drake, Costa Rica," he said through a somewhat weak connection.

"Wow. What's it like?"

"Very tropical. They have a great national park. I went rock climbing and horseback riding. You'd love this place, Jenny."

"We'll have to book our next vacay there immediately," I laughed, only half joking. A trip to the tropics with Nathan sounded like ... paradise.

"How are things where you are?"

"It's great here," I said with as much fervor as I could produce from my drained spirit.

"You don't sound convinced."

I glanced up to see Aunt Maggie heading upstairs, giving me some privacy to speak with Nathan, but with the poor connection, I didn't want to have to raise my voice, so rather than tell him about the ghost sighting, my psychic medium aunt, and my empathic Subway psychosis incident, I decided to focus on a more positive and safe subject: Santa Fe.

After describing the wonder of the town and the Grand Canyon, I told him about our upcoming visit to Ojo Caliente and how my intuition told me that something amazing would happen there.

"I've had some pretty great experiences here, too. I'll tell you all about them when I get home. For now I just want to say Merry Christmas, Jenny. And I deeply miss you. But at the same time..."

"What? Nathan, I can't hear you. You broke off."

"I'm here. I just realized what I was about to say was corny as hell, so..."

"So what? Tell me. I like corny."

I could hear him taking a deep breath before saying, "I miss you completely, but at the same time, I'm comforted just knowing that you exist in the world — and that you're happy wherever you are. There, I said it."

I had goosebumps and was on the verge of tears. It wasn't just what he said, it was how he said it — so rich with tenderness and affection. I wanted to teleport my lips to Costa Rica just so I could give him a kiss. "Merry Christmas to you, Nathan," I finally

said. "I'm so glad you called. It's … really good to hear your voice."
My own voice cracked a little as the tears welled up in my eyes.
"Merry Christmas, Jenny."

December 25

On Christmas day, Aunt Maggie and I shared a lavish breakfast
of smoked salmon, poached eggs with hollandaise sauce, and fresh
brioche. Afterward, I phoned my parents to wish them a Merry
Christmas and was happy when they asked to be put on speaker-
phone so they could talk to Aunt Maggie, too. Although the conversation was a bit stiff and polite, they all expressed best wishes
to one another and said they hoped to see each other again soon.

Before saying goodbye, my dad reminded Aunt Maggie
about 'the package,' and she assured him it was under the tree
as promised.

"What was that all about?" I asked after we'd hung up.

"Your parents sent a gift for you. They wanted to make sure
you had something to open from them on Christmas Day while
you were here."

Taking me by the hand, she led me to the small tree next to
the fireplace, pausing to start a CD of melodic instrumental guitar
carols. It was like a storybook Christmas without the snow.

She took a small package from under the tree and handed it to
me. "From your mom and dad."

I was surprised they had arranged this. I'd assumed we would exchange gifts when I returned from my trip. I was even more astounded when I opened the box to discover a portable digital recorder and a note saying *For your music.*

It was the first time they had ever acknowledged my music or showed any tangible support for it. The love and thoughtfulness I felt in their note swelled in me like an ocean wave. Aunt Maggie reached over to brush the tear from my cheek, saying, "I guess they struck a chord — pun intended."

We laughed as I cried, and then she made me promise to send her some songs after I'd recorded them. I nodded, blowing my nose and tossing the tissues into the fire. It was not uncommon that just a few minutes of intense emotion could exhaust me, and this was no exception. But Christmas Day had just begun, so I tried to boost my energy by switching the CD to something more upbeat. "Mel Tormé?" I asked.

"Best version of 'Sleigh Ride' ever," she shouted. With the jingle of sleigh bells and Mel's velvet voice crooning away, I crawled under the tree to fetch the gift I'd hidden there for her.

"You sneaky girl! Hiding a present under my own tree. You shouldn't have, though. Being with you is all the gift I need."

"Yeah, yeah, yeah. That's what you're supposed to say to your only niece. I want to hear the truth from your lips after you open your present."

She gingerly unwrapped the small, flat box, peered inside, and gasped as she read the name 'Deepak Chopra' on the ticket.

"You got me tickets to see Deepak?" Her voice squeaked like a teenager who just won a backstage pass to a Justin Bieber concert.

"Yes, I did. And what's more, the event is in Boston, which means we get to spend the weekend together."

Now it was her turn to get teary-eyed. She hugged me hard and whispered, "Best Christmas gift ever." Then, reaching for a package under the tree, wrapped in plain brown paper and tied with twine, she handed it to me, saying, "Let this be the first of many Christmases spent together."

When I saw what lay underneath the wrapping, my tears started up again. It was the painting of Ojo Caliente I'd admired in the gallery just a few days ago. "Aunt Maggie ... how did you..."

"I have my ways," she coyly replied. "And don't go saying 'I shouldn't have,' because you're my only niece who's also becoming one of my dearest friends. Enjoy it."

"Always," I said, embracing her with my whole heart and soul.

December 26

The next morning, we woke with the sunrise, sharing some brioche and more of the delicious carob coffee (which I knew Rhonda was going to love!) and laughing at how we'd always remember this year as 'the Christmas of a thousand tears.' With the dishes cleaned up, we went back upstairs to pack for our day trip to Ojo Caliente. Well ahead of schedule, I asked Aunt Maggie if we could take a half hour to do yoga together, feeling that some breathing and grounding would be needed before stepping into the spiritual unknown. On mats laid side by side in front of the large bank of windows, we began a sun salutation flow that elevated me to a place higher than I'd been before. *Moment by moment, breath by breath.* No thoughts of the past few days, negative or otherwise, clouded my concentration; no worries of the future interrupted either. It felt somehow like the grimy film of life was being Windexed off me, and what remained was perfectly clear and bright.

On the drive to Ojo Caliente, Aunt Maggie told me the story of how she learned she was an empath. "I was about your age," she began. "My parents were going through a rough patch, fighting all the time or worse, giving each other the silent treatment — which wasn't so silent to me. I was picking up their toxic energy, and it was so loud, it was like a banging drum. When I was in the room with either one of them, my head filled with horrible thoughts, things I would never have come up with on my own."

"Like what?" I asked, wanting to fully understand.

"Like how my mom wondered why my dad wasn't affection-ate anymore, and how he thought she had stopped taking care of herself."

"So were you reading their minds?"

"No. But of course, there are those who can. Most empaths are just acutely skilled at reading people — you know, their body lan-guage, facial expressions, and tone of voice. We don't even know we're doing it. In any case, I began to realize that I was affected by their emotions to a level far greater than a normal kid should have been; at least far more than your mom seemed to be."

"Was that it? I mean, in terms of your sensitivity?"

"Heck, no," she snorted. "As soon as I picked up on their emotional garbage, it seemed the floodgates opened to the whole world. My emotional pendulum swung all the way from pure joy to the depths of depression and darkness. I couldn't listen to the radio or watch the TV without getting emotional whiplash. If my parents weren't so caught up in their own troubles, I'm sure they would have checked me into the Shady Oaks mental clinic."

"But you said my mom didn't seem affected by any of it?"

"No. She was different, your mom. A bit of a worrywart, but still a 'chin up' kind of girl."

"That sounds like her all right."

"Don't hold it against her," she warned with a wave of her finger. "You can't begin to know her inner workings any more than she can know yours."

"So how did you handle the emotional stuff you were picking up all the time? I mean, did you realize what was happening to you, or did you think it was all in your head or what?"

"I struggled a lot the first couple years. I thought it might have been hormonal, related to my period, like PMS. Terms like bipolar weren't mainstream in those days, or I might easily have been diagnosed — or misdiagnosed — with that type of disorder. The only relief I got was when I was sleeping or alone listening to music. Creative activities seemed to help."

"I totally get that! For me, my music is both an escape and a connection."

"Yes!" she exclaimed, swerving the car a bit to avoid a chipmunk in the road. "Music lets you escape from the external energy pollution, as well as connect with the universe's higher frequencies."

"Exactly. That's exactly how it feels."

"But," she said, "you know what the most powerful thing you can do for yourself is, don't you?"

I shook my head.

"It's your own every day self-love routine." I wasn't sure I understood, so she clarified.

"When you wrote me while I was on the El Camino, you said you sometimes didn't know how you got out of bed in the morning; that you felt lost without any point or purpose to your life."

I nodded, embarrassed that I had revealed my darkest thoughts to her. Then I said, "But that was before," trying to act like it was years ago and not months.

"Before what?" she asked.

"Before I met Nathan and all my new friends. And before you and I became so close."

She reached over and took my hand in hers. It was so comforting and fit so well with mine, it seemed our hands must have grown together like this over years or lifetimes. Her voice, too, was comforting, and the words that passed her lips resonated with such truth, they almost took on an angelic shape and color as they escaped into the air between us.

"The thing is, Jenny, the purpose of your life cannot be a boy or friends or me. You have to learn how to get out of bed so you can be with *you*. *You* must be the point and purpose of your life. Does that make sense?"

She waited patiently while I stared down at our intertwined hands, but I was afraid that if I opened my mouth, my own truth would come out, only the shape and color would reveal something dark and demonic.

I finally swallowed hard, acknowledging to myself that my Aunt Maggie was the one person that required no shielding or bubbles or half-truths either. If I was going to learn from her and benefit from her experience and wisdom, I needed to show her all my broken parts.

"I never told you," I whispered, "what happened before graduation."

Again, she waited patiently as I searched for my words and my courage. I looked down at the floor, then out the window for a good minute or so, until finally I met my gaze in the side-view mirror. At first it seemed like I was looking at someone else, as if my human self just happened to bump into my higher self, and they were surprised to see each other. As I stared at my reflection, a voice in my head said, *I'm sorry*. And another replied back from the mirror, *I forgive you.*

I turned to my aunt and said, "For a brief time I was cutting my arms. Not with a razor. I hadn't intended on killing myself. I just…" I took a slow, deep breath, filling my lungs with as much love and forgiveness as I could absorb from the universe, then

---

exhaled just as slowly and said, "I didn't know how to feel about anyone or anything — except physical pain and physical healing. That seemed all I had control over.

"My parents," I continued, "kinda freaked out and took me to a psychiatrist who wanted me to take drugs, but I resisted and have been able to, so far, with the help of Nathan and my friends."

"So Nathan knows you're an empath?"

Now I broke out in a huge smile and couldn't keep in the laugher. "Actually, Nathan — and all my new friends at school — are empaths. We even have a club, and we meet every month. At first I thought it was some freakish cult. It reminded me a bit of the time you spied on Rick through the kitchen window. But it's really more like a book club without the book."

Aunt Maggie shook her head, looking out ahead to the road as we traveled on the highway in near solitude. "Anything else you'd like to share? Have you been abducted by aliens? Discovered the Lost City of Gold?"

"I'm sorry I didn't confide in you earlier."

"Oh, hush," she interrupted. "I'm teasing. Don't apologize to me or anyone else for sharing or not sharing the personal details of your life. Only you get to decide who you let into your world."

"But I want you in my world! I want you to know everything about me — it's just that I also want you to like me, to love me and not think I'm totally cray cray or one of those immature kids who always needs drama in her life."

"Well, that's just a chance you're going to have to take. It's called trust, and it comes from building relationships — especially good, long-lasting ones."

I nodded, understanding her words, but like reading an instruction manual from IKEA, I didn't yet see how all the parts came together to make the finished product. As long as I could remember, it seemed that relationships ended up with me feeling really bad about myself, and now I realized those feelings were probably more about the other person's feelings than my own. I started to ponder that idea in relation to trust but was cut short when I realized we had reached our destination: Ojo Caliente.

As we pulled into the parking lot of the facility, it was like entering another world. "I reserved the High Desert Getaway package for two," she said.

"Which means what exactly?"

"We get a fifty-minute massage and our own private outdoor mineral pool with a Kiva fireplace for an hour. After that, we have to schlepp it with the common folk in one of the public springs."

"Sounds fantastic," I said, grabbing both our totes and heading inside.

*

In complete contradiction to the El Tovar Hotel, the Ojo Caliente facility was both pleasant and inviting. After signing in at the desk, we were pointed to the lockers, where we changed into our robes and then waited in the anteroom of the massage house that smelled of lavender and eucalyptus and offered sparkling water with cucumber, lime, or lemon slices. I opted for the cucumber. Aunt Maggie chose the lime, because "Cucumber gives me gas," she said, waving her hand behind her bum. I started laughing until I saw the "Quiet Zone" sign over the door.

A few minutes later, we were called in to our respective rooms, and for the next fifty minutes, my body was expunged of its negative, stressful, and toxic energy, leaving me feeling empty, like a room that had been cleared of its clutter. Even my mind was a desolate cavern. No thoughts came to me except that of putting one foot in front of the other as I made my way back to the locker room, where I showered in bliss under the steamy water.

When Aunt Maggie and I reconvened by our lockers, she suggested we soak in our private mineral pool *au naturel* and flashed me her birthday suit under her robe.

"Seriously, you are the most sex-minded person I've ever known — and I'm a teenager! What does that tell you?"

"That I must be doing something right." She winked.

I opted for my modest two-piece suit and followed her out to our private pool. The briskness of the air sent a chill through me, but Aunt Maggie promised the water was comfortably warm.

As I stepped into the pool, the heat penetrated through me with such force, my forehead began to bead with sweat. The water was supposed to be only one hundred degrees, but by the time I was completely submerged, my molecules were melting like butter in a skillet, yet the heat soaked clear into my soul and purged the last traces of anxiety and stress that remained. I closed my eyes and let it consume me. I surrendered to the water, to the sky and sun, the air and the earth, and to my thoughts of Nathan, who caressed my heart and soul with every breath. *God, I wish you were here to share this with me, Nathan.*

Aunt Maggie and I did not utter a word for the next hour. The effect of the pool was so intoxicating, I wondered how we would be able to drive back to her home without getting stopped and checked for sobriety.

Pulling me out of my stupor, Aunt Maggie took my hand, and after we donned our robes, she steered me back to the locker rooms, where she insisted I drink a liter of water, and I insisted she put on her swimsuit before we made our way to the final segment of the day: the Lithia Spring.

I could barely walk, let alone focus on her words as she described the Lithia Spring as having healing powers for depression and also being an aid in digestion.

"The first time I came here, I had a very spiritual experience." She sighed as if reliving the moment. Upon entering the

Lithia Spring area, the smell of salt and something else, perhaps iron or sulfur, filled my nostrils. At first it was biting and offensive. A minute later, however, the odor diffused and became mildly stimulating.

There were only two other couples in the spring, lingering in silence at opposite ends of the pool. Aunt Maggie submerged without hesitation, while I tested the water one step at a time. Still wet from the previous pool, I shivered a bit in the cold afternoon air, knowing it would be warmer in the water but unable to take the plunge.

As I went down the first step, I inhaled deeply and looked up at the sky so dense with cloud layers, it belonged in a Constable painting. With each step I took further down into the spring, I silently prayed ... *I am grounded and rooted in the strength and power of this earth. Goodness and light flow through me from the universe. Its healing powers restore my physical being, and from me, love flows in abundance to all whom I encounter. I surrender myself to the power and destiny of the universe. I commit myself to its eternal energy and light.*

Breathing slowly and deeply, I closed my eyes and felt a strange tingling sensation in my entire body. It was different than chills or goosebumps. Every organ, every muscle and cell seemed to tremble, as if stimulated by a small electrical charge. The feeling was a bit euphoric, not the same as an out-of-body experience (though admittedly, I'd never had one of those myself), but it seemed more like my body was vibrating in harmony with the universe; like my consciousness had called out to the universe, and it replied by pinging me back.

With my eyes still closed, I stood in the water and continued to meditate until I felt another tingling sensation, this time cold and prickly on my face and the tops of my shoulders. I heard someone gasp, and when I opened my eyes, I saw that it was snowing.

Jeannette Folan

*

After we had showered and changed back into our street clothes, Aunt Maggie suggested we head to the lounge for a light snack before going home. It was strange to hear her voice. We had barely spoken in over two hours, and even now, outside of the 'Quiet Zone' of the springs, I was only able to nod.

"You look like you have been seriously unplugged," she said, plopping down next to me on an oversized leather sofa that could easily be my final resting place for the night.

Again, I nodded and let out a wimpy "Uh-huh."

"The springs have that effect," she chuckled. "Are you going to need me to feed you? Carry you back to the car?"

I shook my head while silently thinking how wonderful her idea sounded.

The waiter appeared to take our orders, and Aunt Maggie jumped in. "We'll be sharing an order of the Queso Fundido, as well as the Ojo Fish Tacos. And we'll have a bottle of sparking water. Each."

After the waiter left, she asked, "So can I assume you had a good experience here? Blink once for yes, twice for no."

I smiled and chuckled at her wittiness, surprised I had the strength.

"Ah! A facial expression and an audible reply," she snickered. "Now we're making progress. Seriously, do you want to talk or no?"

"Not yet," I managed, taking a deep breath and feeling the wave of electricity course through me again.

"All right then. Let's just enjoy our meal and this beautiful view in peace and pray that my all-season tires can handle this snowfall."

*

We did make it back to her home without incident, though the snow had accumulated a good five inches since it began two hours earlier. As Aunt Maggie lit a fire in the living room and put on a pot of tea, it occurred to me that this was our last night together. Where had the time gone? My feelings of love and admiration flooded over me, and again, I felt the tingling sensation reverberate through my body. I smiled and nearly laughed out loud thinking that this tingly, pulsing sensation felt a bit like when I was with Nathan.

"Anything you'd like to share?" Aunt Maggie was standing over me holding out a plate of dark chocolate and pear slices.

"I'm too embarrassed to say it out loud," I cringed.

"You haven't been able to say anything out loud all afternoon! I don't want to spend the last night with my favorite niece doing Marcel Marceau impersonations."

"Who?" I quipped.

"Never mind," she said, rolling her eyes. "Kids!"

"I'm teasing," I said, biting into a pear slice that tasted as sweet as honey. "I admit Ojo Caliente took a lot out of me — but in the best possible way. I feel so … what's a good word to describe it?"

"Clean," she suggested.

"Yes!" I laughed. "Very clean and wrung out and renewed and replenished and…"

"And?" She waited, as she always did, with patience.

"And when I was in the Lithia Spring, I felt something extraordinary. This warm tingling sensation filled me from the inside out. It came in a wave, at first when I submerged into the waters and again, several times actually, since leaving the spring. I don't know how I can better describe it than that. It's a pulsating vibe that sweeps through my body and when it happens, I feel peace and … trust."

"Or," she said, her voice low and tender, "perhaps when you're in a mindset of peace and trust, it results in a warm, tingling sensation."

"I thought of that, too, because the first time it happened, I was sending up a request to the universe for goodness and light to flow through me."

"And so it seems it did."

I shrugged. "So it seems."

*

We spent the remainder of the evening sharing random stories of some of our favorite memories. Most of Aunt Maggie's were centered around her time with Rick and her adventures exploring the world. Each destination, it seemed, was accompanied by a mystical event, some small and inconsequential (like her first trip after her breakup when every other man she met was either named Rick or looked a lot like him) and others very powerful and life-changing (like when a shaman told her she would soon live in a land of holy faith, and one week later she was offered a job in Santa Fe).

My memories paled in comparison, mostly involving fleeting moments in my childhood, like when I thought I could talk to the moon or when I stared up at the stars for so long, I thought I had become a part of them.

"Most astrophysicists say that we're all just stardust."

"Hmmm. I like that. It's comforting in a way," I said. "It kinda lifts the pressure off of always thinking I have to become something greater than everyone else."

"Is that how you feel? That you have to live up to someone else's expectations or compete with the rest of the world?"

"Well, let's face it. I mean, I don't know what it was like in your generation, but in mine, success and winning is not really a team event. Because even within the teams you have to compete for team captain, MVP, president, and so on. So those who have natural leadership abilities are given the roles they already excel at, while the rest of the herd go without the opportunities they need to become good leaders."

"Sounds like you've given this some thought. Any experiences in particular that brought you to this viewpoint?"

"Me? No. In fact, from the time I was little, the idea of competing against my classmates and friends appalled me. So I made it a point to never participate in any activity that fostered rivalry."

"None? What about sports?"

"Never interested me. And if you haven't noticed, I'm not the most athletically coordinated person."

"What about intellectual competition like chess, debate or … science fairs?"

"Nope, nope, and nope."

"So here's a question — and I'm not judging. I'm only asking to provoke thoughtful and stimulating conversation."

"Shoot," I said.

"If you don't participate in any competitive activities, how are you challenged to grow beyond your current level of intelligence or performance?"

"I challenge myself to grow beyond by studying more than what they teach in school and by observing and experiencing things for myself instead of living my life on a mobile phone."

"That's an answer. But what happens when you get beyond school and need to survive in the adult world?"

"You mean the 'real' world?"

"Jenny, as you get older you'll realize that there is no place on this Earth that exists without some level of competition. I myself do not thrive on it. But competition is a fundamental part of evolution. And I'm not just talking about Darwin. If we are to evolve, we need to be challenged, and history shows that that usually comes from external sources, not from within."

"So you're saying that you buy into the idea of competition versus cooperation?" I was surprised by my aunt's statement. Of all the people I knew, she was the person I least expected to advocate competition.

"Let's get one thing straight right off." Her words were edgy, but her tone was light-hearted and disarming. "*I* would choose the path of cooperation over competition any day. Yet I also understand the necessity of competition and the value of it at times."

"Such as? Give me one example."

"Such as getting to the moon. If the U.S. hadn't been so hell-bent on beating the Russians, we might still think it was made of cheese! And in the process of winning that race, a long list of spin-off technologies were invented, including the technology for vascular bypass surgeries, firefighting equipment, cochlear implants, de-icing technology for airplanes…"

"Okay, okay, competition might have resulted in some life-changing inventions. I'm not saying that people shouldn't challenge each other, but I don't believe it has to come at the cost of someone else's dreams, hard work, or self-worth. At the core of my being, I know that cooperation will get this world a lot farther than competition."

Aunt Maggie stared at me, shaking her head with a wide grin. "My God, you remind me of myself when I was your age."

"What a nice thing to say!"

We sat for a moment in silence, gazing at the tree and the dying embers of the fire. "Well, we're not going to solve the world's problems tonight. What do you say we turn in and have an early breakfast tomorrow before I get you on that plane back home?"

"Home," I said with a twinge of reticence. "It seems far away and long ago. I feel so at home here. It's going to be like … going back in time or something."

She could tell by my tone that something had taken root here in Santa Fe, here with her, and that leaving now, despite how much I longed to be with Nathan and my friends and family, was like pulling a freshly planted tree from the ground.

December 27

The next morning on the drive to the airport, with last night's conversation still clearly on her mind, Aunt Maggie asked me again about a self-love routine. Seeing my blank expression, she continued. "As an empath, you are like a sponge, right? You absorb the energy of those around you."

I nodded, thinking that a sponge was a great analogy for an empath's life.

"You've told me that you've had numerous experiences where the negative energy of people, and sometimes even objects have affected you, consumed you even."

"Yes."

"So think about how a sponge works. The only way a sponge can absorb anything is if it's dry. If, however, a sponge is full, if it's already soaked up with something, then there isn't any more room for it to absorb anything else. My point is, instead of trying to shield yourself from soaking up negative energy, you need to learn how to keep yourself constantly filled. Filled with self-love."

"Oh..." Her words made me catch my breath. "That's so simple. It makes complete sense!" I started laughing, picturing a human-sized sponge with arms, legs, and my head on top. As I did, I saw a light bulb over my head glowing brighter and brighter, until I had to close my eyes from its intensity and finally doubled over in hysterics at the absurdity of it.

"Are you okay, honey?" my aunt asked with part concern, part sarcasm.

"I'm sorry, I'm sorry." I snorted. "I can't help it. I'm trying to stop…" I was laughing and snorting uncontrollably. "I just feel like I finally got the joke; only it's not a joke, it's my life." Wiping the tears from my face, I realized we were pulling into the airport, and now my tears flowed for our goodbye and the ache I knew I would feel apart from her.

Hugging me tightly, she reminded me it was only two and a half months until we'd see each other again and that it had been the best Christmas she could ever recall.

I kissed her on both cheeks. We were both crying now. Our Christmas of a thousand tears.

Part II:
The Dark And
The Light

January 6

The smell of his skin transported me to another time and place. The familiarity of his hand in my hand, his lips on my lips ... it was like coming to a place I had called home for many lifetimes. Any anxiousness I once felt did not exist now when Nathan was near me. As his fingertips brushed the side of my neck and slid down my shoulder, the sensation of a thousand butterflies flapping their wings tickled me until I smiled and let out a low purr in his ear.

"Shhh," he whispered back, placing his finger gently on my mouth. "Remember...Silentium."

Silentium means *silence* in Latin. It was a game he played with me. One that I'd grown to crave every time we were alone together. I closed my eyes and bit my lip, tilting my body forward expecting to meet his, but like two positively charged magnets, a distance remained between us. How long the resistance would last was hard to tell.

At this moment, Nathan was testing my ability to stay still and quiet as he tickled me with the tip of his tongue. Since returning from our Christmas vacations, things started to heat up between us, but Nathan had expressed his intentions to keep my virtue intact. I assured him that my intentions were the same. As the days passed, however, I became acutely aware of how much more he affected me. And at moments like this, with the weight of his body pursed over mine, I struggled not to throw those intentions out the window.

As if being a teenage empath wasn't difficult enough, I had to deal with the temptation of sex, and as I finally admitted to myself, love.

January 10

It was me who said it first. Although Nathan had expressed to me under the stars that night that he was falling for me, I was the one who said those three big words out loud. It happened in a burst of unexpected happiness. We were out walking on the trails on an unusually warm afternoon the weekend after New Year's. The clouds were layered in a thick, wavy sheet across the sky, reminding me of how the ocean leaves ripples in the sand at low tide. Miles passed as we walked along, sharing every detail of our holiday trips.

His face lit up as I conveyed the sensational and supernatural events in Santa Fe, and likewise, I was mesmerized as he described the coffee plantations, his tour on the rainforest aerial tram, and a helicopter ride over the Poás volcano.

At one point, with our hands intertwined and our faces flushed from the hike, a gust of wind blew a pile of dried leaves down from the crest above us, dousing us like game show contestants getting confetti'ed after guessing the correct answer to the million-dollar question.

The initial flurry startled us both, but as the wind gusted again, causing another blizzard of leaves to pour down on us, we laughed and howled until we were gasping for air, spitting out bits of leaves from our mouths and pulling twigs out of each other's hair. Still laughing, trying to catch my breath, I blurted out, "Oh God, I love you."

Hearing the words escape my lips, I felt both surprised and relieved. I hadn't planned on saying it. I hadn't been waiting for the perfect opportunity to spring it on him. It just bubbled out of me like the laughter we were sharing in that magical moment. As surprised as I was that it came out, a feeling of relief immediately followed. Although I wasn't sure how he would reply, I looked into Nathan's eyes, completely unafraid.

He stepped forward and took my face in his hands. "It's about time you said what I've been thinking since…"

"Since when," I asked, grabbing him playfully by the collar.

"Since the energy of your soul ignited mine back to life."

"Aw, I bet you say that to all the empath girls."

He kissed me fervently and shook his head. "There's only one girl, empath or otherwise, that I love."

When I looked up, I smiled, realizing that the sky was almost completely clear, except for two fluffy clouds.

January 15

It had been almost two months since our last Trinity Empath Club meeting. Although I was looking forward to reuniting with my empath friends, I really just wanted more time alone with Nathan, talking, being close, and playing our Silentium game.

Nathan began the meeting with his usual greeting and wished us all a happy new year. This time, rather than open the floor to everyone's reports, he explained that he wanted to share something from his holiday vacation in Costa Rica.

"I met a couple that practices what is called EFT — Emotional Freedom Techniques or 'tapping.' It's a healing process that engages the energy meridians just like acupuncture does, but instead of needles, you tap with your fingertips. And while tapping, you speak affirmations to clear the emotional block."

"I've read about this for weight loss," Faith interjected. "It's supposed to really control your needless cravings."

I caught myself rolling my eyes, thinking that the craving I had for Nathan right now was not needless and that I wished there were a way to tap away every one of them so I could be alone with him.

"According to Sileny and Machiel, the couple I met," Nathan continued, "EFT can help with a number of issues, including stress, anxiety, sleep problems, pain, weight loss, and ... drumroll please..." Everyone started drumming their hands on the table, and I immediately felt a headache start over my right eye. Nathan gave a hand gesture like a symphony conductor, and everyone thankfully fell silent. "Empath sensitivities!" he announced as if declaring a solution to a world problem.

The group collectively responded with a resounding "Ooo" while I excused myself to find the bathroom and some Aspirin. When I returned a few minutes later, Nathan quietly asked if I was okay. I nodded but found it hard to pay attention. Faith was saying something about the vibrational value of foods, and I immediately felt my stomach turn. As much as I wanted to spend time with Nathan, I finally had to call my mom for a ride home and excused myself from the meeting.

Back home, I climbed into bed still wearing my clothes, not bothering to even brush my teeth. When I heard the phone ring downstairs, I knew it would be my sweet Nathan calling to check on me, but even the sound of his heavenly voice was more than I could bear right now. My head hit the pillow, and I was gone.

February 3

As February began, everything seemed to move in slow motion. With each snowfall, the school, my family and my friends became more weighed down. Everyone's moods and usual lively activities dropped as low as the temperature. Sub-zero.

January had been such a whirlwind. The weather was milder than usual, there seemed to be social events every weekend, and, of course, Nathan and I were in love. The euphoria I felt with Nathan had distracted me from my usual low-grade anxiety. It was blissfully drowned out by his words, his laughter, and joy. On the other hand, the euphoria had also distracted me from being vigilant about my empath exercises. My shielding, grounding, and meditation didn't fit into my new romantic lifestyle. At one point, I even wondered if perhaps the empath traits only presented themselves because something (love and a bonding with others in friendship) was lacking in my life. Now that I had developed such strong social connections, I hardly experienced any of my previous symptoms.

So as each day passed, I interacted more with Nathan, Rhonda, and the others and conversed less with the universe.

February 5

By the end of the first week in February, I felt as lethargic as everyone else seemed to be acting. I figured it was just the winter doldrums, so I didn't think much about it or feel the need to do anything special. But as that first week passed, I slipped very subtly yet quickly into a dark abyss.

The first incident happened as I walked home from school on Tuesday. It was hovering around zero, which meant Mother Nature couldn't decide between snow or rain, so the icy pellets made the roads and sidewalks dangerously slippery.

I had hoped Rhonda could give me a ride, but she was staying late with James for some photography thing, so I had to hoof it home. With my heavy-duty boots on my feet and my iPod earbuds in place, I faced the winter storm and was doing okay until a car skidded off the road and slammed into a mailbox post only three houses up from where I was walking.

Even though I wasn't in danger of getting hit, I was shaken just the same. I think the guy and girl in the car were seniors at Trinity, but I couldn't be sure. It was evident by the way they both jumped out of the car and started yelling at each other that neither had been hurt, so I kept on walking without asking if they needed any help.

A block later, my head began filling with foul thoughts. *That's what you get for driving so fast. You realize you could have hurt me? I could have been seriously injured because you think you're so god-damned invincible and can drive like a Formula One racer. Well, you can't! Far from it! Do you realize how lucky you are that you only hit a mailbox? Do you understand that if a cop had seen you, you would have gotten a ticket for reckless driving or worse?*

As each word echoed in my head, I got madder and madder at the guy. I had half a mind to turn around and give him the other half of my mind. Instead, I dragged myself the rest of the way home, looking over my shoulder every few feet.

February 8

On Monday in social studies class, my mood sank even lower as Mr. Higgins sprang a pop quiz on us about the Civil War. *Who gives a crap about a war that was fought 150 years ago? What the hell am I supposed to learn from this that could possibly help me deal with the messed-up world I live in today, with terrorist bombings and teenage gunmen shooting up their classmates? Why not quiz me about how to protect myself against those psychopaths, you institutionalized robot of a teacher!* I tried to shake off my negative thoughts and concentrate on the quiz, but it was no use. I landed a C minus. My first ever.

*

Time with Nathan seemed to remedy all that ailed me. He even came over to help me with my algebra homework, using kisses as the Y factor to be solved. But that day at lunch in the pit — me with my Ziploc tuna salad and everyone else with sandwiches from the trough — Faith made a joke that my new year's resolution should be to overcome my food phobia. She laughed like it was the funniest joke ever, and a few others, including Nathan, chuckled along with her. *What the hell do you know about me anyway? And who do you think will live longer? Me, eating whole foods I prepared myself or you, shoveling in the processed garbage prepared by minimum-wage workers who probably pick their nose while handling your food as it comes down the conveyor belt?*

I remained gracious enough not to say this out loud. Instead, I snapped up my Ziploc lunch and finished it in the bathroom stall.

*

It was bad enough that these antagonistic thoughts filled my head in the moment, but they also seemed to boomerang back at night when I tried to sleep. Over and over, I would replay each incident, renewing my anger at every toss and turn in my bed and in my head.

When I finally started to fade off to sleep, an image came to mind of a knotted-up ball of yarn. I dreamed that I was tangled up in it, unable to undo the knots, which only got tighter and more knotted the harder I pulled at them.

February 9

As Valentine's Day approached, I could hardly stand to be with anyone except Nathan. Everyone's moods had become almost unbearable, and I wondered if I even wanted to continue having lunch with all of them. I made a point of not saying anything to Nathan about it — these were his best friends, after all — but I was surprised he hadn't noticed or mentioned to me how unusually touchy and irritable they all were lately.

When Rhonda told me she and James were throwing a Valentine's party, I hesitated before saying whether I would go.

"What's gotten into you, Jenny?" she asked while driving me home from school. "You seem so pissy all the time. Everything okay with you and Nathan?"

"Everything is great with me and Nathan! And what do you mean by saying that *I* seem pissy? It's everyone else who seems to be acting like jerks lately. I think that processed cafeteria food might be tainted with something more than just saturated fats and monosodium glutamate."

She looked at me out of the corner of her eye then hit the knob to shut off the radio. Whatever she was about to say was going to be serious. Rhonda never shut off the radio.

"Fess up," she demanded.

"To what?" I snipped back, wishing I hadn't taken a ride from her.

"To whatever has been happening to you that has made you so irritable and snotty."

"Me? Snotty? You've got to be joking. I'm the same person I've always been. I've just gotten a little tired — and yes, irritated — by everyone else's foul moods."

As we pulled up in front of my house, she turned to me and said, "We're friends, right?"

I reluctantly nodded.

"And you trust me, right?"

I thought for a moment about what my aunt said — that trust is part of the process of building good, long-lasting relationships. "I want to trust you," I admitted. "I mean, you've never given me any reason not to trust you."

"And I won't," she said, taking my hands. "So listen to my words and know they come from a loving place." She gave me a half-smile and gave my hands a gentle squeeze. "You are an empath, a human sponge that soaks up all of the energy around you — good and bad. You are right to say that the people around you have been in a foul mood. That's going to happen sometimes. Bad weather, bad economy, bad grades, bad acne."

I smiled at how she made the same reference to 'human sponge' as my aunt had and how, like my aunt, she could always inject levity into any conversation.

"But the thing is, as an empath who has awakened to the knowledge of the universe, you can't just decide to go back to sleep again. As time goes on, you can learn how to turn the volume down, but you can't unplug from who you are, or else…"

…or else I'll end up back where I started or worse, I thought. I hung my head, realizing that she was right. I'd been trying to unplug myself from the empath energy circuit and use my feelings for Nathan as my power source instead. I felt awful. Like someone had just injected me with truth serum that revealed how selfish and weak I was.

"Are you okay?"

I shrugged.

"The good news is that you have more control over it than you think."

I looked out the window as a haze of shields, bubbles, tapping, and meditations filled my vision. It all seemed so exhausting and sometimes even pointless.

"Look," Rhonda said, letting go of my hands and opening the windows a crack to keep them from steaming up. "Up until now, you have been focused on defending yourself against the negative energies around you. And maybe you've tried to get your feet wet in manifesting some positive outcomes for yourself, in your own life. But what you haven't realized is that you can also emit your energy to those around you. What I'm trying to say is that being an empath isn't a one-way street. It's not all about incoming energy. You have the power and control to also send out the energy you choose and influence the balance of energy around you."

My blank look prompted her to continue. "The best analogy I can offer is this: be the thermostat in the room. *You* set the emotional, energetic temperature that everyone else adjusts to. Not the other way around. Does that make sense to you? Do you understand, Jenny?"

I looked at her being so uncharacteristically serious, and I knew I trusted her wholly and completely. I believed that, like Aunt Maggie, she would not judge me but would accept me and help me through any challenge. The hard part was accepting the fact that I needed so much help. I hated admitting that I couldn't handle the challenges in my own life. I had finally been brave enough to get out from under the bed, and now all I felt like doing was crawling back under.

"Are you still processing, Jenny? Because I'm about to run out of petrol here."

February 10

When I woke up the next morning, I got out of bed, grabbed a purple Sharpie from my desk, and wrote on my wall: *FILL UP* and underlined it twice. This would become my self-love routine, my daily checklist. I wrote: *#1 Gratitude Meditation.* Which I would do immediately after peeing and brushing my teeth. There was nothing more distracting than morning garlic breath.

After a ten-minute gratitude meditation that covered practically every person I knew, even Mr. Higgins, I wrote *#2: Self Care: A Divine Responsibility.*

Before dating Nathan, I'd never really cared about how I looked. I always thought it was ludicrous to try mimicking the runway models with skinny bodies, perfect complexions, and pouty lips. I'd convinced myself that dressing down and going without makeup meant I was making a statement that I loved myself authentically. But the truth, I painfully realized, was that I didn't think my looks were worth fussing over.

This morning I'd start by choosing a pair of tights that didn't have holes in them and putting a few curls in my hair. Looking in the mirror, I saw a plain-faced girl with a slightly crooked smile and accepted that she had some work to do, but she was worth it.

#3: Grounding. If I was going to mix it up in this crazy, mixed-up world, I knew I had better do it with both feet rooted firmly on the ground. A five-minute grounding meditation was the best way I knew to ensure I didn't get knocked over every time a jolt of negative energy hit me.

#4: Nutrition. Although I ate very healthily, my range of taste was extremely narrow; plus, I didn't know anything about the vibrational value of foods like Faith described, so I committed myself to expanding my knowledge and my diet.

My social diet needed some expanding, too, so #5 would be: *Kind Gesture.* If I was going to stop being a one-way street, I needed to start putting out some positive vibes, like Rhonda suggested. I imagined I could do that in a number of ways: personally (like helping an old lady cross the street); electronically (sending a loving note via email or text); or spiritually (sending positive thoughts to someone). This morning, I opted to get up close and personal, planting a kiss on my mom's cheek as she came into the kitchen for breakfast and telling her I loved her before heading off for school. By the look on her face, I could tell she was shocked and concerned, which only made me realize how long it had been since I'd told her I loved her. I wouldn't let that happen again.

#6: Connect with Nature. This one would be easy, though sometimes unpleasant. I pulled out my mobile and texted Rhonda, *no pick up today. I'm walking.* Rain, sleet, snow, or hail, me and the mailman were going to do this thing. With today being near zero, I pulled on some extra layers and put earmuffs on under my woolly ski cap. Surprisingly, the one-mile walk was invigorating and cleared my mind exactly the way I needed.

At my locker, I peeled off my clothes down to a knit turtleneck and jeans, leaving so much clothing stuffed in my locker, I could barely get the door shut. When I did, I found Nathan standing on the other side wearing a ski cap and a smile.

"Was that you I saw walking to school or an Eskimo look-alike?"

Jeannette Folan

"Uh, I think the PC term is 'Inuit,' and yes, it was me."

"Did something happen to Rhonda today? Couldn't she drive you in?"

"No, I just decided to walk."

"Well, I certainly hope you'll take a ride home. It's supposed to snow all day. Wouldn't want my princess turning into a Popsicle."

He gave me a quick kiss and took off at the sound of the bell. *Was he just implying I'm too much of a princess to walk home in a snowstorm? Whatever...*

With some kid sneezing and hacking behind me all through first period, a cranky substitute teacher, and yet another inane pop quiz in social studies, I was getting a headache by the start of French class and couldn't see straight when fourth period began, so instead of heading upstairs to consumer ed, I dragged myself to the nurse's office, begging Mrs. Gillespie for some Aspirin.

"You look terrible!" she exclaimed, walking over to wrap her arm around me. "I want you to come in here and lie down."

Without resistance, I went with her into the same room I had occupied on my first day at Trinity. I took the Aspirin she offered, lay on the bed, and closed my eyes. Mrs. Gillespie covered me with a blanket and turned off the light, closing the door behind her.

When I woke up, I saw that it was just after two o'clock. Crap! I'd slept through more than three periods. I grabbed my stuff and opened the door to the main reception area. Mrs. Gillespie greeted me perkily. "Well, look who's finally up."

"I'm late for class. For all my classes!" I yelped.

"Take it easy," she said in a soothing voice. "I notified your teachers that you were ill. You've been excused from classes for the rest of the day, so I suggest you go home and take care of yourself. There's a nasty bug going around the school. I recommend plenty of fluids and rest, Jenny."

"Thanks, Mrs. Gillespie. Sorry for freaking out." I turned to go, looking forward to crawling into my own bed.

"Hold on a minute, dear. I need to call your parents for a ride home. I can't release you without a parent to accompany you."

"I only live a few blocks away, and my parents are both at work. By the time they get here, school will be over. I can make it home on my own, I promise. Is that okay? Please? I just want to go home." I tried to give her my most trusting and beseeching look.

"Well..." She considered my plea for a moment. "Only if you promise to call me as soon as you get home. Deal?"

"Deal." I stopped by my locker, grabbed my coat and hat, and threw on my boots, but left the other layers of winter wear behind. I was too tired to deal with them. As I walked out the main doors, I noticed that more than a foot of snow had fallen since morning. It looked as if the plows had made a pass on the streets, but the accumulation was happening too fast for them to keep up. I trudged down the street, having to lift my feet high with every step, and was exhausted before I had made it halfway home. As my thoughts raced through all of the classes I'd missed and the notes I'd have to get from who knows who, my head started to throb again. What a lousy day this turned out to be.

I stopped and bent over, inhaling and exhaling, willing myself to keep moving forward, but my thoughts anchored me to where I stood. *What is the point of all this? My stupid self-love routine, my empath 'gifts,' my studies and ... my life. What is it all for? Every time I take a step forward, I discover it's off the edge of a cliff. I'm tired of this up and down all the time. Life shouldn't be this hard — even for an empath. What am I doing wrong? Aunt Maggie said I must be the point and purpose of my own life. But what is the point of me anyway?*

As I stood there in the street with sweat pouring down my face, the snow up to my shins, and more falling on me by the minute, I tried to convince myself that I probably just had the flu and that I'd feel better in the morning. But even if I did, the morning was a very long way off, and it didn't seem like it would be any brighter. Right now, as I sank down to my knees, I'd be satisfied just to sleep, just to escape … even for a little while.

*

I awoke in the middle of the night, saw windows where they shouldn't be, and heard a beeping coming from somewhere behind me. I felt a strange pressure in my hand, and when I touched it, I realized there was a tube coming out of it secured with tape.

"Jenny, honey, you're awake," my mom whispered. "Are you okay, sweetheart? How do you feel?"

How do I feel? *How do I feel?* Looking around the room, I realized I was in the hospital and that I felt like I'd been hit by a truck.

As it turned out, I almost had been. Apparently, I was kneeling down in the street only a few yards from the corner, not visible to the snow plow driver making a tight turn with his blade in full swing. Although the truck didn't hit me, the mound of snow it was pushing did, and like an avalanche off a mountaintop, I was buried. The driver immediately called an ambulance and started digging me out.

They were keeping me overnight for observation, making sure there were no internal injuries or a concussion. My mom said, through anxious tears, that I'd been knocked out pretty hard. I looked around the room and started to ask where my dad was, but my throat was dry and scratchy. She gave me a sip of water and said that my dad was out with Nathan grabbing coffees and hot cocoa for everyone.

"Everyone?" I managed to croak out.

"Your entire group of friends from school are out in the waiting room. They got here as soon as they heard what happened and haven't left yet — despite being told that visiting hours are well over with."

The familiar tingles flushed through me, and my eyes filled with tears. What had I been thinking? Why did I decide to go out in a blizzard feeling so sick and knowing I wasn't in my right mind? *Maybe because you weren't in your right mind!* "Duh," I said.

"What was that, dear?"

I shook my head and gave her a half-smile.

"I'm going to get the nurse and then tell your friends you're all right so they can go home now."

A moment after my mom left the room, Nathan walked in. His face was pale and worried, but he looked relieved as soon as he saw me.

"Jenny," he said, taking an unsteady step back. "You're awake. Thank God! I knew something was wrong when you didn't show for lunch. I went straight to the office, and Mrs. Gillespie said you were sleeping. I was worried about you all afternoon, and then when I went back to check on you again before last period, she said you'd gone home…" He paused, and for a moment I thought he was going to cry. "I knew something had happened to you. I could feel it. And I didn't know how I would…"

He broke off again, and I took his hand. "Shhh. It's okay. I'm okay. You can stop worrying now."

"Can I?" He grabbed and held my arm, squeezing it like he was afraid I would disappear. He lowered his head in my hand and sobbed softly. "You don't know what it's like to have someone you love in your arms one day and the next, they're gone. I … I don't know if I can do that again. I don't know if I can do this. I'm … I'm sorry."

Hearing the nurse come into the room, Nathan quickly stood, mumbled "Goodbye" and left.

February 11

I was released the next morning with a clean bill of health but was told to spend the next two days resting at home, watching for any symptoms of a head concussion. What about the one in my heart? Was Nathan just being an over-dramatic empath last night? Or was he breaking up with me?

I looked at the Fill Up routine items on my wall and read them to myself, hoping for something to spark. When nothing did, I crawled into bed and pulled the covers over my head.

Waking after a long nap, Nathan was the first thing that came into my thoughts. I stared up again at the list on my wall. *Nathan cannot be the point and purpose of my life.* As Aunt Maggie's wisdom reverberated through me once more, I pulled off the covers, got into a sukhasana prayer pose, and declared my thanks to the universe. *I am grateful that no harm came to me yesterday and for the concern and care shown by my friends, family, and hospital workers. I am grateful for the chance to begin again — to learn and experience gratitude, patience, kindness, forgiveness — and self-love. And mostly, I am grateful for all those who are teaching me these qualities, who are there whenever I need help.*

I got up from the floor and realized the best person to ask for that help right now was, of course, Aunt Maggie. But first, I tackled #2 on the list, showering, scrubbing my face, putting my hair up in a ponytail, and putting on my new yoga outfit. Next, I took five minutes to do my grounding exercise before heading downstairs for a healthy lunch of avocado and pepper salad on pita. Numbers five and six on the list would have to wait until after my call to Aunt Maggie.

*

"Hello, sweetheart! How's your love life?"

"Aunt Maggie, are you going to tell me that you're telepathic as well as being a psychic medium?"

"The odds of you calling to talk about your love life are as high as a telemarketer calling during dinner. Come on, tell me what's going on. I have a few minutes before my rock-climbing class."

Aunt Maggie listened as patiently as ever as I explained the events of the last few weeks. She gasped when I got to the part about nearly being crushed by the snow plow, and when I finally expressed my confusion and hurt about Nathan, she simply said, "Uh-huh."

"So what do I do?" I pleaded.

"About Nathan or about you?"

Ouch. Her reply stung a little, but like getting a flu shot, I knew it was intended to help me. "So what you're saying is that I need to keep focusing on my own issues and let Nathan focus on his."

"Uh-huh."

"Thanks. You're a woman of few words, but they certainly pack a punch. Enjoy your rock climbing."

"You're welcome, and I will. Love you bunches."

"Love you, too."

*

A few hours later, after completing numbers five and six on my list, I added *#7: Reflective Contemplation.* I sat down on the sofa, wrapped myself in my favorite blanket, and watched the snow fall out our back windows. I was immediately reminded of the same scene at Aunt Maggie's house in Santa Fe on the afternoon after visiting Ojo Caliente. I closed my eyes and tried to relive those magical moments in the spring, conjuring up the same feelings and sensations that had flowed through me.

After ten minutes, nothing. No tingling sensation, no deep rush of peace. Just a low-grade hum of anxiety and fear. How, I wondered, could I access that switch that turned on *The Light* again?

In my contemplation, I considered the two opposites: anxiety and fear versus peace and love. I closed my eyes and imagined what was making me anxious and afraid: *The possible break-up with Nathan and the turbulent road ahead as an empath.* Holding those thoughts in the forefront of my mind, I could feel my body stiffen and my chest tighten, my breath becoming short and strained.

Next, I focused my thoughts on peace and love: My Christmissed night under the stars with Nathan, my sister-like friendship with Rhonda, my friendship with the others at school, my holiday week with Aunt Maggie and all the mystical adventures we shared. As I breathed the memories in and out, I began to feel my body relax, and finally, as I sent loving thoughts to each of those moments and people who shared them with me, the familiar surge of tingles shuddered through my body. I smiled and giggled in glee at my small achievement of finding *The Light* switch.

February 12

On the second day of rest, I grew a bit fidgety from being stuck at home and from not having heard a peep from Nathan. Rhonda had called the night before to see how I was doing and to remind me about the Valentine's party she was having Saturday night. I wanted to ask her if she'd talked to Nathan but didn't dare risk starting rumors about us that I couldn't confirm.

When the day passed without any word from him, I thought about calling but admonished myself that I needed to focus on my issues and let Nathan focus on his. It was good advice. Unless you were in love.

"Hi, Nathan," I said to his voicemail. "I had hoped you'd stop by or maybe call so we could talk about what happened and..." I lost my momentum. "...and um, talk. Please call when you get this." I hung up feeling a pang of anxiety coming on but tried to defuse it with positive thoughts. *Nathan, whatever fear you are having about us, trust that we will be guided to the safe, loving destiny we are meant to share.*

The rush of warm tingles came on again but was interrupted by the vibration of my phone. "Hello, Nathan," I said with a mixture of excitement and dread.

"Hello, Jenny."

The airwaves between us went silent, and I wondered for a moment if the call had been dropped.

"Hello?" I said again. "Are you there?"

"Yes, I'm here. I just got your message. I'm out having dinner with my folks." More silence. "They say 'hello,' by the way."

He sounded so stiff and awkward, I knew whatever he wanted to say to me wasn't something he could express in front of his parents, and that meant it probably wasn't good.

"Hi to them back," I finally managed to reply.

"Is it okay if I call you when I get home?"

"Sure," I said. "No problem. I'll be here."

And with that, he hung up.

*

I kept the phone nearby all night waiting for him to call, but he never did.

February 13

The next morning, I was more determined than ever to work through my self-love Fill Up routine, and by late afternoon I had added two more items to the wall. The first was *#8: Celebrate Myself & Life*. Despite how confused and gloomy I was about the no-show from Nathan, I realized that his calling or not calling couldn't change who I was. I was still me, I was still here, and I was thankful for it. It was time to fill up my sponge with joy and celebration, and the best way to do that today was to dance, which prompted #9 on the list: *Music*. I had neglected my music, any music, for too long, and like exercise or meditation, music had a positive physiological and mental effect on me.

Cranking up my R&B hits on my iPod playlist, I took off my socks, put my hair up, and grabbed my favorite dance partner, Mickey. Before the song got to the second verse, I heard a knock on my bedroom door and found my mom on the other side, swaying her hips and snapping her fingers in the most goofy but adorable way.

"I was going to tell you to turn down the racket," she shouted, "but then I realized 'September' is one of my favorite songs." And so for the next two and a half minutes, we danced and celebrated life together.

*

I decided that whether or not Nathan called, I was going to go enjoy myself at Rhonda's party. I knew most of my friends would have a date, but some wouldn't, and I didn't want to let the uncertainty of my future happiness with Nathan interfere with the certainty of my own happiness today. *Yay for me!* In the back of my mind, of course, I also knew that I was dying to see him, to talk to him, to kiss him, and dance with him. Even if he did show up at the party, there was no guarantee he'd feel the same.

I got dressed, picking out black leggings with a flared red print top and black cuff boots. I took some extra time to roll my hair, applauding myself for keeping up with item #2 on my list. *Who am I kidding? I'm just trying to look good for Nathan.* No matter, I was ready to go — and I did look pretty good.

In a surprise turn of events, my parents said they would be happy to drop me off at Rhonda's but that I'd need to find my own ride home because they had decided to go out for dinner and a movie. I couldn't remember the last time they did anything for Valentine's Day. Maybe the dancing this afternoon had loosened my mom up a bit.

*

When I got to Rhonda's, the party was already going strong. I immediately began looking around for Nathan, weaving through the crowd like a dog latching on to the trail of a scent. I felt a hand on my shoulder and spun around to find Rhonda holding out a glass of punch.

"Happy V-Day, girlfriend. Glad you could make it! I assume this means you're feeling better?" I could barely answer before she threw her arms around me in a bear hug. "Don't ever scare me like that again. You hear me?"

I nodded, looking over her shoulder at a figure I thought was Nathan.

"He's not here, as far as I know. And he didn't return my voice mail either. What's going on with you two anyway? Is that why you've been acting so strange lately?"

Before I could answer, another hand gently clasped my shoulder, and when I turned around, I was surprised to see it was Adam.

"Happy Valentine's Day, Jenny. I'm happy to see you're safe and sound. That must have been really scary being trapped under a mountain of snow like that."

I shrugged, noticing that Rhonda quickly departed with Adam's arrival. "I blacked out as soon as it hit me, so I don't really remember anything."

"Well, that's probably for the best," he said. Then he raised his glass to mine and said, "To your health."

I had always been suspicious of Adam, but tonight he was sending out positive vibes. Although I wanted to break away and continue my search for Nathan, Adam took my hand and nodded toward the dance floor. "How 'bout it? One dance?"

I agreed, figuring it would do me good to focus on myself and the music for a few minutes. To my surprise, a few minutes turned into twenty, and I was desperate for something to drink.

"Let me refresh your drink," Adam said.

"Sure." I followed him off the dance floor, again searching the crowd for any sign of Nathan.

"Here you go." Adam handed me a fresh plastic cup filled to the brim with a red punch. I took a few gulps, thirsty from all the dancing and asked, "What's in this stuff?"

"Nothing too strong. Mostly fruit juice and some Red Bull with just a little kick." He put his hand gently on my back and steered me in the direction of the back porch, which was semi-enclosed and had a small wood-burning fireplace that roared against the quiet of the winter evening.

A few other friends from the club were gathered around the fire, and for the next few hours I got lost in their laughter and company. Adam was especially attentive and jovial. He went out at one point to grab a pitcher of punch to refresh everyone's cups and brought back a bag of Valentine's marshmallows — a hideous blood-red shade — to roast on the fire.

Faith, who I sensed had a crush on Adam, asked him to repeat what he'd told her in school on the day I got plowed under. I looked at him quizzically, not sure if I wanted to hear what he was about to say.

"I don't know if it's appropriate, guys," he said, looking directly at me.

Everyone chided him, and I finally gave him a brief nod in approval.

"Um, well, it was seventh period, and the snow had fallen a couple feet by that time. I was sitting in class when I heard a voice in my head say 'I'm late for class.' Then I heard, 'I can make it home on my own.' It's not always easy for me to determine who these thoughts are coming from." He said this with a humble-ness I hadn't seen from him before. He continued, "Almost fifteen minutes later, I felt freezing cold. And hopeless. I was shivering and lost in a very dark place. The one thought that continued to resonate in my head was sleep. All I wanted to do was sleep."

Adam turned and looked at me. His eyes were soft and questioning, as though asking me if he'd said too much.

Everyone else was looking at me, too. I felt naked, completely vulnerable with no words to confirm or deny Adam's recounting of the event. Finally, digging deep into the calm and peace in my heart, I said, "Well, I'm thankful to be here with my friends."

The group cheered and raised their cups in a toast as Adam leaned over the hugged me in what felt like a gesture of sincere friendship. I hugged him back, my head slightly fuzzy from the punch and my heart wholly empty from Nathan's absence. I tried to shake off the fuzzies and asked Adam for the time, remembering that I needed to arrange for a ride home.

"It's still pretty early," he said, not actually answering my question. I reached into my purse and looked at my mobile. It was well after eleven. And there was a text from Nathan: *I'm sorry. Happy Valentine's Day.* That was it? Sorry for what? I wondered. For not showing up at the party? For not calling me back as he promised? Or for breaking up with me? I felt a rush of anger. He seemed to be behaving like a coward. How could he be afraid to confide in me, no matter what the problem was? I'd never given him reason to believe I was one of those girls who would freak out and go ballistic every time something wasn't going her way in the relationship. So why didn't he trust me enough to share his feelings with me?

"You're anxious to go," Adam said. "And I'm guessing that you need a ride home?"

Maybe Adam wasn't the phony telepathic that Rhonda thought. He seemed to be exceptionally good at reading my thoughts tonight.

"Yes. I do need a ride home, but I can call a cab, really. You should stay and hang out."

"Jenny, I don't mind leaving. And if you're worried about my driving, I can assure you I haven't had that much to drink. It would take a lot more than a few cups of Rhonda's Red Love punch to put me over the limit. Besides, I consider you precious cargo. I wouldn't put you in jeopardy like that."

The way he looked at me when he said 'precious cargo' made my knees a little weak. I knew that my hurt and anger at Nathan were fueling my interactions with Adam tonight, but from a purely logistical perspective, Nathan wasn't here, and Adam was. And I needed a ride home.

Before we left, I sought out Rhonda to tell her I was going.

"With Adam?" she hollered.

"Yes, with Adam. He's not as bad as you said — or as I originally suspected. He's been really nice to me all night..."

"Yeah, only because he knows Nathan isn't here, and he's hoping to put another notch on his stick shift."

"Very funny. But I don't think it's like that. He hasn't done anything out of bounds all night. We've just been hanging out like the friends that we are. Okay?"

"Twenty bucks says he tries something on you before you're home."

"I'll take that bet. And if Nathan does happen to show up..."

"No worries. My lips are stapled shut. Good luck."

"And good night." I hugged her tight as we both said "I love you," then as I turned to go, she stuck something in my hand. It was a mini blare horn, often used at parties for fun, but also intended to scare off unwanted predators.

"Just in case," she said, pumping her finger as if to demonstrate how to use it. I rolled my eyes and fled the party before she said something to make me change my mind.

*

"How often are your thoughts preoccupied with being an empath?"

The question, especially coming from Adam, caught me off guard, yet I heard myself drone out, "Allllll the time."

"Yeah, me, too. Well, not as much as when I first 'awakened.'"

He said the word with obvious sarcasm, so I asked him frankly, "For being an empath, you seem to not take any of it seriously. It's like you almost don't believe in it. What's up with that?"

"I don't know. I guess it's because I wish I wasn't an empath. I mean, my thoughts are hardly my own — literally. Before realizing what was happening to me — I mean about being telepathic — I believed I was a really negative person, a bad guy."

"Why would you think that?" I asked, surprised by such an intimate confession.

"Because my head was usually filled with bad thoughts, worries and dark shit. And I used to think it was all me. You'd be surprised at the kind of negative thoughts most people have, Jenny. But our friends at the school and you, especially you, are the exceptions."

I could feel my face blush against my better judgement. Every feeling I'd had about Adam up until tonight had been apprehensive and skeptical. I wasn't sure what to think about him now; if I should trust my initial gut instincts or allow for the possibility that he might actually be an okay guy.

"I know," he said with some hesitation, "that I can come across like a jerk sometimes. I don't mean to; it's just a defense mechanism, I guess."

As we pulled up in front of my house, I thanked him for the drive home, and though I wanted to keep talking to him, I could feel the blare horn bulging in my coat pocket, reminding me to err on the side of caution instead of throwing it into the wind. So I said goodnight and opened the car door.

"Thanks for a great evening," he said. "Maybe we could hang out again some time."

And that was it. I was home safe and sound — and twenty bucks to the good.

February 14

On Sunday morning I got up early, feeling a bit muddled. Whether it was from the Red Bull punch, the time with Adam, or my growing distress over Nathan, I wasn't sure. But I forged ahead with my day, working through my self-love list, which landed me in a hot bubble bath around ten o'clock. More and more I found that a hot shower or bath rejuvenated me, washing away whatever negative energy I had accumulated. For whatever reason, water seemed to have a therapeutic property that soothed my soul.

I had just closed my eyes, sinking into a serene meditation, when a knock came at the door. My mother opened it a crack and said, "Sorry to disturb you, but Nathan is downstairs asking to see you. Should I tell him you'll be down or..."

"Yes, of course! Please ask him to wait."

As I dried off and scampered over to my bedroom to throw on some clothes, my heart pounded in anticipation of what he would say — and what I would say in return. Although I had been angry with him for the past couple of days, my deeper feelings were only of concern and love. No matter what he was going through, I wanted to be a positive influence in his life. And so I held that intention in my mind as I headed downstairs to meet him.

"Hey, I'm so glad you came," I said, hugging him like a friend instead of a hurt, anxious girlfriend.

He hugged me back, and though it felt half-hearted, I tried not to let it sway my positive thoughts. "Do you want to come in? We can go downstairs or..."

"No. Thank you. Actually I was hoping we could take a walk. Do you feel up to it?"

"Sure," I said, though I dreaded piling on the layers of winter clothes. I told my mom I'd be back soon and asked if she'd start a pot of hot water for some tea when we got back.

Once outside, I realized it wasn't as cold as I'd anticipated. It was actually pretty comfortable. The mood between Nathan and me, however, was not.

"So I guess you're wondering why I'm here," he said, walking stiffly a couple of feet away from me.

How was I supposed to answer that? He was my boyfriend (at least he was supposed to be), and so showing up to see me shouldn't be a big deal. But if he wasn't my boyfriend anymore, and he'd showed up to see me, then yeah, I guess I'd be wondering why he was here.

Taking my silence as the obvious confusion it was, he continued, "I wanted to apologize for the way I behaved that night at the hospital. I was confused and ... not thinking straight."

Good. Confused and not thinking straight was what I needed to hear.

"I'm sorry if I stressed you out ... you know, more than you already were."

I waited for more. There must be more to his explanation, or confession, or whatever this was. But nothing came.

"So where does that leave us?" I couldn't believe I had the guts to ask straight out, but not knowing was worse than hearing the truth.

"Well, first I want to explain the reason for my not calling you back and not coming to the party last night. After seeing you in the hospital and feeling so terrible for so many different reasons, I decided to go and visit my friend — my mentor, Richard, who I told you about. I left Friday night right after having dinner with my folks, and I just got back this morning. That's why you haven't heard from me. I wasn't..." He shrugged and searched my eyes for some reaction. I had none, because he still hadn't answered my question.

"So anyway, I spent some time with Richard. We talked a lot. And I think I'm okay. I mean, I think I'm going to be okay."

I looked at him then looked away. Finally, I looked back at him and said, "You still haven't answered my question. Where does that leave us?"

He stepped closer to me and took hold of my arms. "Jenny, again I want to say how sorry I am…"

"Enough with the apologies!" I shouted, losing my patience and my temper. "Why can't you just answer my question?"

"Because," he said, "I don't want to hurt you."

"So that's it. You're breaking up with me for real?"

"No!" he wailed. "I'm not breaking up with you — exactly. I just … I just need some time to…"

"To work through your issues." I finished his thought.

"Yes. The biggest, the only issue right now is how live and love without being afraid of losing you all the time."

"But Nathan, you're not going to lose me. I have no intention of going anywhere."

"That's not the point, and you know it!" Now he was the one losing his patience. "I told you, I don't know if I can afford to get that close to you … or anyone really. I thought I could, but the closer we got, the bigger my fear got. That day in the snowstorm, you could have been killed, Jenny."

I started to protest, but he put his hand up to stop me.

"Look, you have a lot of stuff to work through, too. Think about it. How can I be assured that you're not going to do what my brother did? You told me you've had thoughts about it. That you'd been cutting yourself and…"

"That's not fair!" I shouted. "That was a long time ago. Okay, maybe not that long; but it was before I met you, before I understood what was happening to me. Now I have tons of support. I have our friends and my aunt and you. It's made all the difference in my life. I never even think about hurting myself anymore."

"No?" He looked at me with a mix of anger and pity. The blood drained from my head, and I suddenly felt woozy. "So what was that whole thing about last week then? I mean, exactly what state of mind were you in when you decided to kneel down on the street corner in the middle of a snowstorm, knowing full well you could be hit by a car — or worse, a snow plow? Huh? Are you going to try to convince me it was all just a freak accident? That you were happily meandering down the street on your way home when suddenly…"

"Enough!" I yelled. "Enough." I stood there frozen in the truth about myself with nowhere to escape. He was right. I was careless with my life that day, because I didn't want to make the effort to go on. In my mind, it had been only a fleeting moment of weakness. Yet that moment had nearly cost me everything. And apparently Nathan's everything as well.

"Okay, Nathan. I get it. You don't want to be the boyfriend of a semi-suicidal empath. Good decision." I wasn't trying to be flippant about it. If it was over, I just wanted it to be over. I wanted to go home and start grieving or meditating or throwing things. I turned to leave, but he caught my arm and pulled me close to him.

"I am not breaking up with you forever, but we do need a break; a time-out to get our bearings."

"Get our bearings about what?"

"About how to proceed with this relationship in a way that is healthy for both of us."

"Oh, well when you put it that way…" I didn't know what else to say. He made sense. And I knew that he was speaking the truth — not just his, but speaking the universe's truth, as well — because a wave of tingles came over me so forcefully, I felt I'd been washed ashore, as if a tide of truth swept me back on to solid ground, and in that instant, I knew I would be okay. With or without Nathan, I would find my way.

I hugged him wholeheartedly and said, "You're right. I understand. Thank you." And I turned for home.

February 20

It was weird seeing my friends at school all week and not knowing what to say about me and Nathan. I assumed by the way they looked at me with concerned eyes and avoided mentioning his name that they all had heard about our 'time-out.' Adam, interestingly, had been popping up in school all over the place. Everywhere I turned, it seemed he was there. At my locker one morning, he showed up with hot cocoa, telling me he'd thought I might need it, since the walk to school must have been brutally cold. It was. A record minus three degrees!

The next day before lunch, he caught me on the way to the library, asking if he could join me to tell me about a Netflix movie he'd seen called *Frequencies*. It was about relationships being determined by the frequency at which a person resonated. Apparently, lower-frequency individuals didn't mix well with high-frequency ones. Adam's point was that while the movie was well made, the central theme was nothing more than an analogy of the class system based on paranormal intellect instead of wealth. I had to admit that conversations with him were stimulating, both from an intellectual and emotional perspective.

The next day, he caught me coming out of gym class on my way home. "Can I give you a lift?"

"If by 'lift' you mean a ride home, no thanks. I enjoy the walk."

"And if by 'lift' I mean a joyful elevation of your spirits, what would your answer be?"

I laughed. "Okay, so I've been a little down lately, and I'm sure you know the reason why, so let's not get into that."

He crossed his heart, saying, "Empath's honor. I just thought maybe you could use a friend and a little cheering up."

I considered that I probably could use a friend and a little cheering up. I just wasn't sure it was a good idea that Adam provided either. On the other hand, he'd been really nice company the past week, and since I knew my intentions were above-board, I decided to let Adam drive me home after all.

"I just need to do one thing before we go. Can you give me ten minutes? Meet me back here?"

"Absolutely," he said. "Your chariot awaits."

I pretended I hadn't heard that last comment and quickly made my way to the administrative office in search of Mrs. Gillespie. She'd sent me a note a couple days ago asking that I stop by, but every time I did she was either in a staff meeting or with a student. Thankfully, she was there now and looked extremely relieved to see me.

"Jenny," she said, coming out behind the counter to give me a hug. "I feel so terrible about what happened."

"It's okay, Mrs. Gillespie. I'm fine."

"I know you are now, but if I hadn't let you go that day…"

"Really, it was my fault, not yours. I deceived you into thinking I was feeling well enough to walk home on my own. The fault is mine."

"I'm just so grateful," she said with her eyes brimming over. "I knew it was the wrong decision as soon as your friend came in here asking about you."

"Yeah. Nathan told me he was checking on me."

"Not Nathan. Your other friend, Adam."

"Adam came in here asking about me?"

"Yes. He was so worried. I know he's one of your friends. I just told him the same thing I told Nathan. I hope that's okay..." She suddenly looked very worried herself realizing that she'd not only broken a school policy by allowing me to leave that day, but she had also broken a privacy rule.

"Please don't be concerned about it. You meant well. I'm just curious ... what did you tell him?"

"Only that I had offered to call your parents, but you said that you were really tired and just wanted to go home and thought that you could make it on your own — so I released you."

"I see. Well, thanks for taking good care of me. I would have been in much worse shape if you'd have just thrown some Aspirin at me and kicked me back to class. Honest."

She shook her head, knowing my words were more kind than true. As I left the office, I realized the sad and disappointing truth about Adam. Maybe he was an emotional empath like the rest of us, and maybe he got lucky that night with the mind-reading stunt, but no way was he really telepathic. The only reason he knew about my state of mind that day was because he had gotten inside information from Mrs. Gillespie.

When I returned to the student parking exit, Adam was waiting with a cool, confident smirk. "Ready to go?" he asked.

"Actually, Adam, I've changed my mind. I really just want to be alone right now." I turned coldly without further explanation and made my way home.

*

Rhonda was the only friend who made sense to me right now. She was a great comfort and even told me that she and James had

gone through a similar time-out period and that it was 'brilliant.'
But she warned it was crucial that I used the time to do my home-
work and not just sit around waiting for the time-out to be over.
I presumed by 'homework' she didn't mean algebra and biology.

Taking her advice, I immersed myself in the sea of my self-
love practice, taking long walks on the trails where I would do
my gratitude and grounding meditations, reflective contemplation, and sometimes even dance to music out in the middle of the
frozen pond. Mostly, I loved watching the clouds. They calmed
me in a way that made me feel the universe had painted the sky
with them just for me to enjoy.

*

As the first week of the time-out ended, I added a final item
to the list, *#10: Learn from the Masters*. Since last summer, when
Aunt Maggie left me a copy of her *Shambhala Sun* magazine, I had
been writing down a list of books that were recommended. *The
Magic Path of Intuition* by Florence Scovel Shinn; *Positive Vibes* by
Gordon Smith; *Entanglement: A Tale of Everyday Magic* by Gregg
Braden; *Meditations to Live More Fully, Deeply and Peacefully* by
Denise Linn; *Spirit Junkie* by Gabrielle Bernstein, and almost
every book written by Deepak Chopra or Dr. Wayne Dyer.

If I started reading now, I might get through the list by my
fiftieth birthday. I've always been a slow reader, but thankfully,
most of the books were available as audio downloads, so I ordered
my first one — *The Tao of Pooh* by Benjamin Hoff — and began
listening to it on my walks to and from school.

February 27

I found that the messages in the book often fueled a great deal of introspection, and somehow it made me feel connected to the author, and even distantly to all those people who were enjoying it like me somewhere in the world. What surprised me most was that out of all the books on my list, this one spoke to me at such an immediate level, with such a childlike perspective, it was as if the universe had picked it for me personally.

The only downer was that every chapter made me want to call Nathan and share everything I was learning and discuss the multitude of questions that came with it.

As I lay in bed that night, I imagined Nathan's hand in mine. I felt the warmth and comfort. I smelled the sweet vanilla scent of his skin and heard his breath escape through his soft lips. In my mind's eye, I could see the tenderness and goodness in his eyes, his face, his smile. I smiled back at him there in my mind, and for a brief moment, I let go of my fear. As I did, I felt my spirit rise up above me. I pictured its soft, glowing light radiate down upon us. Then Nathan's spirit rose up, too, and together they hovered over us like two guardian angels. The peace I felt as I drifted off to sleep was deeper than I'd ever known before.

February 28

I loved Sundays. And today was going to be an even more awesome one than usual. After going through my routine, I would enjoy brunch with Rhonda downtown, and later in the afternoon I would call Aunt Maggie and finalize our plans for our weekend together with Deepak.

As I heard Rhonda honk in the driveway, I grabbed my purse and hollered up to my mom that I'd be back in a couple of hours. I could hear Trevor Davis blaring from Rhonda's car stereo as soon as I opened the front door. Rhonda was like the Pig-Pen of noise pollution, and I only hoped my neighbors would be tolerant.

"What up, girl?" She greeted me with an air-kiss when I got in the car.

"I've been surprisingly good but missing you a lot. We hardly get any alone time now that you don't chauffeur me to and from school anymore."

"Yeah, but all that brisk air is good for the complexion."

As we drove along the streets heading downtown, I was mesmerized by how everything looked. Old houses, new houses, big and small cars, fancy storefronts and grungy ones, rich people and homeless. All the things we label and categorize, dropping them in our personal buckets of good and bad, like and dislike.

"Earth to Jenny." Rhonda stuck a wet finger in my ear. "You look like you've been put into a trance."

"Sorry. I was just thinking."

"About?"

I shook my head. "Nothing specific. Just some book I'm reading. It suggests we try looking at the world without judgement or attachment."

"I see. So what … are you planning on becoming a Taoist now?"

"No. Why?"

"Because I recognize the philosophy of the Tao Te Ching when I hear it."

"You do?" I gaped at her with my jaw in my lap.

"Uh yeah, I do. And that face you're wearing right now … very judgmental. Come on," she said, pulling into a parking space. "I can't discuss the Tao on an empty stomach."

The Artemisia Cafe was low-key and had a cozy, intimate feel. Rhonda gave her name, and the smiling host seated us in the corner table by the window.

"I already know what I'm having," she said, tossing the menu aside, "and it's incredible."

"You do? But you said you've never been here before."

"True, but there is such a thing as a website and, hold on to your hats … an online menu." She waved her mobile in my face, teasing me.

"Ha-ha. Okay, so I don't use my mobile for the Internet."

"Or apps," she pointed out. "Or games. Or taking pictures."

"No, that's not true! I took a picture at your Valentine's party."

"Oh, you mean you and Adam did a selfie together?"

"No. And don't bring up Adam, okay? I actually took a picture of the whole group when we were roasting marshmallows."

"Don't bring up Adam?" she squawked. "Why, did I just win my twenty bucks back?"

I really didn't want to replay the whole story and bring a downer to our perfectly playful brunch date, so I changed the subject, and thankfully, she didn't push it. "So what are you having that is so incredible you had to pick it out before we even got here?"

"Bangers and mash. A proper British breakfast right here in our humble little American town. You should try it."

"Okay, I will!"

After the server took our orders, I told her in more detail about the last two weeks, my Fill Up list, my meditations and reading, and also about the upcoming visit with Aunt Maggie. "I really wish you could meet her. I'll make sure you do on her next visit. And also … I really want to thank you for that speech you gave me in the car that day about how being an empath isn't a one-way street. It hit home with me. So thank you."

She smiled. "Well, there was a street, and you did get hit, so that makes sense."

"Did anyone ever tell you, Rhonda, that you suck at accepting thanks?"

"No. I think you're the first one, actually, and for that, you should get a prize. Oh look! Here it comes now."

When the plates of food were put in front of us, my appetite disappeared. "This is bangers and mash? Seriously? Sausages and mashed potatoes for breakfast are what you consider incredible British fare?"

"Don't diss it 'til you've tried it."

"I have tried it," I quipped. "For lunch and for dinner. I just never thought about consuming a nine-hundred-calorie meal for breakfast before."

"Well, technically this is brunch, so … bite me. And enjoy!"

*

When we got to the serious talk, I asked her straight out if Nathan had confided in her at all about me, about our time-out, and specifically if there was ever going to be an end to it.

"He hasn't talked to me, but I think he and James have gone out a few times. I could ask him if you want me to, but he and Nathan are pretty tight, so I don't think he'd feel comfortable."

"No, no. I get it. That's good. It's all right."

"Are you all right? I mean, you seem like you're pulling it together with your Fill Up routine and the reading and everything. Don't let the anxiousness about Nathan interfere with that, because you know you can't hide your feelings from the universe, and it only sends you back what you send to it. It's a two-way street there, too."

"In theory," I said, "I know you're right, but putting it into practice is hard. I feel like I've got my end going pretty strong, but whenever I think about being with Nathan, I go weak. But the thing is…" I couldn't find the words to make my point.

"Yes, darling, what is 'the thing'?"

"There is an expression. Maybe it's not an expression, but it's a quote from somewhere, and it says 'you gotta learn to love what's good for you.'"

"Hmmm. I'm pretty sure that's a line from *Twilight: New Moon*, if I'm not mistaken."

"Stop making fun of me! My point is that Nathan has never not been good for me. I mean, he's such an incredibly good guy!"

She looked at me with so much compassion, I thought I would cry. "I hear what you're saying, Jenny, but despite how good Nathan is as a person, being in such an intense relationship with him was distracting you from being good to yourself. So perhaps Nathan isn't the subject in question, but rather the intense relationship — with anyone — that isn't good for you. At least not right now."

I considered her words. I knew they were truthful. Not just because of the tingles that shuddered through me as she said them, but because as I reflected, I was reminded that the more attention I gave to Nathan, the less attention I gave to me. Damn. I hated that my first real relationship was a failure on my part.

"Hey, Jenny," Rhonda interrupted my thoughts. "Don't beat yourself up about it. I can see the bruises forming under your eyes. Really. You're an incredibly good person, too, who's had some incredible challenges handed to her. Cut yourself some slack. Stay focused on yourself. Keep sending the love out to the universe. And have faith. It will all work out."

"Wow, that's got to be a record for the best one-liner motivational speeches ever."

"It was sincere," she said, raising her glass of orange juice to mine.

"Can I tell you something else?" I asked hesitantly.

"If you tell me you're pregnant, I'm going to lose my bangers and mash all over this table."

"No! It's nothing like that! It's just that, along with all the meditations and self-love exercises I've been doing, I've also been trying some manifestation exercises. You know, about me and Nathan."

"You mean like having sex? Are you trying to manifest your way out of your virginity?"

Sometimes Rhonda was impossible to have a conversation with. "I mean that I focus on us being together again. I visualize him thinking about me, missing me, picking up the phone and calling me to say..."

My purse began to vibrate. I grabbed my mobile and looked at the screen, shoving it in Rhonda's face so she could see the caller's ID. Nathan.

"What do I do now?"

"Um. Answer it would be my advice."

"Hello," I said tentatively.

"Hi, Jenny. It's me, Nathan." It was silly for him to say so, considering that he knew I had caller ID, along with the rest of the mobile users on the continent.

"Hi. I was just thinking about you," I said.

"And obviously I was just thinking about you." A long silence ensued.

We weren't going to get very far if our conversation continued like this, so I said, "What's up? Why are you calling?"

"That's a good question. I was wondering if we could get together and talk."

"He wants to talk," I whispered to Rhonda.

"So … talk!" she mouthed back.

"Okay, Nathan. We can talk."

"How about this afternoon. On the trail? We could meet at the park entrance. Two o'clock okay?"

The memory of the last time we walked there together stuck in my throat, but I finally said, "Sure. I'll meet you there."

*

As two o'clock approached, I felt myself becoming more anxious about my meeting with Nathan, but like Rhonda said, the universe only sends you back what you send to it, so I quickly shifted gears, doing a gratitude exercise about my love for Nathan and his love for me. *Guide me to be a strong and loving girlfriend, to listen with an open mind and open heart and to respond with kindness and a sensible attitude to the health and happiness of us both.* As I breathed in and out deeply and steadily, I felt the peace I had begun to recognize and cling to these past few weeks. It told me that no matter what happened in this moment, I could feel safe in the moment after and the next.

When I met him at the trail's head, I was not hesitant or fearful. I greeted him with a hug and told him how happy I was that he called. He smiled and said how good it was to see me. "You look fantastic, like you've been on a vacation or something."

I shrugged. "Must be all those massages and tanning sessions."

"Yeah, right. Well, it's really good to see you. I'm glad you agreed to meet me. I've been doing a lot of thinking the past few weeks, and I'd like to ask you something."

"Yes?" I said, my heart suddenly fluttering off the peaceful scale and moving onto the marathon-running scale. I took a deep breath.

"My friend, my mentor, I should say, Richard, is coming into town this week, and I'd love for you to meet him. It would mean a lot to me."

"Oh," I said, unsure of how his invitation fit into the equation of our relationship.

Sensing my uncertainty, he said, "I know things are 'off' with us right now, and I have to be honest and say that I don't know when it will be the right time for us to be 'on' again, but you still mean a lot to me, Jenny. I want you to meet him, and him to meet you, because you are two of the most important people in my life. So what do you say?"

"I say … I'd be honored." I was disappointed we weren't 'on' again, but it was enough for now that he wanted to include me in his life at any level. And being asked to meet his mentor was no small thing. I smiled at him nonchalantly, but in actuality, I couldn't push away the thoughts of his mouth pressed against mine.

"I'd like to arrange a dinner for us next Friday night. Is that good for you?"

"Sure. That sounds great. What time?"

"We'll pick you up around seven o'clock."

"Okay. I'll be ready. And thanks so much for asking."

We walked back to the park entrance in silence, but the energy between us was suddenly as loud as thunder. It vibrated through me so powerfully, I caught myself counting 'one-two-three' waiting for the lightning strike. "What did you just say?" he asked.

"Nothing," I mumbled, giving him a quick hug before walking the few blocks home.

March 4

The week progressed slower than the chapters on the world wars in social studies class. Although Adam had tried to interject himself in my days like he did the week before, I was careful to keep him at a distance while not rebuking him too harshly. I was also careful not to slip up and say anything to Rhonda about Adam's deceit regarding my snow plow incident and his alleged telepathy about it that day. I didn't think it would serve any purpose to confirm the perceptions she already had about him. Plus, I knew she'd ask for her twenty bucks back.

When Friday finally came, I felt calmer than I thought I would. I was actually more excited about the idea of meeting Richard than I was about having dinner with Nathan. Go figure.

When Nathan rang at the door, both my parents greeted him like a long-lost son, and I had to pry him away before they got too embarrassing. I had decided not to tell them about our time-out until I knew whether it was permanent, but they could tell something was going on, and I guess I couldn't blame them for being anxious about it. I certainly was.

Richard was waiting to greet me at the car, which Nathan told me was an S55-e, the top-of-the-line hybrid car from Mercedes. It suited him. His thick hair with streaks of gray and strong face exuded a classy, gentlemanly quality, while his eyes had a down-to-earth, boyish, mischievousness.

"It is lovely to finally meet you, Jenny." He shook my hand then made sure we were all buckled in before quietly speeding off to a fine dining restaurant called Grace, which Richard told us was a restored church from the 1850s. When we entered the building, I was mesmerized and emotionally moved by the atmosphere of the place, with the gigantic stained-glass windows and oak woodwork archways that supported the entire structure.

Once seated, Nathan reached across the table and squeezed my hand as if he understood how great an effect this former spiritual place was having on me.

"So Jenny, Nathan tells me you are quite a gifted empath."

"Gifted is not the word I would use," I replied, shooting a look of disbelief to Nathan.

"I understand your reticence in accepting your unique skills. I felt much the same when I was your age."

"You mean that you're an empath, like us? And you knew when you were really young?"

"Yes, I did. Only there weren't any of the resources available like there are now; although, in my opinion, the mainstream population is still a ways off from much-needed communication and education in this area."

"So how did you deal with it? How were you able to understand what was happening to you?"

"Like you, I was fortunate to have a circle of friends who were supportive and curious enough to 'put themselves out there,' I guess that's the expression you kids use these days."

"What do you do now, if I may ask?"

He chuckled. "You mean how do I cope with being an empath, or what do I do for a living?"

"I'd like to know the answer to both, but I meant to ask what you do for a living, whether you are still a counselor?"

Nathan chimed in, "Richard is the director at the Center for Anxiety and Related Disorders at Boston University."

"*One* of the directors," Richard corrected humbly. "And I'm only there part-time. My other work involves research with empaths, discovering why empaths are different from other people, whether it's hereditary or environmental, whether it should be classified as a disorder or a treatable psychological condition, how many people are empaths and ... things of that nature."

"That's so cool!" My face lit up. "What have you discovered so far?"

"That we need to do a lot more research."

I laughed at his joke, but the harsh truth was that it would probably be years before anything definite was known about the biology or psychology of empaths. In the meantime, all I could do was take advantage of the resources I had. "I'm curious," I asked Richard, "whether my defensive feelings will ever go away. It's exhausting always having to be on guard all the time."

He nodded with a kind smile. "Shielding yourself from the world isn't the answer. Living defensively isn't a life. I can help you shift that perspective if you'd like. Perhaps you and Nathan would consider coming down to my office in Boston for a few days; that is if your parents would approve, Jenny?" I nodded and thanked him as our meals were served.

As the evening went on, Richard shared some of his early empath experiences. "The first time I realized I was different from my siblings or my friends was when I was eight, and my mother was in labor, about to deliver my baby sister. Every time she would have a contraction, I would double over in pain, screaming, 'The baby's coming! The baby's coming!'"

We all laughed heartily. "So you're a physically receptive empath?" I asked.

"Yes, among other types."

Nathan glanced at me with a look that suggested I should change subjects. "How did you become Nathan's mentor? I mean, I know you were Daniel's counselor, but..." By the looks on both their faces, I could tell I'd avoided a pothole and run straight into a ditch. They gestured to each other as if to say 'You tell her.' Finally, Richard began.

"It was just over five years ago. Daniel was not well, as you know. His parents brought him to the local psychiatric center for counseling, and I was consulting on the case because the case manager had a 'gut feeling' about Daniel and thought he might need more than traditional therapy. So I met Nathan in the family session, which is the first meeting I generally conduct so that all members of the patient's family have an opportunity to build trust with me and share their perspectives and concerns about the patient."

When I looked at Nathan, he had the saddest expression, and I wondered if this was bringing back too many painful memories for him. Richard must have noticed it, too, because he paused before continuing. Nathan glanced at him and briefly nodded, but Richard gestured for Nathan to continue instead.

Nathan shook his head as if shaking off a memory. Then he said, "After the family session was over, Richard asked me to stay behind. We talked some more about Daniel, and finally," he hesitated and swallowed hard, "Richard asked me to pull up my sleeves."

My effort not to look stupefied failed. I knew what he was about to say, and I didn't know if I wanted to hug him or scream at him.

"When Richard saw the marks on my arms, he realized that I was in the early phases of what he called 'empath labor.' He explained that it was the first stage of awareness and that, while it's considered a growth spurt spiritually, it often results in self-injury and mental trauma."

He looked at me then, beseeching me to have compassion and forgiveness for not having shared with me the experience that I had so cautiously and trustingly shared with him about myself. Although I did feel immense compassion for him, I also felt a little betrayed. Realizing the significance of this moment, however, I finally reached across the table and took his hand in mine.

Nathan gave a half-smile and continued. "It was then that Richard and I began our own counseling sessions. He taught me what it was to be an empath, how my brother had undergone the same process — though the mental trauma of it was still affecting him. He cautioned me about the importance of staying connected to life with all its joys and sorrows. I admit that part would have been much easier if I hadn't had to watch my brother slip away so violently."

"And I'll always be sorry for that," Richard said.

"I know, and thank you. I told Jenny before, my family all knows there was nothing you could have done for Daniel. He had given up, had 'unplugged' long before you had a chance to help him."

This moment I was witnessing between them seemed somehow sacred. I felt like an interloper in their friendship. Yet just as I thought of excusing myself from the table, they both reached out to me, and the three of us clutched our hands together with genuine affinity and affection.

A full minute passed as we sat breathing and connecting, when I finally said to Nathan, "Why didn't you tell me?"

"I don't know." He shrugged. "Maybe because I thought I could help you more if you didn't know, or maybe I was afraid of what you'd think of me if you did know."

"That sounds like a purely ego-driven mentality, Nathan," I gently retorted.

"Ha!" Richard exclaimed, giving me a thumbs-up.

"Yes, it was," Nathan agreed. "And what I'm beginning to understand now is that we probably could have helped each other more if you knew the whole truth about my past."

Richard nodded and laughed. "It reminds me of a story I heard on a television show I used to enjoy called *The West Wing*. It goes something like this: a guy falls into a hole, a really deep hole, and he can't get out. He hollers up for someone to help him, and a doctor walks by and says 'Hey buddy, what's wrong?' The guy says, 'I'm stuck down here in this hole. Can you help me out?' The doctor writes a prescription, tosses it down in the hole, and walks away. A while later, a priest passes by, and the guy shouts up again, 'Hey! I'm trapped down here in this hole. Can you help me?' The priest kneels down, says a prayer for the guy, and moves on. Finally, one of the guy's friends walks by and says, 'What's going on?' The guy says, 'I'm stuck. Can you help?' So the friend jumps down into the hole with him and the guy says, 'Are you crazy? Now we're both stuck down here.' And the friend says, 'Yeah, but I've been down here before, and I know the way out.'"

Nathan and I dropped our heads while Richard sat quietly waiting for us to say something. Finally, we looked at each other with tears streaming down our cheeks and reached out, holding hands like we were grasping for each other's lives. We tried not to make a spectacle of ourselves, but the poignancy of Richard's anecdote moved us beyond control.

Moving in closer to me, Nathan whispered, "Jenny, I love you."

"I know. I know you do. And I love you."

Our evening with Richard ended in more tears, warm embraces, and the promise to see each other again soon. Richard suggested we all meet for dinner when I was in town with Aunt Maggie next week. I thought it was a fantastic idea. I knew Aunt

Maggie would have so much in common with Richard, and if they hit it off, maybe she would be even more motivated to come up this way and visit.

March 5

Nathan came over the next day, and although we both were careful with our words and expressions of affection, it wasn't out of fear. We were instead being mindful of the precious and fragile gift we were holding — each other.

"I knew Richard would love you," he said as we sat feet-to-feet on the sofa under the blankets.

"You think he loves me? He's a bit old for me, isn't he?"

"True. Plus, I'd have to challenge him to a duel, and I'd hate to have to kill the guy. He is my mentor, after all."

"What makes you think you'd win?" I kicked him gently under the covers.

"Because of what would be at stake. Seriously, Jenny, what I've really learned from these past weeks is that it all starts right here," he said, tapping his chest. "I was so caught up in trying to teach you what I know and to position myself as the wise sage that I missed the part about still having a lot to learn myself."

"Hey, we're only teenagers, right? Gifted empaths or not, we aren't supposed to have it all figured out. What I learned from these past weeks is that allowing myself to get so lost in our rela-tionship — no matter how beautiful it may be — was like a form of self-sabotage. I was neglecting myself to the point where I think you started not to even recognize me anymore; to the point where I didn't recognize myself anymore. That probably doesn't even have anything to do with being empaths; I think that's a pitfall for anyone in a relationship."

"But it's certainly more challenging when you add the empath factor!"

"I know, I know. Yet everyone has a past and emotional junk they're dealing with. I don't think it matters what kind. I guess what I'm trying to say is that sometimes I think it's easy to hide behind the empath label, believing that a lot of the garbage we feel and the challenges we face aren't our responsibility, you know? Like somehow we feel less accountable for our thoughts, feelings, and behavior because we've convinced ourselves that it's not really our stuff; that's it's all coming from the negative, dark energy around us."

"Whoa. That's intense and ... kinda depressing," he said, the familiar sadness showing in his eyes.

"Sorry if I'm getting too heavy. We can change topics if you want."

"No, it's all right. Please don't feel you have to hide your thoughts from me because I'm too fragile or whatever."

"Well, sometimes it's the kinder thing to do. Not dumping on someone who is already buried under a pile of mud."

"True. But I can see your point. It doesn't matter if it's a bad childhood, a dead brother, an illness or being an empath. We're responsible for our own happiness. Period."

As we looked at each other at opposite ends of the sofa, months after having fallen in love, it felt like we were seeing each other for the first time. Not as Nathan and Jenny, but as two human beings just trying to figure out how to make the most of life on this earth.

March 7

After school, I phoned Aunt Maggie, apologizing for not calling her the previous weekend to discuss our trip.

"Life happens," she said casually.

But when I told her the reason for my missing our call, that Nathan and I had met, talked, and reconciled, she shrieked so loudly, she startled the birds out on the feeder. "So I get to meet him when I come into town?"

"Actually," I said with my ear still ringing, "I not only want you to meet him, but I wonder how you feel about being set up on a blind date of sorts?"

"Are you trying to pimp me out to one of your friend's divorced fathers?"

"Not exactly. He's Nathan's mentor, someone who was close to the family when Nathan's brother was ill."

"Have you met him?"

"I have, and I can tell you that he's handsome, he's about your age, a good conversationalist, drives a hybrid car, and overall, I think you would have a lot in common." I giggled under my breath at how intrigued she would be when she found out about his empath research.

"Well, I consider you a good judge of character, so I guess it's a date."

"Terrific. Your plane gets in around six o'clock, and my train gets in before eight. How about if we meet at the hotel? I booked a funky boutique hotel called EnVision — I thought it sounded like us. After we get settled, we can go find somewhere casual to have dinner. We'll do the lecture on Saturday, dinner with the guys on Saturday night, and have all day Sunday to walk around or do ... whatever. Sound good? Any questions?"

"Just one," she said. "Does this guy you're setting me up with look like he'd be up to playing some nug-a-nug?"

"What are you talking about?"

"You know ... shake the sheets, dance the Paphian jig, make whoopee, take a turn at Bushy Park."

"Aunt Maggie ... you need help. See you in a few days. Love you bunches."

"Love you, too."

March 9

The only thing that made waiting for Friday tolerable was that I had a date with Nathan Wednesday night. His parents were taking us to the new brick-oven pizza place, Flatbread Company. Although I had spent time with them when I was over at Nathan's house, this would be the first time we were going out for dinner together. I felt a bit tense, though, and didn't know if that was me projecting my energy onto them or vice versa.

Despite how often I grounded myself or did any number of calming and self-love meditations, I still sometimes felt like either my circuits were overloaded or I was flatlining. The feeling usually only lasted a short while, but it bugged me that I didn't have any control over it. One minute I was strong and joyful, the next was like I hit heavy turbulence in a little prop airplane.

I made a note, *overloaded or flatlining*, in my journal, excited that Nathan said we could go down to visit Richard and that he'd work with us on whatever issues we had.

When the doorbell rang a few minutes later, my heart jumped and butterflies tickled my stomach. I greeted Nathan at the door with a kiss on the cheek, and he returned it with a smile that calmed my nerves.

The drive to the restaurant was filled with flurries of small talk about the weather, school, and local events. I didn't contribute much to the conversation; instead, I observed the candid way they communicated as a family and wondered if it had always been this way or if losing Daniel had shifted them past the typical strenuous relationship between parents and teens.

Once in the restaurant, we each ordered our own gourmet brick-oven pizza with the promise to share a slice around the table. It was just before the pizza came when Mr. Leeds said directly to me, "We're concerned about you, Jenny. I can't hide that fact. When Nathan told us how you ended up in the hospital we … well, to put it plainly, it stirred up a lot of emotions for us. I know Nathan has already voiced these concerns to you. We," he said, reaching across the table for his wife's hand, "just wanted you to know how we felt. We try not to be overprotective of Nathan, but that doesn't mean we don't still have some sleepless nights."

Nathan looked at me questioningly, waiting for my gracious or defensive response, unsure which was coming.

"I completely understand. And I hope it might help you sleep a little better knowing that Nathan and I are maintaining a healthier balance to our relationship. I'm also working very hard on maintaining my own personal balance."

"Yes," Mrs. Leeds replied, "he said you hardly see each other at school and that you'll be keeping your dates to twice a week."

Nathan laughed. "It's the 'Jenny diet.'"

"Good thing it's not a pizza diet," his dad jeered as four large platters were set in front of us. We carried out our plans to try one slice of each other's pizza and voted that we each liked a different one best. Nathan's mom and dad liked the ones they ordered the best — pepperoni and onion for him and roasted tomatoes and mushrooms for her. "That's what happens after fifty-some years on the planet. You know what you like."

Nathan and I were the opposite. He loved the ingredients I ordered best: portabella mushroom and artichokes with oil and parmesan instead of tomato sauce. And I went crazy for his: sun-dried tomatoes, spinach, mushrooms, and ricotta cheese.

"The only thing this is missing is a little roasted garlic," I said, inspecting my slice so closely, the waiter immediately sprang on us to make sure I hadn't found a hair in my food. "And the only thing missing from yours," I said, pointing to Nathan's slice of my pizza, "is shaved black truffles."

Mocking me, Nathan held up his slice in the same way and said — doing a terrible impersonation of me — "The only thing this is missing is shaved black truffles, green olives, and red peppers. No, wait! Red *roasted* peppers and flecks of twenty-four-carat gold!"

Everyone laughed good-naturedly, and then, catching me completely off guard, Nathan leaned over and gave me a full-on open-mouthed kiss right there in front of his parents. He pulled away and smiled at me. "Nothing missing from that."

I felt myself flush bright red with the heat of embarrassment and quickly excused myself from the table in search of the bathrooms. As I snaked my way through the tables to the back hallway leading to the restrooms, I ran smack into Adam.

"Wow, Jenny. What a surprise — a very nice surprise," he added.

"Yeah. Nice to see you, Adam. Guess this is the popular new place in town. Are you here with anyone from the gang?"

"No," he said, looking somewhat uncomfortable that I asked. "Just a friend. No one you know, I don't think. What about you?"

"I'm here with Nathan and his folks."

"Really?" His tone was pure shock, but he quickly recovered. "I'm sorry. That came out wrong. I was just under the impression you were seeing someone else now ... an older guy maybe? Anyway, my mistake. Again, it's really good to see you. Enjoy the rest of your night." He squeezed my shoulders and stepped past me, leaving me standing there wondering what the hell that was all about.

After I used the washroom, I headed back to the table and spotted Adam in the corner near the wood pile. The girl he was with was a senior. I recognized her from photos in the school newspaper and spotlight boards in the hallways. I could see her hand was across the table, stroking Adam's arm. She seemed pretty casual about it, like it wasn't a first-time thing. So much for being just a friend. Before I looked away, however, I noticed that Adam had pulled his arm away, and he gently shook his head at her. Huh. Weird.

Back at the table, I sat down, saying, "Now that that embarrassing moment has passed, are we ordering desserts?"

"My dad beat you to it. He ordered one of everything and is looking forward to hearing what is missing from each." Everyone laughed again at my expense. I was glad to be a part of such a close, happy family. It made me wonder how much the traumatic events in our lives impact who we are.

"Penny for your thoughts," Nathan said.

"Oh, I'm sorry. I zoned out there for a minute." I tried to snap myself back to the topic of desserts when it occurred to me that if Nathan could have an open, respectful relationship with his parents, it probably meant I could, too. So I took the plunge. "Actually, I was thinking about how fun and joyful you guys are, despite having gone through such a life-changing tragedy.

Whereas my family doesn't have half the joy and laughter, yet we've never experienced an illness or any death at all." I shrugged. "It just seems strange to me."

When Nathan's parents turned to each other, the look of compassion and communion they shared was so powerful, I felt a surge of tingles and began to weep.

Mrs. Leeds smiled at me. "Losing Daniel and the process of losing him, of watching him become lost to us and not be able to control any of it, it was life-changing in the most profound and consuming way imaginable. But we knew we had a choice. We knew losing Daniel would change our lives, but we had to decide if we would allow it to change us. Because," she continued, looking at me now with intent, "life is ten percent of what happens to you and ninety percent how you react to it."

"It's like I always say," Mr. Leeds added through moist eyes. Then the three of them sang in unison, "You can't eat arsenic to keep away the rats."

"I don't get it," I said, feeling a bit foolish.

Nathan mocked his dad now, speaking in the tone of a nerdy professor. "I believe the meaning of the proverb Professor Leeds wishes to bestow upon you — and has bestowed upon us most generously for almost a decade — is that living life with fear in your heart won't stop bad things from happening."

"Go ahead and make fun," his dad replied, "but it's true!" He motioned for the server to put the dessert plates in the center of the table. Everyone grabbed their forks and began digging into the dish closest to them. "Another soon-to-be famous expression," Mr. Leeds continued, "is *don't hide under your umbrella on the chance it might rain.*"

Everyone nodded as if in deep contemplation, when in fact we were working out which dessert to try next. Nathan nudged me while spooning some whipped cream gingerbread into my mouth, saying, "I think that last comment was directed at you ... or me ... or probably both."

I looked at his dad, who gave me a half-smile and a knowing wink. "Those sleepless nights I told you about are sometimes because of the monsters hiding under the bed with you."

*

As I lay in bed that night, his words echoed in my mind, and I couldn't help but wonder if my parents had sleepless nights, too. I'm sure they were worried when I was in the hospital, and of course, they worried like any parents did about drugs, drinking, sex, and the general dangers that lurked in the world. But did they lie awake at night, afraid I might cut myself again? Did they think it was a mistake that I didn't take the meds or go to counseling?

With those thoughts tumbling in my head, I was the one who didn't get any sleep that night, and the next morning I looked like a zombie myself.

March 10

Although the time-out with Nathan was officially over, I continued to spend most lunch hours in the library, studying, reading, catching up with Rhonda or today, as it turned out, Adam.

"What's up, Jenny?"

"Not much. Just doing some studying. Algebra. Yuck."

"Well, I happened to ace algebra, so if you need any help..."

I immediately thought back to the night Nathan helped me with my algebra by demonstrating the equation using kissing as the Y factor.

"You're blushing." Adam chuckled. "Was it something I said?"

"No, no. It's just hot in here." He looked at me bundled up in a turtleneck, a bulky cardigan, and a winter scarf draped around my neck.

"Okay," he said dubiously.

"Hey, as long as you're here, I wanted to ask you about what you said at the restaurant about my dating an older guy."

"Yeah, I'm really sorry about that. It's like I said before, sometimes I get thoughts, and I'm pretty sure I know where they're coming from, but I'm not always right."

"So, just out of curiosity, what thoughts exactly were you having about, you know, this 'older' guy?"

"Um, how do I explain it? You were thinking about being out on a date, and a few days later, your thoughts seemed preoccupied about him romantically, and the idea of seeing him again seemed to really excite you. That's it."

"I see," I said, though I didn't really. I wondered if this was just another of Adam's phony attempts at showing off his 'telepathy,' when it suddenly dawned on me — Richard! I hoped I hadn't said his name out loud, and thankfully I hadn't.

The look on my face must have shown some emotion, however, because Adam said, "Hey, please don't think I'm trying to spy on you with the whole telepathy thing. I swear. I'm not that good. What I mean to say is that I would never intentionally invade your thoughts. But I'm beginning to understand that..." leaning in to whisper, he said, "the closer I am to someone, the stronger the telepathic connection seems to be."

It reminded me almost exactly of what Nathan had said to me that day we walked to the market last September. Not wanting Adam to see my perplexed expression, I excused myself to return to my studies. As I sat there reflecting on all that had transpired with Adam, I concluded that he probably did have some telepathic abilities after all. There was no other way he could have known the things he did about Richard and my 'excitement' over him, which was really just a projection onto my Aunt Maggie and the anticipation I had about them meeting. What was probably really happening with Adam, I decided, was that his telepathic abilities were as mature as he was. Not very. But like Rhonda had said that night in the café, he was harmless enough.

March 11

After school, I raced home to throw the last few items in my suitcase and waited for Rhonda to give me a ride to the Amtrak station.

"You must be so excited," she said. "I wish I could meet your aunt. She sounds the coolest."

"She is. I don't know what I'm more excited about, spending time with her, going to the Deepak event, having her meet Nathan, or having her meet Richard."

"Don't get too carried away about the matchmaking. My mum once did some matchmaking back in England with her best friend and her cousin. It all seemed to be going well until it wasn't, and then neither of them ever spoke to her again."

"I'll keep that in mind," I said, still envisioning Aunt Maggie and Richard falling madly in love and living together just a few hours away from me.

On the train ride to Boston, I continued listening to *The Tao of Pooh*, and just like the 'awakening' process Nathan and I had talked about so many times, I felt as if I were remembering something I had already been taught. One story in the book really hit home with me. It talked of a great waterfall that plunged for thousands of feet, so deep that no living creature could be seen in the churning waters below. One day, K'ung Fu-tse (Confucius) saw an old man being tossed around in the turbulent waters. He called to his friends, and together they tried to rescue the old man. By the time they reached the water, the old man had already climbed out onto the bank. Confucius rushed over to him and said, "You should be dead, but you are not. What power do you have?"

The old man replied, "Simple. I taught myself to become one with the water. Instead of fighting against it, I go up on and down with it. That's all."

That's all? Could it be that the secret to life is to go with the flow and not struggle against it? I'd like to think it was that simple and that I could teach myself to live that way as well.

When we pulled into the Boston station, I grew more charged up about seeing Aunt Maggie. The cab ride to the hotel seemed to take forever, but as soon as I entered the lobby, her smiling face was there, welcoming me into the sunshine of her soul.

*

We found a little Cuban place a few blocks from our hotel called The Old Havana and for the next few hours, we laughed and talked as if not a minute had passed since our time spent together over Christmas. We had a good laugh about Adam, too. She said she had a brief fling with a guy a lot like Adam in her first year at college and that I was better off 'skipping the appetizer,' as she called it.

"You already have a full plate with your boyfriend, Nathan. I hope you're not tempted by some flaming saganaki."

"That's an interesting analogy, Aunt Maggie, but I can assure you, no flashy dish is going to distract me from Nathan. Speaking of dishes," I teased, "are you looking forward to meeting your date tomorrow night?"

"You bet I am. It'll be fun. But I see that gleam in your eye, Jenny. Don't go getting any big ideas about my falling head over heels for this guy and moving my butt out here to the cold tundra of the northeast."

"Farthest thing from my mind," I said with my fingers crossed behind my back.

March 12

On Saturday morning, we woke early, got bundled up, and strolled along Huntington Avenue until we found a greasy spoon for breakfast called The Robinwood Café. Our conversation over blueberry pancakes and herbal tea was minimal. I think we were both mentally preparing to receive the spiritual wisdom of Dr. Chopra.

Coincidentally, another couple that came in for breakfast was also attending the event and mentioned to us that if we walked across the street, we could catch the number 39 bus, which would leave us only ten minutes from the auditorium. We rode the bus in silence, staring out the window as we passed little shops and apartment buildings. We passed our hotel, too, then turned onto Huntington Avenue. I laughed out loud when I spotted Jenny's Laundromat right next to Maggie's Hair Salon but was a bit confused when we made a stop at Harvard Medical School. I thought Harvard was in Cambridge? Another stop was made at the Massachusetts College of Arts & Design and finally the Museum of Fine Arts, which was where we got off the bus and continued up to Krentzman Quadrangle at Northeastern University.

"How typical of academics to call it a quadrangle instead of just naming it a square like everyone else," I said.

Aunt Maggie smiled and took my hand as we strolled through 'the quad' and found ourselves standing in front of a building called the Sacred Space. The building was used for worship services, meditation, and yoga, and as we stood there, we could hear and feel the sacred Om sound resonating from within. We closed our eyes and joined in for a long and powerful Om. I silently recited: *Moment by moment, breath by breath. Let our journey today lead us to a greater understanding of our higher selves.* Hand in hand, we continued on to our destination, Blackman Auditorium.

The thousand-seat facility was filled to capacity, and the air buzzed with a joyful expectancy. We found our seats and whispered to each other about how many books Deepak had written, how many of his PBS specials Aunt Maggie had seen, and whether it was true that he got $25,000 per appearance.

When Deepak took the stage, he began by telling a Zen story about two monks watching a flag wave in the wind. "The first monk says, 'The flag is waving in the wind!' The second says, 'No, the wind is moving.' Their teacher comes over, and they pose the question to him. 'Which is moving, the flag or the wind?' He answers, 'Neither. Only consciousness is moving.' As consciousness moves," Deepak affirmed, "it imagines the world into existence."

For the next two hours, he explained in simple yet eloquent terms the three domains of existence. The physical domain is the visible universe. It's the three-dimensional place where our five senses experience the world. It's predictable, following the laws of physics. The second level of existence is called the quantum domain. It consists of information and energy, our mind, thoughts, and ego. Because everything is made up of energy — molecules and atoms — all of us are actually connected to everything and everyone else. Together, our minds created the physical world into existence.

Although I hadn't yet taken physics and was having a hard enough time with algebra and biology, my mind exploded like fireworks with all the information and enchantment of the universe.

The third level of existence, Deepak explained, is the nonlocal domain. It is called nonlocal because it is not restricted by location. It is not here or there. It simply is. This spiritual domain is what organizes everything else. Essentially, the nonlocal domain is the soul of the universe, and it exists in all of us. If we are able to tap into it, then our potential to make miracles is unlimited.

*

As we broke for lunch, my aunt asked me what I thought of the lecture so far. "It's overwhelming," I said. "I'm going to need a while to digest all of this."

"Join the club. I've been digesting it for years and still can't wrap my head around it sometimes. The theory of it is ... beautiful. Putting it into practice, however, can be an ugly mess."

Her words comforted and scared me at the same time. If she, my aunt of great wisdom and experience, was floundering with these profound truths about the universe, what hope did I have of employing them in my own life?

Our options for lunch were limited, since we had less than an hour before the second half of the lecture began. There was a Taco Bell and two Mexican joints around the corner, but Aunt Maggie worried about the effects of that cuisine, saying that her gaseous qualities could be felt in any level of existence.

We finally opted for a Middle Eastern restaurant on the other side of Huntington Avenue called Boston Shawarma. We talked about the nonlocal domain over chicken kabobs and grabbed a water to go before heading back to the auditorium.

*

The second half of the lecture was deep, but thankfully lighter than the first. It outlined spiritual coincidences, or synchrodestiny as he called it, as they related to the three domains of existence. He then offered practical tools for harnessing those coincidences by using meditation and mantras.

The exercises he shared were based on seven principles of synchrodestiny. As he spoke, I felt that familiar buzz come to life in my body. This was who I am, and I knew it in every fiber of my 'local' and 'nonlocal' being. By the time the lecture was over, I was exhausted. I felt like I had run a marathon. My aunt, quite the contrary, looked as stunning as if she just came off a model's runway. We walked next door to Starbucks to grab a tea for the bus ride back to our hotel.

"I should have gotten a real coffee," I whined. "I'll never make it through dinner tonight."

"So take a nap when we get back to the hotel. I was thinking I might take a cold shower. I'm doing the thirty-day challenge."

"Of course you are."

"It has some pretty amazing health benefits, some of which even apply to empaths."

"Such as?"

"Such as improving emotional resilience, reducing stress, depression, and boosting your immunity."

"I'll give it some thought," I droned, trying to work up the energy to sip my tea.

"Boy, that lecture really did zap you, huh?"

"How did you notice?"

"Come on," she said, grabbing my hand as we approached our stop. "We'll do a clearing meditation, and then I'm putting you to bed for a couple hours."

"But we don't have that much time together," I whined. "I don't want to sleep through your visit."

"And I don't want to spend the rest of my visit with a zombie empath who's too stubborn to take care of herself."

"Point taken."

Back in the hotel room, we got into some comfy clothes and found a nice spa soundtrack on my iPhone. Sitting in a relaxed position, she took me through a glorious meditation with a rainbow of colors that emanated from my crown chakra, my root chakra, and finally, my heart chakra. Ten minutes later, I was flat-out on the bed sleeping like Snow White dreaming of her Prince Charming's kiss.

A few minutes before six o'clock, I awoke feeling light and refreshed. Somehow, Aunt Maggie had convinced me to try the cold shower, insisting it would energize my body and mind in a delightful way.

"Since you are a newbie, gradually turn the cold up, spending only the last minute at the coldest temperature."

Seven minutes and thirty-two seconds later, the scream coming from the bathroom should have caused someone to call the cops. I could hear Auntie Maggie howling with laughter outside the door.

I shouted out, "Why do I have a feeling you're about to yell 'April Fools'?"

"Just wait, you'll see how great it feels by day seven."

"Ha!" I bellowed back. "Fool me once, shame on you. Fool me twice, I'll be in the ER with hypothermia."

*

When I opened the door to the bathroom, I saw my aunt shimmering before me in a handkerchief blouse dabbled in shades of purples and grays. With black flared pants and heeled boots, she looked like a celebrity on the red carpet at a movie premier.

"Aunt Maggie, you look … stunning."

"Thank you," she said sincerely. "Do you think it's too much?" She twirled around so the layers and wisps of fabric billowed and swirled with her.

"I can't decide if you look like an angel or … or an Ice Capades dancer."

"Aw … that's not very nice; but touché, my dear."

"Sorry. I was just getting you back for the cold shower. Honestly, you look bewitching."

"Thank you. I'm very much looking forward to meeting your Nathan. And I hope whoever he's bringing to meet me likes ice skaters."

A half hour later, I was ready to go, wearing nothing special except my smile. I had an ear-to-ear grin the entire cab ride, which landed us at the restaurant at ten minutes to seven.

Deuxave was a French fine-dining establishment, not one I could have afforded on my allowance, but Nathan said that Richard was picking up the tab since Deuxave was his pick for our night out. As we stood at the hostess's desk, I marveled at the high ceilings with accented stonework, beige tones, and modern light fixtures. It was the kind of place everyone wished they could have a piece of for their own home.

When the host greeted us and asked what name our reservation was under, I stammered, realizing I didn't know Richard's last name. I offered Nathan's instead, and luckily, the host confirmed and led us to a table next to the expansive curved windows overlooking Commonwealth and Massachusetts Avenues; hence the name Deuxave.

No sooner had we sat down than Nathan arrived, giving me a tender kiss and a warm hug to Aunt Maggie. "It's so nice to finally meet you," he said. "Jenny talks about you all the time. I feel like I know you already."

My aunt chuckled. "Likewise. I feel very close to you, too."

Turning to me, he said, "I got a call from Richard. He should be here soon. I took a cab over from the train station rather than wait for him to pick me up. You never know about the traffic around here, and I didn't want to keep you ladies waiting."

"You're quite the gentleman," Aunt Maggie said.

"I get it from my dad. So tell me how the lecture was. Is Deepak as cool in person as he seems on TV?"

"Totally as cool," I said. "He wasn't putting on a show, if you know what I mean? He let the ideas and the words stand on their own. And I never got the impression he has the attitude like, 'it's my way or the highway.' I think if someone argued against his philosophies, he would respond with the graciousness and love that he so clearly has manifested through the synchrodestiny principles he advocates."

"Jenny," my aunt said, reaching over and squeezing my hand, "you are so articulate for such a young woman. You astound me."

We chatted about the seminar for a few more minutes until I saw over Aunt Maggie's shoulder that Richard had finally arrived and motioned for Nathan to make the introductions. Nathan stood and extended an arm toward Richard as he reached the table, then gestured toward my aunt. "Richard, I'd like you to meet Jenny's aunt, Maggie. And…"

"Holy shit," my aunt said before Nathan could finish the introductions.

"I don't usually elicit that response," Richard replied, "but under the circumstances…"

My aunt got to her feet and stared at Richard. Her look was so forceful, I thought for a moment she was going to spit at him. But then he put his hands on her shoulders and said, "Maggie."

And she sighed. "Rick."

*

It took a full ten minutes for us all to get our bearings. We shooed away our server twice as we digested the reality of the situation. Richard was Rick, Aunt Maggie's former fiancée from back in college.

Under the table, Nathan and I clutched hands, realizing we were just spectators in this drama, awaiting the next line from one of the lead characters. It was Aunt Maggie who finally spoke up. "The last time I rode an emotional rollercoaster of this magnitude was … well, you remember when," she said, gesturing to Richard. "Despite my abundance of emotions, I am at a loss for words, so perhaps…"

Richard broke in. "Perhaps it's best if I leave and allow you to enjoy your evening." He started to get up from the table as Nathan and I sent compassionate, pleading looks to them both.

"Oh, sit down, Rick," she scoffed. "What I was about to say was that perhaps we should just enjoy our meal. That's all."

Nathan and I exchanged looks of cautious optimism.

"I'd like that very much," Richard said, taking his seat again.

*

I didn't know how my aunt did it; how she could keep her cool, make small talk, and look like she hadn't a care in the world, while the love of her life, whom she hadn't heard from or seen in thirty years, suddenly showed up as her blind date.

At one point, Nathan leaned over and whispered in my ear to 'act as if.' But I had no idea what he meant by that. Act as if they just met for the first time? Or act as if they were old friends? Or act as if her heart wasn't broken? Every time I started to say something, I caught myself. No words seemed natural or right to me. I was completely frozen.

At some point in the middle of the first course, it dawned on me that my problem was that I was still in a matchmaker mindset. This whole past week, I'd been imagining myself posing clever and engaging questions, weaving adorable anecdotes in the conversation about my aunt while Nathan did the same about Richard. Shifting to another mindset was like trying to find a rainbow on a white wall. My mind was blank.

"Are you okay, Jenny?" my aunt said, snapping me out of my blankness. "You haven't said much since we got here."

Tell the truth or let it go? Tell the truth or let it go?

"I apologize. I don't know what to say. I mean, literally ... I have no idea what words to speak at this table right now."

Richard shifted his gaze to his wine glass, but my aunt shot me a look that said 'Are you kidding me? If I can sit here and make conversation, you darn well can muster up a few words yourself.'

All of the sudden I got the nervous giggles. I don't know if it was the irony of the situation, my aunt's look, or Nathan's fingernails digging into my knee, but the laughter came out of me in such a flood, I gave myself the hiccups and had to excuse myself from the table.

*

As I bent over the bathroom sink, splashing water onto my face, I wasn't surprised to see my aunt coming through the restroom door. I thought for sure she was about to dish out the words that went along with that cantankerous look from the table, but instead she threw her arms around me and cried.

"How did this happen? How can this be happening?"

I tried to soothe her, saying, "Shhh. We'll figure it out. It'll all work out." She clung to me as if I were the adult and she was the child. So I put on my adult hat and asked, "Do you want to leave?"

She shook her head, wiping her tears on my shoulder.

"Would you rather Nathan and I left so you could be alone with him to talk?" There was a hesitation before she shook her head again.

"Would you like it if we stopped acting as if everything was okay and just talked openly about the elephant sitting on top of our dinner table?"

That got her to laugh, and as she pulled away from me and dried her tears on a hand towel, she said, "I think I'd like that very much. But…"

I waited patiently for her to finish her thought.

And waited.

And waited.

Finally she murmured, "But what if he doesn't like elephants?"

"Aunt Maggie, if he is half the man you've described him as, he will feel the same relief you do. And he will respectfully and honestly share his thoughts and feelings with you. If not, if he's changed from the man you once knew and loved, then you'll know, and the elephant can be stuffed and mounted over your fireplace."

"How did you get to be such a wise soul?" she said, hugging me again.

"It must run in the family."

*

Back at the table, Nathan and Richard looked like two defendants awaiting the jury's verdict.

"Nothing to worry about, gentlemen," I said. "I just inhaled a piece of elephant."

Everyone, including Aunt Maggie, looked mortified, and I wondered if humor was the best way to approach this matter. So as our second course was served, I regrouped and started again.

"I apologize for my earlier remark and for the nervous laughter. And the whole hiccupping episode. But I wonder," shooting a glance over to Nathan, "rather than *acting as if* the past between you two didn't exist, what if we talked about it as if it really did exist?"

My little speech was rewarded with silence. But I saw Aunt Maggie glance at Richard, and his eyes met hers compassionately. I decided another nudge might do the trick.

"I know, Richard, that you and Nathan are very close. The same is true for my aunt and me. So if there were ever a time and place for this reunion to happen, it's here in the company of two people who love you very much."

Richard turned to my aunt and said, "She reminds me a lot of you."

"She does indeed," my aunt proudly replied.

And so for the next hour, the four of us ate the elephant one bite at a time. We laughed at the exchange of stories and playful barbs tossed back and forth between Aunt Maggie and Richard. At some points, when it seemed a more private memory was being shared, Nathan and I quietly conversed between ourselves until a subtle cue let us know we were welcomed back into the discussion.

At one point, I overheard Richard say that he'd been married, but that his wife had died, though he didn't say how. Though my aunt expressed her sympathy, I could tell there was a spark of hope in her eye that hadn't been there earlier.

*

By the time dessert was served, it felt as if we were four old friends catching up, having some laughs and sharing a meal together. The ease and joyful flow of our conversation had hit a stride, and I was most pleased when the topic of Richard's work finally surfaced.

"I work at Boston University at the Center for Anxiety and Related Disorders."

My aunt nodded expectantly.

"Tell us about your other work," I prompted.

"Oh, that. Well, my independent research involves the study of how some people — empaths — are able to feel the emotional state of another person at the energetic or vibrational level. What I'm trying to do is to help define if there are variable levels of empaths and to study how they cope, what psychological issues they face, and possible therapy options."

I caught Aunt Maggie's eye and threw her a 'how freaky is that' look.

"And what have you discovered thus far?" my aunt asked.

"Funny," Richard replied, "your niece asked me that very question not long ago. And I'll give you the same answer — that we need to do a lot more research."

"What are the odds there would be four empaths dining together like this?" I asked, looking back and forth between Aunt Maggie and Richard, urging them to make the connection.

"Four?" Richard asked, looking at my aunt, whose thoughts were somewhere else at the moment. "Well, if you're asking about the percentage of the population who could be classified as empaths, the stats we have indicate about three percent, but the similar class known as highly sensitive people account for as high as fifteen to twenty percent."

My aunt shook her head. "I think she meant to say 'How cool is it that all four of us are empaths.'"

"Ah, yes," he replied, a bit embarrassed. Then, turning to my aunt, he said, "How cool indeed."

Something had shifted in my aunt's demeanor. I could see her withdrawing a bit, and Nathan sensed it, too.

"Knock-knock," Nathan said.

"Who's there?" we all replied.

"Dewey."

"Dewey, who?"

"Dewey have to say goodnight already?"

The lame joke still brought hearty laughter around the table and brought us to a light-hearted close of our evening. As Richard was paying the bill, I motioned for Nathan to join me out front so that Aunt Maggie might have a moment alone with him.

*

"I cannot believe this is happening!" I squealed once we were outside. "It's fate. There's no other explanation for it. The universe wants to reunite them." I jumped up and down with such glee, I could feel my four-course French meal coming back up my throat.

"Slow down," Nathan warned. "You're getting a bit over-excited, and I have a feeling we're both going to need to be the level-headed ones once we get out of here."

"So what's the game plan?" I asked. "I mean, should we persuade them to meet again tomorrow, or what?"

"Breathe, Jenny," he said, clutching my shoulders. "You've been on quite a rollercoaster yourself tonight, no doubt absorbing a lot of their emotional energy along the way, just as I have. So maybe we should take tonight to be good listeners and not give our opinions on anything. Agreed?"

"But what if she asks me a question? What if she wants my opinion?"

"The standard reply to all questions is this: what do you think?"

"That's it?" I wailed. "What do you think?"

"It's psychology 101. Most people don't want to be given advice, they just want to work through their own issues while you sit by and listen. Can you do that?"

I could see Richard and my aunt coming through the door, so I nodded and kissed him eagerly, asking him to text me before he headed home.

*

On the cab ride back to our hotel, I tried to do as Nathan suggested — just listen. But Aunt Maggie had gone quiet, and so I stared out the window, watching Boston roll by, waiting for a sign to tell me what to do.

She still hadn't spoken a word by the time we got to our room. She grabbed her robe, went into the bathroom, shut the door, and turned on the water. I heard it running steadily for ten minutes, but there were no signs of other activity. No toilet flushing, humming, crying, nose blowing, puking, or other bodily functions. Finally, I buckled and said into the door, "Aunt Maggie, are you okay? Please say something."

No reply.

"Really, come on. You're starting to scare me. Just say 'okay' if you're okay."

Still not a sound.

"Aunt Maggie, I'm telling you now that if you don't acknowledge me by the count of five, I'm coming in."

"One."

"Two."

"Three."

"Four."

"Five."

When I opened the door, I couldn't have been any more surprised, and neither could she. We both screamed in unison, holding our hearts, trying to breathe without hyperventilating.

There she was, sitting on the edge of the tub up to her knees in cold water, wearing only her bra and panties and earbuds.

"Jesus Christ on a cracker, Jenny, you scared me half to death!" She pulled out her earbuds and slipped on her robe.

"Well, you've been in here for almost twenty minutes, and I got worried, so I was talking to you through the door, and when you didn't answer me I..."

"You what? Thought I was drowning myself?"

"No. But maybe you'd had a heart attack or something!" I shouted defensively.

"As a matter of fact, I nearly did when you came storming in like Rambo!" she shouted back.

"Who?" I screamed.

Still huffing and puffing, we scowled at each other until we finally broke into laughter.

"We make quite a pair," she said when she finally caught her breath. "Go on, get out of my bathroom so I can get ready for bed in peace."

Once we were both tucked into bed, I asked her, "Is there anything you want to talk about?"

"I'm still processing."

"Well, I'm here if you need me."

"Good night. Love you bunches."

"Love you, too."

March 13

"So here's the deal," she said, standing over my bed like a boarding school master. "Rick expressed to me last night that he'd like to see me again. He offered to take me to lunch today, but I explained it was my last day here and I intended on spending it with you."

I was about to interrupt and tell her it was okay if she wanted to see him, but she held up her hand and continued. "So he asked if I could change my flight and stay on another day or two."

"Are you?"

"That's one of the things I was meditating on last night when you decided to crash in on me. Come on, lazybones, why don't you get up and we can talk over breakfast."

*

As we strolled down the block, I could feel Aunt Maggie's trepidation and confusion. Although I was eager to put on my matchmaker hat again, I remembered what Nathan had said last night about most people wanting to work through their own problems, so I rehearsed the mantra in my head: *What do you think?*

After we placed our orders, she began. "That was a lot to take in last night, and I'm glad you were there. If I'd had run into him alone anywhere else in the world, I think I would have turned on my heels and fled as fast as my feet would carry me."

I nodded and kept listening.

"What I painfully realized as the evening went on is that all these years I'd been sure that my feelings for him were resolved. If you'd had asked me back at Christmas how I would feel if I ever saw him again, I would have waved my hand and said 'Ancient history' or 'Life goes on' or some other flippant remark. But if I'm really honest with myself, I'd admit that I haven't been drinking my own Kool-Aid."

"I have no idea what that means," I said.

"It's an expression. Obviously one from before your time. Basically, it means that I've been walking around in a t-shirt that says 'I've moved on,' but secretly it's his t-shirt I'm wearing."

"Don't tell me you still have one of his old t-shirts."

She laughed and smiled as big as the sun, and it eased my heart to see how she allowed humor to help keep balance in her life — even at the most serious of times.

"I learned how to get on with every other part of my life except one."

"But you date, and you've had lots of relationships since him, haven't you?"

"I've had lovers and companions and friends, but I haven't had *Love*. I've never gotten on with the love part of life."

I let her words linger in the silence as we ate and watched the traffic out the window. Then, seeing as it was such a sunny day, we decided to walk the two miles to the Museum of Fine Arts.

Inside, with its high ceilings, beautiful light, and affecting works of art, it was the perfect place for us to spend our last day in Boston together. When we paid our admission and looked over the map, we were overwhelmed by the decision of where to begin. There were four levels that housed over fifteen collections and myriad traveling exhibits ranging from the Italian Renaissance to Hiro photographs, jewelry, textiles, and musical instruments.

"What do you say we start somewhere romantic?"

"Impressionism?" I asked.

"There's nothing quite like it," she said. "Do you want to get the headsets for the audio tour?"

"If you want, but I'm okay just seeing the stories for myself."

"I like that idea. Who needs a history lesson on a Sunday anyway?"

As we entered the gallery, the first piece that grabbed my attention was a Renoir that hung across the room. The colors were lively, yet the mood of the painting captured a playful tenderness between its subjects — a man and young woman dancing at a café.

"It's called 'Dance of Bougival,'" my aunt said, coming to stand beside me as I gaped at the painting. "It is actually one of my favorites, from long ago, anyway. Rick once gave me a print of it for our apartment just after we moved in together."

I wanted to ask her if she'd made a decision about staying to see him, but I sensed she wasn't ready to talk yet. She just stood in front of the painting for several minutes, lost in the story it told of her own life, until finally she said, "Time to move on."

We chatted casually as we made our way around the collection, pointing out little details in the scenes or emotions captured and conveyed more honestly than any photograph could. "That's why these artists are called the masters, I think."

"What do you mean?" I asked.

"Because they command us to feel, and we obey."

*

After leaving the Impressionist gallery, we moved on to Asian art, then on to the Contemporary collection, ending up at the museum's café and wine bar just in time for a light lunch. "I won't keep you in suspense any longer," she said once we'd settled at our table.

I looked up at her and held my breath.

"I've decided to go back home as scheduled."

"Oh," was all I could manage to say without risking running off at the mouth about what a mistake I thought it was. But after a moment, I said, "May I ask why?"

"Yes, you may." She smiled. "I feel that while our meeting last night may have been a fated event, it doesn't mean that its purpose was for us to automatically be together again. It could have been fate giving me a nudge to finally deal with the elephant I shoved in the closet thirty years ago."

I nodded and waited for more.

"I think we both need some time to sort through not only our feelings from the past but also our desires for our futures. Despite my admission this morning about never having gotten on with love in my life, I'm not a hundred percent sure I want to at this point. And who's to say he wants to commit to another relationship?"

"Do you think he would have asked you to stay if he didn't?"

"I think it's possible that last night he found a hundred-dollar-bill in his pocket he'd forgotten about, and now he wants to spend it, just like any human being would."

"Aunt Maggie, that's a cynical side of you I've not heard before."

"I didn't mean it to come out that way. What I'm trying to say is that taking some time out to consider what's been presented to us is the healthiest choice, and if we both feel like we're ready to reinvest in each other, he can get on a plane and come out to see me. That's all."

A rush of glee spread through me, and I giggled. "Aunt Maggie, I think you're playing hard to get!"

She waved her hand and scoffed, "Don't be ridiculous. I am not."

"If you say so," I teased. "But tell me this: do you think it is at all possible that, like any human being would be, you're simply afraid to get hurt again?"

"Let's put it this way," she said, leaning in. "The last time I cried over a man was thirty years ago. And it was the same man! So I think it's safe to assume that fear is playing a big part in my decision." She leaned back and saw me raising my eyebrows. "I'm not saying 'no,' I'm just saying 'not now.' If something is meant to come of this, then the universe will make it happen despite my fear."

"Or stubbornness," I added.

"Hey," she said, changing the subject, "do you mind if we get out of here? Museums tend to zap my energy after a while, and I'd really like to see this church downtown. We could take a cab there and find a spot to grab a bite before we have to head out."

"Ohhh ... I don't want you to leave. This flew by too fast."

"I know it did, and I was thinking that from now on we should never say goodbye without having our next visit planned or, you know, at least tentatively scheduled."

"That's genius!" I cried, throwing my arms around her. "Can I come back to Santa Fe? I could stay as long as you want me to over the summer. School lets out mid-June. Hey, would you mind if maybe Nathan came out for a while, too? We could all go hiking in Colorado! It can't be more than like an eight-hour drive, right?"

"S-l-o-w d-o-w-n. You're like the Energizer bunny on Red Bull. But I do like the sound of it, so let's pencil it in and work out the details next time we talk."

"Yippie! I'm going back to Santa Fe! I'm spending the summer with you!" I threw my arms up in the air. I didn't care if anyone gave me sideways looks; my joy could not be contained.

*

The fifteen-minute cab ride took us to the Old North Church, which was apparently Boston's oldest surviving church building from 1772. "Doesn't this place have something to do with Paul Revere?" I asked.

"You know your history better than most," she praised. "The Redcoats are coming! The Redcoats are coming!" Taking an information sheet from the table inside, she read, "This is the location where the famous 'One if by land, two if by sea' signal was sent from."

"So what made you want to come here? Because of the history of the American Revolution?"

"Please..." she chortled. Then turning me around by the shoulders, she pointed to a sign that read: *Behind the Scenes Tour: Bell Ringing Chamber and Crypt — next tour starts in 10 minutes.*

"You want to go to the crypt? Uhhhhhh," I whined.

"Boston is said to have some incredible spirits. There are roughly 1,100 bodies buried here; some were even key people in the Revolution."

"Good for them. Do we really have to go down into a creepy crypt?"

"I don't know what you're afraid of. Nothing is going to hurt you."

"Says the woman who won't spend one day with the ex-love of her life."

"Fine, I won't force you to go; but would you mind if I took the thirty-minute tour to check this out?"

"Go. Please. Knock 'em dead."

"Really? Knock 'em dead?" she quipped. "Is that the best you can do?"

"I'm just saying ... I wouldn't be caught dead down there."

She nodded. "That's better."

"And although I don't want to beat a dead horse, I think this tour might wind up on a dead end."

"Okay. That's enough."

"I'll be right here waiting for you." I waved as she disappeared with the small tour group. "Even if you're dead last to come out of that crypt."

I couldn't be sure, but I think I actually saw her give me the finger from around the corner.

*

As I waited in the small lobby, I tried to call Nathan, but his phone was off, so I sat quietly reflecting on everything Aunt Maggie had said about love. Fifteen minutes later, I started to get panicky. I felt overheated, even though I'd taken off all my winter wear, and I felt a bit queasy, too. Although I knew some fresh air would do me good, I really just wanted to find my aunt and tell her we needed to go.

I quietly explained the situation to the woman at the welcome desk, asking her if I would be permitted to go find my aunt on the tour. She gave me a compassionate smile and pointed downstairs. Just my luck, they did the bell-ringing chamber first and were now down in the crypt. I unsteadily made my way down, down, down into a dark ante-room made of crumbling brick walls and low-arched ceilings. I'd never been claustrophobic before, but I had a sudden urge to escape back upstairs and wait for my aunt outside.

Don't be afraid. Nothing is going to hurt you. I kept repeating that to myself as I followed the sound of a voice coming from one of the crypts ahead. It was so cold in this part of the building, I was sorry I had left my coat in the lobby. By the time I found the tour group, my teeth were chattering and my arms were wrapped around me so tightly that they ached.

The room, if it could be called that, where the tour was gathered was narrow and long, and it contained a dozen or more coffins, some laid side by side, while others were stacked awkwardly as if someone couldn't decide on how to arrange the furniture. It reminded me of a scene from an old vampire movie, and I had to fight back the wave of a nausea as images of the walking dead filled my vision.

I spotted Aunt Maggie in the middle of the group and cleared my throat to try to get her attention, but she was too enthralled by the tour guide's story to notice me. When I opened my mouth to call her name, nothing came out. I was still as a statue now, frozen in place with my shoulders hunched up to my ears and my heart pounding through my toes. *Please, Aunt Maggie, please turn around and see me.*

A split second later she did and came pushing through the others, taking my face in her hands, saying, "Jenny, what is it? Are you all right?" Before waiting for an answer, which I couldn't provide anyway, she put her arms around me and whisked me back up the stairs, grabbing our things from the coat rack in the lobby and pulling me out into the brisk afternoon air.

"You look as white as a ghost, Jenny. Are you okay?" She helped me on with my coat then put on her own and held me close to her, trying to warm me as best she could.

When I still didn't answer her, she held me tighter and spoke softly in my ear. "I think I know what happened. The cold you are feeling and the silence you can't seem to break … you've absorbed the energy of some of the spirits here. It's not uncommon for empaths, even ones that aren't mediums. But it will pass, Jenny. We just need to get your energy cleared, okay?"

Again, she didn't wait for a response but began the meditation with her arms still wrapped around me. "Imagine a hole opening slightly in your crown chakra like a gateway for positive energy to come in. A stream of white pure light flows down from above, down through to your root chakra, down to the soles of your feet and into the earth. As you take a deep breath in, draw the positive energy from above, and as you exhale, send the intention to release the negative and foreign energy out of your body, down through your feet, releasing it completely from your being.

"Good. Do it again. Inhale the positive light from above. Exhale and push the negative energy down and out. Once more."

As I exhaled the last time, I felt the comforting tingles resonate through me, and although I still was a bit weak, I finally felt free to speak again. "I told you those places creep me out."

"Next time, I'll listen. Promise."

We stood there a few more minutes, absorbing the freshness of the air and taking in the beauty of the church grounds dappled with snow that glistened in the afternoon sun.

"The clouds are so mesmerizing," I said, stretching my neck around in every direction. "Look there! That one looks like a smiley face, and next to it is one that looks like Casper the ghost!"

"You're adorable." She laughed, taking me by the arm, strolling to where the Freedom Trail crossed the grounds of the church. "I heard the Italian restaurants around this neighborhood are to die for, pun intended. Do you feel up to an early dinner, or would you rather go back to the hotel?"

"Um, I think I'm okay. Just a little freaked out, but I'm kinda getting used to weird things happening when I'm with you. It's like you're a magnet for the supernatural."

"I've been called worse."

"So were you able to, you know, talk to any ghosts back there?"

"Nothing worth mentioning," she said in a tone that I recognized as being more kind than truthful.

As we walked along the Freedom Trail, I realized that for the first time, I had handled a traumatic empath event relatively well, all things considered. My recovery was quick, although perhaps not complete, and while I had a strong urge to take a shower, I didn't have any urges to run, faint, cry, barf, or throw myself in front of a snow plow. All in all, I was rather proud of myself.

"So tell me," I asked, "is this place we're going to dead ahead?"

"You're going to start that again, are you?"

"I'm just asking 'cause I'm really dead on my feet — and hungry."

"I've created a monster!" she hollered. "I have no idea where we're going. Let's just look up this street and see what we find."

Crossing the trail was Hanover Street, where there appeared to be two restaurants in sight, one to the left across the road and another to our right. "You pick," I said.

She steered us to the right and into a casually decorated restaurant called Maurizio's. Being early for dinner, the place was nearly empty. The manager greeted us warmly and said we could sit wherever we wanted. We took a table that looked onto the kitchen, nestled along a wall and an ornate wrought-iron staircase.

After the manager gave us our menus and took our drink order, I said, "Did you notice? The manager is a dead ringer for Mel Gibson."

"Uh-huh, and right now I wish you were brain-dead."

"Aw … that's not nice. And here I was going to give you a compliment and say that you look drop-dead gorgeous today."

"I'd agree with that," a voice said from the direction of the stairs.

When Aunt Maggie turned around and saw Richard's warm, smiling face, she said, "You've got to be kidding me."

*

"What the hell are you doing here?" It came out harsher than I'm sure she intended, and for a moment I thought Richard was going to throw up his hands and leave. But I guess he knew her flippant style well enough, because it didn't seem to faze him.

"I'm having dinner with my nephew," he said, indicating a geeky-looking teenager a few tables away.

"We didn't see you when we came in," she said in an accusatory tone.

Richard laughed softly and shrugged. "I was downstairs in the restroom. Washing my hands. Combing my hair. Thinking of you."

251

She looked over at me, her eyes a mixture of antagonism and fondness. Before she had a chance to hammer him again, I said, "Would you and your nephew like to join us?" I clenched my fists under the table in anticipation of her rebuttal, but none came.

"If that would be acceptable to you, Maggie, I would like that very much."

She gave a mild shrug of indifference but met his eyes with surrender. As he stepped away to tell his nephew about the arrangement, I leaned in and whispered, "What's that you said earlier about the universe and your fear? I think it's universe 1, Aunt Maggie 0."

*

The conversation was a bit clumsy at first. We kept bumping and tripping each other up, until finally Aunt Maggie called over the manager and ordered a Chianti for her and Richard. "Make 'em doubles," she chortled.

"What are you doing here with your uncle?" I asked the geek, whose name was, appropriately enough, Norman.

"I'm in from Worcester to tour a few campuses. I'm hoping to get a full ride to one of them."

"Which ones are you looking at?"

"Boston U, Harvard, and MIT."

"Wow. Congratulations," I said, hoping my envy wasn't too obvious.

"Well, I haven't been accepted yet, but thanks."

When the wine was served, Richard raised his glass in a toast and said, "To the fates that brought us together." My aunt met my eyes, and I saw hers were full of anxious hope and desire.

By the end of the meal, I noticed that my aunt had let her guard down considerably. Maybe it was the wine, but the feistiness she conveyed gave me a glimpse of what she must have been like as a young woman. It made me smile, and I said a silent thank-you to the universe for taking over the matchmaking duties.

When Norman excused himself to use the restroom, I did as well, giving my aunt and Richard a few private minutes to themselves. This was like having déjà vu, only with Norman instead of Nathan. I reached into my purse for my phone, thinking I would send him a quick text with the latest news of the Maggie and Richard dramance, but when I saw the time, I hustled back to the table and announced that we had to go. We still had to get back to the hotel and pack up our bags. The front desk staff had been good enough to allow us a late checkout, but I couldn't afford to miss my train, since there wasn't another one until tomorrow.

Richard offered to drop us at the hotel, and there we said our goodbyes to him and Norman. I told Richard how much I looked forward to visiting him soon, and Aunt Maggie gave him a casual hug before turning to go into the hotel.

"That was rather chilly," I said as we walked up to our room. "I'm sorry if that sounds judgmental, but after seeing how relaxed you were with him tonight and how much chemistry there was across that table, I guess I expected your farewell to be more ... I don't know, romantic or promising or something."

"That *is* being judgmental, Jenny. You should work on that. But you're also very perceptive. The fact is, we weren't saying our farewells. I decided to stay for a couple days and see where we're at."

"Aunt Maggie!" I cried, throwing my arms around her. "I'm so happy for you. I think I'm going to cry."

"I'll be honest," she said with a little quiver in her voice, "I thought I was prepared for just about anything life could throw at me, but this has knocked me off my feet."

"I think you mean swept you off your feet."

She smiled, looking like a young girl again, her face filled with vulnerability. I suddenly realized that in all my excitement, I had overlooked the possibility that she could get seriously hurt.

"Stay cool," she said (which meant don't hound her about Richard). "I'll call you when I'm back home."

It was hard to say goodbye, but at the same time, I was already excited about seeing her in the summer and also eager for her to spend this time getting reacquainted with Richard.

*

The train ride home was quiet, and the gentle motion and rhythm hypnotized me into a light slumber. As I lingered in that space between consciousness and sleep, I conjured up the image of Nathan and me playing the Silentium game. He was leaning into me against the wall with one arm on either side of my head, like he was doing a standing push-up. Every time he leaned in, he came just a little closer to my mouth and held himself there a little longer so that I could feel his breath on my lips and the warmth from his body radiating toward mine. Just when I thought he was going to tease me indefinitely, he leaned in even farther and bent his head in as if to whisper something, and then put the fleshy part of my ear in between his teeth and bit down. It was gentle at first and then a little harder, until I finally broke the silence with a loud whimper and he pulled away.

"That's not fair," I whined. "I want a do-over."

"No can do," Nathan said. "We gotta leave now."

"Where are we going?"

He gave me a look of kindness and concern. "Aunt Maggie's memorial service," he said.

I sat up so fast in my seat, I startled the man across the aisle. I got up and rushed to the bathroom, feeling like I was going to be sick to my stomach. I splashed the 'do not drink' water on my face and looked in the mirror. I hated myself for having dreamed something so awful about Aunt Maggie. I knew sometimes that dreams came up out of worries and fears, but I was also becoming more aware of how often dreams held a sign that foretold the future. I considered for a moment trying to analyze the dream to see if I could come to some other conclusion as to its meaning but decided instead to go back to my seat and finish the train ride in wakeful silence.

March 14

The next day at school, I raced to the pit to see Nathan and find out if he'd heard from Richard. I had filled him in last night on everything that happened since we parted in Boston (with the exception of my horrible dream on the train).

"Anything?" I asked, popping open my pasta salad.

"Only a quick voice mail that your aunt is leaving on a twelve thirty flight tomorrow."

"No other update on their relationship? No hint of how everything is going?"

"Nope. And I don't think he's going to call me to talk about that anyway. And I'm not calling him, so you can stop working up that pouty princess look. No matter how adorable it is, I'm no poking my nose in my friend's affair."

"Who's having an affair?" Rhonda asked, her head whipping around when she heard the word.

"My friend, Richard, from Boston and her Aunt Maggie," Nathan announced so the whole table could hear.

"No way!" Rhonda shouted. "How did it happen?"

So Nathan and I spent the rest of the lunch hour bringing her and the rest of our friends up to speed. Some shook their heads in disbelief while others nodded as if approving the universe's choice to reunite them.

"Jenny's going stir-crazy waiting to find out whether fate is going to win this one or not," Nathan said.

"Who can blame her?" Faith said. "I'd be trying to text them both for hourly updates if it were me." Even I thought that was way overboard but appreciated her sticking up for me.

"I know a way we can make the time go quicker," Nathan whispered. He was millimeters away from putting my ear between his teeth, and I lied and told him I didn't hear what he'd said just to feel his breath on my neck again.

"Come over tonight," he urged with a hunger in his voice that made my whole body quiver. "We can have an early supper with my parents before they go out for their bridge game." He twitched his eyebrows up and down and turned on his sexiest grin.

"Do you think we should?" I asked somewhat coyly. "I mean, we just saw each other over the weekend, and I don't want us to get … consumed again." *Please say yes. Please say yes.*

"I think we should see each other tonight, and then we'll wait again until Friday night when we have our club meeting at my house." He was still talking in his low, teasing whisper, as if I needed any enticement to his offer.

"Okay. Sounds like a good plan. You know, I just realized that I missed the February meeting."

"You didn't miss much," Rhonda said, leaning in so only I could hear her. "Adam gave us a presentation on angels. It was … heavenly." She fanned herself and batted her eyelashes, then rolled her eyes in sarcasm.

As the period bell rang, Nathan gave me a little bite on my lower lip and said, "I'll get to the rest later."

*

I could hardly concentrate in my classes for the rest of the day thinking about Nathan, and twice caught myself caressing my own lips with my eyes closed. Not funny. If anyone had seen me, or worse, taken a picture or video, I would have ended up on the Trinity High twit-twat board.

When the final bell rang, I sprinted to my locker and got out the door before I even had my coat on. Something was pushing me, driving me forward with an excitement that was out of my control. I knew the cause was Nathan and the thought of spending hours alone in his house, biting my ear, my lip, my ... *Stop!*

Although my mood was nothing like the 'snow plow' day, it had the same tone of surrender, as if I'd given up my own will and allowed my behavior to be controlled by outside forces. I stopped walking, put my book bag down in the melting snow, and lifted my head to the sky. *Sever the cords that bind me to all people, places and things that do not serve my greater purpose and highest good. Protect me from all negative energies and low vibrations, whether they be of this universe or beyond. Guide me to my highest existence, freeing me from the thoughts that keep me rooted in fear. Let me now feel the light of the universe flow down through my chakras and into my feet, where the energy forms roots of strength, vitality, and balance. I am connected to the earth, grounded in its power and positive energy. I feel the connection, I breathe the power, and know its strength.*

Taking a few more deep breaths, I strolled home completely relaxed and grounded.

*

After doing my homework and some laundry, I worked through my self-love list with renewed joy. When my mom got home from work, I told her about the invite to Nathan's house for dinner and asked her for a ride over there. She agreed and suggested I bring the pecan pie she'd bought for our own dessert that night.

"You guys keep it," I told her.

"No, I'd rather you take it over there. It makes a nice impression to bring something when you're invited to dinner."

"If you're sure…"

"Absolutely. Oh, and don't forget the whipped cream."

Visions of whipped cream on Nathan's lips and tongue distracted me from what she said next.

"Did you hear me, Jenny? I asked if you were going to need a ride home."

"Um. I'm not sure. Can I call you after I get there?"

It was still before six when she dropped me off, but dinner was nearly on the table. Mrs. Leeds thanked me profusely for the pie, and I tried not to giggle when she shook the whipped cream can and said, "Yum."

We shared a hearty late winter meal of slow-cooker beef stew and talked about our favorite card and board games. Nathan's parents had joined a bridge club two years ago and still considered themselves novices. Nathan and I both agreed that Speed and Joker Rummy were our favorite games. "Not to mention Silentium." He smirked at me across the table.

As soon as his parents left, Nathan and I cleaned up the dishes, packed up the leftovers for the fridge, and put the pie in the oven to heat up. Then he took me by the hand downstairs, spread all the blankets and pillows on the floor, and said, "Lie down."

He grabbed the remote and put on the fireplace channel. "Oh my God, is that actually a channel dedicated to showing a burning fireplace? And that's all it does?"

"Yup. If you prefer, I can switch to the fish aquarium channel."

"No, that's okay. Really."

He plopped down beside me and propped himself up on a mound of pillows. "Hi." He smiled.

"Hi, yourself," I grinned.

"Can I get you anything? Are you warm enough?"

"With this roaring fire, how could I not be?" I giggled.

"I was thinking we could try a new game tonight."

"Are you going to teach me how to play bridge so we can partner up with your parents?"

"Ha-ha. That would be fun. But the game I have in mind is more like rock, scissors, paper, only with slightly different objects."

"What objects are those?" I asked, totally intrigued by his imagination.

"Mmm. Actually they are more like body parts instead of objects."

"Even more interesting. Go on…"

"You know in rock, scissors, paper that rock breaks scissors, scissors cuts paper, and paper covers rock, right?"

"Yup. I remember the rules."

"Well, in this version, rock represents the head and face; your lips, eyes, ears, neck…" He touched each part with the tip of his finger as he spoke, sending goosebumps down my body.

"And scissors?" I gulped.

"Scissors are legs." He mimicked his scissor fingers walking along my leg. "So anything below the waist counts for scissors."

"I see," I said, feeling a pulsation growing inside me.

"And paper is, well…it's the entire body. Anything is game."

Suddenly I was more nervous than excited, and I squeaked out, "Can you please clarify that?"

"I mean any part from head to toe is game."

"Game for what? What is the objective?" I asked, trying to sound more seductive than scared.

"If your paper covers my rock," he whispered, "you get to do whatever you want for one whole minute anywhere on my face or head."

"Anything I want?"

"Anything."

"And if your scissors cut my paper?"

He didn't answer but gave me a deep, sexy stare, and I could feel perspiration starting under my arms and down my back. Maybe that fireplace wasn't so ridiculous; it seemed to have some powerful subliminal effects.

"Ready?" he said, sitting up and facing me with serious competitive eyes.

"Don't make me laugh." I poked him.

"On the count of three. One, two, three." He had paper, I had rock. "Good start," he said, reaching for his phone and setting the timer for one minute.

"For you, maybe." I pouted.

"Oh, I think you won't have any complaints about losing in this game. Come here, you." He turned me around so my back was to him, and for the next sixty seconds, I got a sensual and relaxing head and neck massage that put me in la-la land.

When his mobile timer beeped, I frowned. "Do-over!"

"If you're lucky," he teased. "Let's go again."

Round two: he had rock, I had scissors. The look in his eyes was almost demonic. "Uh-oh." I squirmed at the thought of what he was about to do and started kicking my feet at him, but he grabbed me by the ankles and in one swift pull had me laid out flat across the blankets.

"Close your eyes," he said.

"You never said anything in the rules about having to close my eyes," I argued.

"Don't you trust me?" he asked, half playful and half serious.

"It's more a matter of trusting *us*, I think. What if you start something we don't want to stop?"

"That's what the timer is for." He grinned. "Now close your eyes."

I did as I was told and squirmed again when I felt him peel my socks off.

"Don't move." For a full ten seconds there was nothing but anticipation heightened by the sensitivity of my nerve endings, making me twitch and tingle in response to his *not* touching me. Then it came. The touch of a feather on the sole of my right foot. It tickled, and I reflexively pulled away, but he took my foot in his other hand and held it there while he stroked the feather again, this time across my toes. He repeated the same gesture on my other foot just as the timer started to beep.

"That was torture," I moaned when he pulled me up to a sitting position. "I was so afraid I was accidentally going to kick you in the face."

"Thank you for not accidentally or purposefully kicking me in the face. Wanna go again?"

I nodded and was confident that this time I would win. And I did! Rock to scissors. It was revenge time! I stripped off his socks, rolled up his pant legs a few turns, and then used the tips of my fingers to brush his skin so delicately, I could feel that I'd only come in contact with his hairs. Then I used the backs of my fingers, running the tips of my nails up the bottoms of both his feet at the same time, starting at the heel and stroking up to his toes again and again. He cried 'uncle' just as the timer sounded.

"You're right," he gasped. "That was torture. I think it was even more intense than the feather because of the energy in your fingertips." He took my hand and touched each of the tips of my fingers with his lips. The physical sensation was nice, but the visual stimulation of watching his mouth envelope my fingers was bringing on another round of perspiration.

"Is it getting hot in here, or is it just me?" Putting my fingers a little deeper into his mouth, he said, "Should I put out the fire?"

I closed my eyes. "No. And you don't have to change the channel either." More than a full minute passed before it occurred to me that I was anticipating an alarm that was never set. "Hey, are we still playing the game, and if so, we should really set the alarm, don't you think?"

"Holy crap!" Nathan bellowed and bolted for the kitchen, throwing open the oven door. Although the crust was nearly burned, the pie itself was okay, and after gingerly removing it from the pan, we cut one large slice for us to share.

"I'll bet the kitchen timer went off at the same time as our alarm downstairs, so we didn't hear it."

I laughed. "Or maybe we were just too distracted to notice."

"So are you a fan of whipped cream?" he asked, shaking the can teasingly in front of me.

"Pile it on!"

As expected, he squirted an obnoxious amount onto our pie plate, then pointed the can toward my face and pulled the trigger. To his surprise, my mouth was wide open, awaiting his sweet assault. His face erupted in a devilish smile as he squirted a mound of whipped cream into his own mouth before bending down to plant his lips on mine. The sticky-sweet cream was everywhere now; in our hair, down our shirts, up our noses. We kissed and laughed and kissed again until it all had melted from the heat of our breath and our desire.

"I don't think I want to stop," I said between kisses, my legs straddling his over the chair. He didn't say anything but ran his hands from my knees, up along my thighs, following my curves until he reached my lower back. As he found his way under my t-shirt and felt my bare skin against his hands, his kisses became deeper, more giving and more taking.

"Jenny?" he whispered.

"Yes, Nathan?"

He pulled away just long enough to look into my eyes, saying, "I don't think I want to stop either."

I pulled him to me again, biting and sucking his lip and putting his hands back under my shirt. This time, his kisses were more controlled, almost pained, as if it were torturing him to kiss me.

"Where's the goddamned timer when you need one!" He stood up suddenly, nearly knocking me to the ground, and stormed down the hall into the bathroom. I sat in shock for a moment before realizing what might have happened.

I was about to head down the hall and coax him back out when my phone vibrated on the table. The display said 'Mom.' Darn, I'd forgotten to call her about a ride home. Not knowing when Nathan's parents would be back or when Nathan might emerge to ask, I told my mom to come get me in half an hour.

"Na-than," I called through the door. "Are you coming out soon?"

The door opened, and I was met by a defeated, mopey face. "Here I am," was all he could say.

I buried my face against his chest, feeling his body heat through his shirt. He put his arms around me and sighed. "Well, at least I made good on my intentions. Your virtue is still intact."

I smiled. "Come on. Help me clean up the mess in the kitchen before my mom gets here."

As we said goodnight at the front door, I leaned into him and whispered, "Rock-scissors-paper will never be the same for me again. I love you."

*

That night in my dreams, I was flying over houses and trees, not in an airplane but with my own body, like a bird. Sometimes I felt a rush of anxious adrenaline as I swooped down to the treetops or careened around the tall buildings. But mostly it was invigorating. At one point I looked up at the sky, and from the corner of my eye, there appeared to be a giant dove coming out

263

of one of the clouds. I tried to turn back to get a closer look, but it was already gone. After a few minutes of joyful bliss, I began to wonder what my purpose was here. I didn't seem to have any destination or specific direction. Was I supposed to be looking for something or someone?

As my invigorating feeling began to shift to uncertainty and then to worry, I lost my balance and knocked into a light pole with my arm, which sent me into a series of somersaults that finally landed me flat on my back in what appeared to be a huge parking lot. When I turned around to get up, Rhonda was standing over me. She looked down and calmly said, "Boom."

March 15

After waking from my dream, I couldn't fall back to sleep again. I tossed and turned, listened to my meditation playlist on my iPod, and focused on my breathing, finally trying a visualization trick I had read about by picturing a waterfall. But every time I felt I was slipping away into slumber, my head went *boom*. Finally, a little after six o'clock, I got up and put on a yoga DVD in the sunroom.

By the time I needed to get dressed for school, I was ready to go back to bed. My muscles ached, and I felt a bit foggy and detached. Recognizing these signs, I paused and did a grounding routine then stuck my iPod in my coat pocket for an extra music boost on my walk to school. It was a milder day, and I hoped we wouldn't be hit by any late-season snowstorms, an unfortunately common occurrence in this part of the country. Looking up, I saw only a flat, grayish-brown sky, a sure sign that some weather was on its way.

Upon entering the school, I noticed it was unusually quiet. The raucousness in the halls was replaced by murmurs and whispers, and I wondered if something had happened I wasn't aware of. The last time I remembered the mood being this low was after Mrs. Lockhart died in the roof collapse. God, I hoped nothing as sad as that had happened again.

As I headed to my first period class, I spotted Rhonda around the corner and caught up with her to see if she had any insight about the mood. "There's a storm coming," was all she said, as if that explained everything. I continued to feel slightly on edge throughout the morning, and as I made my way to the pit for lunch, I experienced a sort of split vision. It wasn't double vision. It was more like when an old TV's reception would be interrupted by a thunderstorm, splitting into a bunch of horizontal lines that divided and reconnected in opposite directions.

Nathan gave me a concerned look when I sat down at the table, and once everyone was present, I asked if any of them had been feeling anything weird with the energy today. Adam spoke up first, explaining that the combination of the low-pressure system from the west and the cooler system from the northeast was causing unusual atmospheric pressures and electrical variances. He continued to say that we could expect some extreme storm activity today, and that we'd see the effects in everything from our pets to our electronic devices.

"Hey," Rhonda whispered in my ear, "if his weather predictions are anything like his telepathy, I'll start packing for an outdoor picnic." Although Rhonda's side comments were always funny, I felt bad that she wasn't discreet about them in front of Adam. It was too obvious that she was talking about him behind his back, and I wondered if it bothered him that she did that — or that I was the one at the receiving end of her inside jokes.

Faith brought up the fact that it was also a full moon, and perhaps the incoming storm coupled with that was causing some disruption in the energy fields. After a few more random comments were made on the subject, everyone returned to their usual gossip about school and upcoming parties.

As I sat there nibbling at my chickpea salad, a wave of nausea swelled inside me, and I mumbled, "I'll be right back." I dashed to the bathroom and got there just in time to lose my lunch — and breakfast, too, it seemed. Clammy perspiration covered my face, and I used the sleeve of my sweater to wipe it dry, wondering if I could have a touch of food poisoning.

I closed the lid on the toilet, sat down, and shut my eyes, breathing deeply and intentionally into my heart and root chakras. But something strong and tumultuous was passing through me, and I felt myself sinking, dropping in time and space like one of those parachute rides at the amusement park. This was more than a flu bug. Without intending it to, the title of the book we were reading in English class popped into my head: *Something Wicked This Way Comes.*

Tears started flowing down my face, accompanied by tiny gasps of fear and panic. I couldn't see whatever monster was coming to attack me, to eat me alive, but I could feel it near. I tried desperately to remain as quiet as possible in case someone came in and decided to report an 'incident' to one of the hall monitors.

Please protect me from all negative energy and low vibrations, whether they be of this universe or beyond. Please protect me ... please protect me ... I didn't know anymore who I was praying to, but I felt the strong urge to go on as long as I had breath.

"Hello, Jenny, are you in here?" Rhonda didn't have to wait for my reply. She knew my hiding places. "Are you okay?"

I tried to say 'Yeah, I just need a minute to myself,' but it came out as, "I'm not sure."

She located my stall and stuck her face under the door. "Let me in." My hands trembled as I worked the lock. Rhonda immediately knelt at my feet, pulling a stream of tissue from the roll, wiping my eyes and face.

"Tell me what brought this on."

"I don't know," I cried. "I didn't feel well when I woke up this morning, and I got a little dizzy on my way to the pit…" I was sobbing heavily through my words, but Rhonda coaxed me to breathe and continue. "Then, when we were all talking about the storm and energy, I was getting nauseous and … it's like there's a tornado inside me. Please tell me what's happening." I sobbed as she held me and rocked me slowly.

This was worse than the snow plow day or even the cutting days. I wanted to shut down completely. I thought that if I didn't unplug, I'd blow a fuse big-time. Then suddenly I remembered Nathan. "Oh, Rhonda," I cried. "You can't tell Nathan. Please promise me you won't tell him I'm in here or that I'm not well, okay? Do you promise?"

"Shhh." She hugged me again. "I'll do whatever you ask. But Jenny, why don't you want Nathan to know? Maybe he can help."

"No. You don't understand. If he thinks this is happening again, he's going to be too afraid to be with me."

"Again? You mean the day you ended up in the hospital." She said it as a statement and not a question.

A moment later the bathroom door was flung open and Faith called out, "Jenny, Rhonda, you should come out here. Something is happening."

Rhonda walked over to her. They were speaking in hushed tones, but I could still hear bits of their conversation. "Everyone is worried" … "Don't understand" … "Some disturbance." Rhonda sent Faith away and then came back to me.

"Whatever you're feeling is contagious. The whole gang is now picking up on it, too, which I'm guessing could mean a global event of some kind."

A nanosecond after I felt relief that I wasn't alone in my craziness, I was terrified at what might be happening that would put all of my friends in an energy tailspin. Clearly, this was bigger than a library roof collapsing at our local high school.

"Don't you sense anything, Rhonda?"

She shrugged. "Nothing really unusual, but I've had a bit of a headache off and on day. You know … *boom, boom, boom.*" She gestured like a bomb going off in her head.

Suddenly, I was even dizzier than before as the implication of what she said sank in, but before I could explain my fears, the P.A. system jolted to life. *Attention all staff and students. Please remain in your current location until further notice. No one is to leave the building. Monitors should keep the halls clear.*

Rhonda dragged me out of the stall and back to our table in the pit. I was still worried that Rhonda would say something to Nathan, but as she sat us down, she said, "Jenny's been feeling it pretty strongly — whatever *it* is." Instead of worried or judgmental looks, they all turned to me to ask what I was sensing.

A few moments later, James said, "Hey, I found something on the local feed." We all waited in anticipation of what he was about to announce. Although I felt better being around my friends instead of holed up in the bathroom, my head was starting to spin again, and the nausea was back, too. *Boom, boom, boom* went the echoes, so loud they drowned out what James was saying. Like a slow-motion movie scene with the sound turned off, I saw everyone's faces morph into fear, shock, and terror.

I turned to Rhonda, shaking my head in confusion. "What did he say? What's wrong?"

She took me by the shoulders. "There's been an explosion in Boston. At the airport. They don't know if it's a single plane or a terrorist attack on the airport or what."

I looked past her to where Nathan sat, staring at me wide-eyed as the information clicked in his head. Then we both gasped the words, "Aunt Maggie!"

The entire cafeteria was now buzzing as kids read the reports on their mobiles and called home to check on their loved ones in Boston. Just like the day of the roof collapse, the rumors varied from an accidental plane crash to a copycat 9/11 terrorist attack.

I tried to leave the pit, thinking I could clear my head with some quiet in the bathroom, but the monitors wouldn't let anyone leave without clearance from the front office. I knew Aunt Maggie was already gone from the hotel, but I called there anyway to confirm while Nathan tried to call Richard's mobile. When that got us nowhere, I phoned my mom at work, asking her to call the school office and have me excused. I was surprised that she not only readily agreed but sounded so worried herself, she said she was leaving her office and would meet me at home shortly.

Nathan promised to keep trying the number he had for Richard and to call if he heard anything. He said he'd be over as soon as they released everyone from school, but that it might not be until after last period. Everyone hugged me and wished me the best as I dashed out of the pit and raced down the hall to my locker then to the admin office for my release slip.

I was about halfway home, sprinting as fast as I could in my Ugg boots on the sloshy pavement, when I suddenly stopped in a frozen pose on the sidewalk, like I was six years old playing a game of Red Light, Green Light. I dropped my bag on the sidewalk and looked up at the dark sky, feeling a somber gravity rush through me.

With the light and goodness of the universe, I send a protective shield to my Aunt Maggie, wherever she may be. Guard her from harm and all negative energy. Bring her to safety.

I stood there repeating those words again and again, and when I finally opened my eyes, I saw that the dark cloud directly in front of me had taken the shape of a cross ... or maybe it was a plus sign. I took a deep breath, grabbed my book bag, and ran the rest of the way home with agitation growing in the pit of my stomach.

*

The reports on the Boston networks were all the same. An explosion at the airport ... one or more planes involved ... damage to the terminals ... multiple injuries and fatalities. A knock at the door startled me, but I was immediately relieved to see it was Nathan standing there huffing and puffing. "Did they close the school?" I asked.

"No. They sent everyone to their next class, but I decided to ditch and come help you find your aunt."

"Aren't you going to get in trouble?" I asked, though I was relieved to have him here, trouble or not.

"Don't worry about it. Let's just focus on the crisis at hand, okay? My dad texted me the other numbers for Richard. You try his home, and I'll try his two offices. Last time I called his cell, it was still turned off."

In the midst of leaving messages across Boston for Richard, my mom came home and phoned Aunt Maggie's house in Santa Fe. "I just don't know what else to do," she cried, hanging up when her voice mail picked up.

"It's okay, Mom," I consoled her through my own tears. "We'll find her." I glanced at Nathan with skeptical eyes, but he conveyed a spark of confidence and hope in his that triggered something in me, too. "Listen, we know she checked out of the hotel this morning for a 12:30 p.m. flight connecting through Chicago. According to the news reports, the first explosion was around that time, but what if her flight was already off the ground? She could be in the air right now! We need to find out where that flight is."

We all crowded around my laptop, impatiently waiting as the network connection chugged along at slug-speed. CANCELLED. The flight showed as cancelled, along with every other flight scheduled after hers. There was an audible thud as our hopes crashed to the ground.

The travel alert at the top of the page read: *Be advised that no flights are operating in or out of Boston Logan Airport until further notice. To inquire about the status of any flight, please check our website at www.massport.com/logan-airport or call 1-800-235-6426.*

"What do we do now?" my mom asked, looking at Nathan and me as if we were in control of this thing. Nathan's phone rang, and I jumped like I'd just gotten an electrical shock. It wasn't from Boston. It was Rhonda calling to say she and James would be over shortly. I had a feeling she was finally tuning in and was going to tell us something more than we already knew. I crossed my fingers for luck and tried to calm my anxiousness with some deep breaths.

When they arrived, we headed downstairs, asking my mom to keep tabs on the news reports and to holler if anything changed. I filled the others in on what little we had discovered, then Rhonda suggested that we pool our focus, that perhaps if we all tried to plug in to Aunt Maggie's energy together, it might be stronger than each of us doing it alone. "What have we got to lose?" I shrugged.

I pulled up a picture of my aunt on my phone and put it on the middle of the table. "Should we hold hands or something?" I asked.

"It's not a séance, Jenny," Rhonda snorted, "but on the other hand, it couldn't hurt." So we joined hands and closed our eyes as Rhonda instructed us to picture my aunt in various places throughout the city. We imagined her in a hotel room, a taxi, a restaurant, a shopping mall, on the street, in a plane, and finally in the airport. The whole process took five minutes, and when we were done, Rhonda asked each person to say where they felt the strongest surge of energy.

James said the airplane. Nathan said an airplane, too. Rhonda and I both nodded — airplane. "So what do we do now?" I asked, feeling my heart sink and my mouth go dry.

"The good news is, we all felt her energy, which means she is probably safe, even if she is stuck on an airplane." I nodded, trying to convince my doubts to believe in my intuition. "The question now is," she continued, "do we sit here and wait or do we go and try to find her?"

"You mean like go to Boston ourselves?" I asked.

"Absolutely. You know it won't do us any good trying to call the airport; even if we got through, they won't tell us anything we don't already know from the news. I have updates set on all social media feeds for the airport, so we can follow that while we drive. Worse case, we find out she's run off to Vegas with her new boyfriend and we turn around."

"And I left messages with all the numbers I have for Richard," Nathan added, "so if he calls from Boston, we can meet up with him. Maybe he can help us navigate the city or whatever red tape we might run into."

"You guys are amazing," I said. "Let me go and try to explain this to my mom."

*

After ten minutes of serious disputing, pleading, and a promise to call her every hour, my mom hugged us all goodbye, and off we went in search of my aunt.

Diary of a Teenage Empath

As we drove down Highway 95, Nathan continued to try all of Richard's numbers. "I feel somehow that if we can find him, we'll find her."

"I know what you mean," I said, curling up close to him on the back seat. "When I focus on her, I immediately imagine him there, too. It's like they are one energy now."

"Maybe he found her!" Nathan exclaimed. "Maybe that's why we're feeling them connected."

"Mmm, maybe," Rhonda chimed in. "But why wouldn't he call and tell you? I think it's more likely that he is putting his energy out there, too, just like we're doing in an effort to find her. You said he is a multi-sensory intuitive, right?"

"Yeah," Nathan replied. "He has pretty extensive skills, which, I might add, would come in very handy now, so I say we should focus our efforts on finding him, which might be easier anyway."

I looked uncertainly at Nathan, but he assured me it was the more effective way to reach Aunt Maggie. I didn't know what was right. I wasn't sure where to start looking, who to look for, or why we'd decided to drive two hours to what was certainly going to be a traffic and pedestrian madhouse. Confusion, fogginess, and fear clouded over me, and just like the dream where I was flying, I felt now like I was falling, and my focus on Aunt Maggie was getting smaller and dimmer.

I closed my eyes, breathing stillness into my mind. *Shhh. Just breathe. Inhale the light of the universe ... hold it inside ... and exhale the darkness. Inhale the power of the earth ... hold it in your being ... exhale the fear. Inhale the wisdom of the world ... hold it in your mind ... exhale all doubt. Just breathe.*

Through the insides of my eyelids, I saw a splash of color. Just like when Nathan did the manifestation exercise with me, tiny flashes of light flickered in the margins of blackness, followed by swirls of purple and green. The purple swirl became more whole and circular now, with uneven edges like a paint splatter. Radiating out from behind it was another circle, this one a neon lemon-lime color. Both shapes pulsated and moved across my field of vision until they disappeared off my peripheral horizon, only to reappear on the other side. I watched them rising and setting like my own personal sun and moon. I noticed right away that with each pulse, they glowed a little brighter, and the splatter-like edges changed a bit. My anxiousness was changing, too. I was so calm, I thought I might fall asleep, as if I were going under hypnosis. I remained in this trance-like state, quiet and still as a statue, watching the colorful dancers swirl around me.

Who are you? my inner voice said. I don't know what made me ask that question, but a smile suddenly spread across my face, and a warm elation tingled through me.

Are you here to help me? I felt a bit silly talking in my head to colorful floating dots like they were my imaginary friends, but the more I talked in my head, the faster the pulsating images grew, so I tried again. *Am I doing the right thing going to Boston to look for my aunt?* Now the circles were becoming larger then smaller and larger again. *What else do I need to know?* In a flurry of neon, they shrank to miniature size and whirled away, leaving only a flat black emptiness. I focused a moment, searching for any more signs of them, but they were gone.

When I sat up, I ran my fingers through my hair, trying to rejuvenate my brain cells into life. Nathan said, "Hey, sleepy, I thought you'd be out for the whole trip. We're almost there. Are you okay?"

"Listen guys," I said, feeling a renewed confidence. "We were on the right track when we collectively focused on her and unanimously felt her presence on that airplane. But then we started spinning our wheels again, dispersing our energy over social media, Richard's location, and all the phone calls to him and whether we will even get into the airport. We're acting like we don't have any power here, but we already know where she is. We need to focus all of our energy — our manifestation skills — on having her with us again. Forget everything else. If the phone rings, fine. If a news report comes in, good. That will happen independent of our efforts. Our efforts must be spent on the certainty, the knowledge that Aunt Maggie is on flight #1240 to Chicago. Agreed?"

Three heads bobbed silently up and down as we exited the highway for Logan Airport.

*

Upon entering the airport property, we were immediately met by a police blockade. They were flagging everyone over to a service road that, according to the Google map on James's phone, would send us right back out to the highway. "Roll down your window," I instructed Rhonda.

Before I could formulate a convincing speech, the cop stuck his head in and told us we'd have to use the service road around to the other side of the airport. We knew it was a lie, just a way to deflect people, to keep them driving around in circles and avert unnecessary traffic and chaos. And it made sense, but not for us.

"Hello, Officer," I said in my most mature, confident tone. "We are here to pick up my aunt, who sustained some injuries. There apparently aren't enough ambulances for everyone who needs one, so we were instructed to pick her up at the infirmary ourselves. Can you direct us to the fastest way there, please?"

The cop looked completely bewildered and apologized for not knowing where to direct us to, but he suggested we try parking in the long-term lot and hoofing it from there. "If anyone gives you any trouble inside," he said, "tell them to page Officer O'Malley #6781."

"Thank you, Officer," we all said in unison.

"How the hell did you do that?" Rhonda shouted, banging her hand on the steering wheel for emphasis. "That was brilliant!"

I didn't answer. Instead I closed my eyes and was welcomed again by the purple and neon orbs floating in my vision. *I don't know if you had anything to do with that, but if you did, thank you.* A smile spread across my face, and I felt butterflies in my stomach that invigorated my hope of finding Aunt Maggie.

It took us a while to find a parking spot, and before we got fifty feet from the car, it started pouring rain. If we didn't want to get drenched, we were going to have to navigate our way through the parking garage. "According to the airport diagram, she would have left from Terminal B," James said.

"I feel like we should split up," Nathan urged. "I'll take James with me, since I can spot Aunt Maggie quickly, and you take Rhonda with you."

"And we can communicate via text every fifteen minutes." James added.

I was about to go along with the idea when I felt a strong pull to stay put. "Hey, guys, I don't think we should split up. We've done well pooling our strengths and energy, so I don't think now is the time to weaken that by going off in different directions. I don't know what we're going to find in there, but I'd guess we're going to get bombarded with all kinds of negative shit. I mean, it affected me pretty badly from over a hundred miles away. Now I'm about to walk into the front lines of this thing, and although I don't know what awaits me, I do know that I need to be surrounded by my friends ... all of my friends together."

"Agreed," they all said, moving in for high-fives.

"So where should we start?" James asked.

I closed my eyes and focused on the corridor ahead for Terminal B, then shifted my attention to the other directions. "It's like I first said. I think we need to find the infirmary."

Inside the airport, it was freakishly quiet, despite the sea of people filling the chairs, lining the walls, and huddled in groups like they were having a campfire. As we made our way down the corridors, we caught bits of conversations that, pieced together, revealed that the devastation was not an act of terrorism. Apparently, one of the planes landing at the airport was struck by lightning, causing it to lose control and careen into the airport terminal. Although somewhat relieved by the news, I felt no less frantic about finding my aunt.

I scanned the bank of windows and found what I was looking for: the information kiosk with a large map of the airport. The infirmary was located at the far end of Terminal A on the lower level. We walked swiftly but calmly, not wanting to bring too much attention to ourselves. About a hundred yards from the infirmary, we were stopped by one of those post-and-pulley barricades and a sign that read *Only people needing medical attention beyond this point.*

I looked up ahead and was shocked to see that the fifty-by-three-hundred-foot corridor was now, in fact, the infirmary. Rows of people were sitting or laid out along either side of the hall while airport staff bustled about like they knew what they were doing, when it was obvious they were just making people comfortable until they could be seen by real medical staff. Some of the people we could see appeared to have only superficial cuts, but some were bleeding badly, with towels or t-shirts soaked in blood. Most likely, those who had been badly hurt were already taken to the hospital. I closed my eyes, hoping Aunt Maggie was not one of them.

I motioned to one of the guards who wasn't of the airport variety but rather a full military guard with a semi-automatic gun and a stern face. I pitched him the same story I had used earlier, even dropping O'Malley's name for good measure. The guard shook his head. "You can't enter the barricade. People released from the first aid area will be sent to that exit." The way he pointed to a small opening in the barricade fifteen feet away made me want to snap one of the straps off its post and point out that the barricade system he was so stringently protecting was the same one we had in our local movie theater.

Despite having been confident up to this point, I began to wonder if we shouldn't be looking for Aunt Maggie somewhere else. Or maybe ... maybe she needed to look for us. I grabbed Nathan's hand while Rhonda and James followed us to the information kiosk in the middle of the terminal. Behind the counter was a middle-aged woman with a gentle face, so this time I decided to try a softer approach.

"Pardon me, but we're a bit lost. We were supposed to meet our aunt, who is rather old and no doubt scared with all that's gone on, but we're having no luck finding her. Could we please have her paged?"

"We're really not allowing general public pages at this time," she said like an automated voice recording on a customer service line. So much for reading her gentle face. But I latched on to the word 'really,' which meant there might be room for exceptions, so once again, I dropped Officer O'Malley's name and badge number.

"Who am I paging?" she asked with an empathetic look. I scribbled the name on a piece of paper and handed it to her.

"Thank you," I said as my friends nodded and expressed their appreciation, as well.

"Paging Maggie Stewart ... Maggie Stewart. Please meet your party at the information desk in Terminal A or pick up a red courtesy phone to be connected." She repeated the page, and we thanked her again then stood waiting impatiently for a reply. Each second that ticked by seemed like a minute and each minute an hour until finally it seemed a week had passed. At last, the phone rang.

"Hold, please," the attendant said, handing me the receiver.

"Hello?" I gasped. "Is that you, Aunt Maggie?"

"Jenny? I could hardly believe when I heard my name being paged, and yet somehow I knew you'd find me."

"I found you. Where are you? I'll come get you."

"We're in the first aid area on the lower level. If you go past…"

"I know where it is. We were trying to look for you there, but they wouldn't let us in. Wait. You said '*we're* in the first aid area.' Are you with Richard?"

"Yes. We were on the plane together. We were just about to pull away from the gate when there was an explosion, and then another and another." She was starting to cry, and I wanted to hug her through the phone but needed her to remain calm so we could coordinate the rescue.

"Aunt Maggie. Please just breathe and listen to me. Are you and Richard okay? Are you hurt?"

"I'm okay. A few cuts and bruises, but Richard is…" She broke off.

"Keep breathing and focus on what I'm saying, okay? I need you to go to the entrance of the first aid area. There's a guard there where it's roped off to the public. Go and wait for me there. Can you do that?"

"Yes. Please come get us."

*

I handed the phone back to the woman behind the counter and ran with my friends to the other side of the terminal. We stood in front of the guard area again, waiting anxiously for a sign of Aunt Maggie. "Richard was with her on the plane," I explained to Nathan. "I don't know if he's injured or not."

"There she is," he shouted, pointing to a woman I would hardly have recognized as my vibrant, carefree aunt. The guard attempted to block us again, but my aunt gave him a gentle nudge and threw her arms around me over the barricade strap that divided us.

"Aunt Maggie, you are hurt!" Her left arm was in a makeshift sling, and her head and face had several cuts. It looked like a black eye was forming, too.

"It's nothing. I'm okay, really. But there's something wrong with Richard. He took a bad bump to the head and has been in and out of consciousness for the last hour."

"Sir," I said to the guard. "Our aunt and uncle need help. We have a car and request permission to take them to the hospital ourselves. Clearly there isn't enough medical staff to handle everyone who needs help."

"Only individuals with medical release forms are allowed to leave the first aid area."

"And how do we acquire one of those?" my aunt asked in a less than gentle tone.

"You will get one after you've been seen by one of the medics."

"We've been waiting for over three hours to be seen by a medic," my aunt pleaded.

"Please," I begged. "With all that's happened today, surely you can see that we are only here to help our family, who are innocent victims in this tragedy and who need medical attention they can only get if they are given the freedom that you help provide to them and this country." I knew I was going way over the top, but hoped that my words were humble and patriotic enough to persuade him.

Finally, he said, "You can wait with your family inside the first aid area," and held open the barricade strap like it was the door to Buckingham Palace.

Aunt Maggie grabbed my hand and led us to the far end of the corridor, where some cots had been set up for those with more serious injuries or the elderly who could not comfortably rest on the concrete floor. When Nathan saw Richard, his face went pale. He dashed to his side and took his hand. "Richard, it's me, Nathan. How are you feeling?"

Richard's eyes fluttered open and then closed again. Aunt Maggie said he'd been doing that for almost an hour, that he hadn't spoken for a while and that she couldn't get any of the medics to come look at him. Nathan and I moved closer to him now, trying to assess his condition, though clearly we had no training or special gifts in this area. But one of us did. "James!" I called over my shoulder. "Please come and take a look at Richard. See if you can find out what's wrong." We moved out of the way as James hesitantly kneeled down by Richard's side.

"Is he a healer?" my aunt asked.

"Yes," Rhonda replied. "A very good one."

James glanced over at Rhonda with a dubious look but turned his focus quickly back to Richard. He moved his hand slowly over Richard's body, ending up at his head. "He has a concussion and…"

"And what?" Nathan asked, his face creased with concern.

"And maybe a small brain bleed, I think."

Aunt Maggie gasped and buried her face against me.

It was hard for James to say those words and harder for us to hear them. He looked defeated, but Rhonda put her hand on his shoulder and said, "You can do this."

James bowed his head, and with his hand on the back of Richard's head, he silently mouthed the words of a healer's prayer. Instinctively, we all joined hands around him, focusing our positive energy on Richard and on James. With my eyes closed, I imagined the hot electrical current running from Richard's brain to James's hand. Just as Rhonda had explained it to me when James helped his foster father, I pictured the bright light radiating from above to his crown chakra then down through his body, his arm, and his hand where he held Richard's head. Minutes passed as James mouthed his healing prayer, looking up to the ceiling then back down to Richard, until finally he let out a deep sigh.

"Excuse me." A voice broke the silence from behind. "Please step aside while I examine this man." The medic, who looked more like a boy scout, bent over Richard with his stethoscope and pocket light. Richard blinked awake and followed the medic's finger right, then left, then right again. He sat up and took deep breaths as instructed, and we all breathed with him. As he lay back down after the exam, he reached for Maggie's hand, looking suddenly content and bright.

"Your vitals check out," the medic said. "How are you feeling?"

"Like today's my lucky day." Richard winked at James.

"I think you took a nasty bump to the head," the medic continued, "and I recommend you go to one of the local clinics for an X-ray to be sure you don't have a concussion. Will you do that?"

"He will," my aunt replied, staring down Richard before he could retort.

"Okay then. I'll sign off on both your releases."

March 16

"How did we do that?" Nathan asked, holding my hand as we walked along our trail. "How did we, against all odds, force our way into a disaster zone, find your aunt and Richard, and then save him from a neurological trauma?"

"Just lucky?"

"You and James are the heroes, you know. Richard might not be with us if it weren't for you two."

"I admit," I said somewhat sheepishly, "it was the first time I felt that my empath skills really were a gift and not a curse."

"You were magnificent," he said, kissing me. "Thank you for not giving up on your wicked empath skills."

"Speaking of which, have you ever experienced or heard of any optic visions like … like floating shapes and colors? Purple and neon? Sort of pulsating and … I don't know how to describe it, really." I felt somewhat foolish for bringing it up, not sure myself that it wasn't just a side effect from my headache or the massive stress, but Nathan was my touchstone now for the reality of my empath existence and beyond.

He shook his head and smiled, putting my hand on his heart. "You never stop amazing me. You're incredible."

"What makes you say that?"

"What you described. I haven't experienced it myself, but Richard has. He once told me about colorful visions like that."

"And? What did he say about them?"

"Well…" he hesitated, then finally blurted out, "They are not of this realm. Jenny, you've been connecting with another dimension."

THE END

Jeannette Folan

SACRIFICE ME (Jenny's Theme)

Blow out the candle, it won't do any good anyway
It's too dark to leave now, and yet there's not light enough to stay
When push comes to shove, will they show you the door?
With all that you've paid, it'll still cost you more
The hard fact of life is that none of it's free
Sacrifice me ~ Sacrifice me

Empty your pockets and think of something clever to say
There's too much to handle, perhaps we should just call it a day
When push comes to Love, will you show me the door?
With all that I give, you can't take anymore
So when the times comes to make your decree
Sacrifice me ~ Sacrifice me

It's hard enough to be normal
As if anyone possibly could
So I'll stay in my head
And hide under my bed
And pretend to be all that I should be
Sacrifice me ~ Sacrifice me

Light me a candle, you know there's nothing left you can say
There's no one to blame here, in time you'll see it's better this way
When push comes to shove, I will walk through that door
With nothing to lose, I can't win any more
The answer to how I will ever be free
I will sacrifice me ~ I will sacrifice me
Sacrifice me ~ Sacrifice me

JENNY'S SELF-LOVE ROUTINE

Jenny's self-love routine includes many elements that are helpful for all highly sensitive people and empaths. To learn more about these and other tools and exercises, sign up for the blog at EmpathDiary.com.

#1 Gratitude Meditation

#2 Self-Care: A Divine Responsibility

#3 Grounding

#4 Nutrition

#5 Kind Gesture

#6 Connect with Nature

#7 Reflective Contemplation

#8 Celebrate Myself & Life

#9 Music

#10 Learn from the Masters

In Appreciation...

As with any creative endeavor, there are many people who contribute to the idea, the process, and the finished product. Some have played a key role since the beginning of our lives. Others touch us only briefly but leave a lasting imprint on the people we are to become.

In the making of this book, those individuals I am grateful for include my friends, Nathalie Lefrense and Yvonne Czarniak; my sister, Cindy Busch; my professional advisors/editors, Madison Arsenault, Allister Thompson, Dianne Gaudet, and Laura McCallum; my spiritual advisors, Stephanie Atwater, Barry Nahirnak, Bita Bitajian and Dr. Maggie Pattillo; Alison Gerard for her clever doodles; Taryn Kawaja for her beautiful recording of "Sacrifice Me"; Lil Thomas, Benjamin Marmen and all of the artists whose music helped bring the book to life. And to my husband, Bob, who remains my most valuable teacher.

References

The author wishes to credit with gratitude the following sources of material, and also offer references to places and people in this book to inspire further reading.

Page 22
The Way, directed by Emilio Estevez (Los Angeles, CA: Icon Productions, 2010), viewed on Netflix.

Page 30
Melvin McLeod, "Educating the Heart," *Shambhala Sun*, January 2007, 58-65.

Page 32
T.S. Eliot is quoted from quotes found on Goodreads (http://www.goodreads.com), accessed January 31, 2016.

Page 63
The quote from Dr. Wayne Dyer was found at https://rayhemachandra.com/2015/09/05/wayne-dyer-interview/

Page 76
To learn more about Dr. Elaine Aron and HSP related research, visit https://www.psychologytoday.com/articles/201107/ sense-and-sensitivity

Dr. Aron's website: www.hsperson.com
Dr. Aron's book: Dr. Elaine Aron, *The Highly Sensitive Person* (New York: Citadel Press, 2012).

Page 78
To learn more about the HeartMath Institute, watch the film: *I Am*, directed by Tom Shadyac (Homemade Canvas Productions, 2010), viewed on Netflix.

And visit the HeartMath Institute website: *HeartMath Institute*. HeartMath Institute, 2016. © (www. heartmath.org)

Page 91
The Secret, directed by Drew Heriot (Prime Time Productions, 2006), DVD.
For information about the law of attraction, visit http://www. thesecret.tv/.

Page 91
Visit www.quantumjumping.com for more information on this topic.

Page 94
For more information on Dr. Denis Waitley, visit www.waitley. com. See also *The Secret*.

Page 97
Dr. Michael Smith, *Empath Intuition* (Akasha Entertainment, LLC, 2009), CD.

Page 130
For information about the El Tovar hotel, visit http://www. hauntednorthamerica.org/hauntedlocation.aspx?id=395

Page 168
For information on EFT Emotional Freedom Techniques, visit https://goe.ac/history_of_tapping.htm

Page 197
Frequencies, directed by Darren Paul Fisher (United Kingdom: Incurably Curious Productions, 2013), viewed on Netflix.

Page 213
Aaron Sorkin, Peter Parnell, *The West Wing,* season 2, episode 10, directed by Thomas Schlamme, aired December 20, 2000 (John Wells Production, Warner Brothers Television).

Page 226
Benjamin Hoff, *The Tao of Pooh* (New York: Penguin Books, 1983).

Page 228
Deepak Chopra, *The Spontaneous Fulfillment of Desire: Harnessing the Infinite Power of Coincidence* (New York: Random House, 2003).

*All of the restaurants, museums, hotels, and buildings mentioned in this book are real places.
**Please note that the urls featured here are subject to change or removal.